She was definitely not his aunt Bertie

Michael fought the urge to step back and check the house number on the trellis over the entry. He didn't need to. The three-story brick home was as familiar as his own home in Chicago.

The flame-haired woman guarding the door looked ready to slam it in his face, and from her proprietary stance he knew instantly that history had repeated itself. This one might be infinitely more appealing than the last moocher his aunt had taken in, but he'd make sure she was on her way by nightfall.

"I'm Michael Wells, Bertie's nephew. And you are…?"

"Lauren McClellan, your aunt's assistant."

"Well, Ms. McClellan, I'm staying here for the summer, and I'll be doing some remodeling of the carriage house for my office. I'll be happy to settle up with you, so you can pack your things and—"

"That's not possible, Mr. Wells. I'm responsible for this place. And I can't let you do anything without Bertie's permission."

She was good, Michael thought. He could *almost* believe she had his aunt's best interests at heart.

Almost, but not quite…

Dear Reader,

In *The House at Briar Lake*, a disillusioned lawyer searching for a quiet life in a small resort town ends up sharing a house with a woman who has a dark past, a troubled daughter and a menagerie of epic proportions. The situation is challenging enough. Add a miniature goat with a penchant for roses and adventure, plus two vagabond cockatiels, and life becomes even more…interesting.

I've always loved stories in which two people with impossible differences are able to move past them and find everlasting love. This story is about healing, and finding trust, and the formation of family bonds. I hope Lauren, Michael and little Hannah will touch your heart as much as they've touched mine.

I love to hear from my readers. Please write me c/o Box 2550, Cedar Rapids, Iowa, 52406-2550.

Roxanne Rustand

My web sites are:
http://www.pobox.com/~Roxanne.Rustand;
http://www.superauthors.com

The House at Briar Lake
Roxanne Rustand

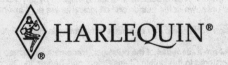

HARLEQUIN®

TORONTO • NEW YORK • LONDON
AMSTERDAM • PARIS • SYDNEY • HAMBURG
STOCKHOLM • ATHENS • TOKYO • MILAN • MADRID
PRAGUE • WARSAW • BUDAPEST • AUCKLAND

ISBN 0-373-70946-3

THE HOUSE AT BRIAR LAKE

Copyright © 2000 by Roxanne Rustand.

This edition published by arrangement with Harlequin Books S.A.

Visit us at www.eHarlequin.com

Printed in U.S.A.

DEDICATION

For my late father,
who didn't get to see my first book in print.

And for my husband, Larry, and children Andy, Brian
and Emily. Your love and support mean the world to me.

ACKNOWLEDGMENT

Special thanks to Kathie DeNosky, Diane Palmer
and Monica McLean—you three are the best!

Countless thanks to Zilla Soriano, Harlequin Superromance
editor, whose tact, vision and editorial skills
have been a continued blessing.

And many thanks to attorney Bill Roemerman,
elementary school teacher Peggy Lehman
and Dennis Gardner, DVM,
for answering my endless questions.
Any mistakes are mine alone.

CHAPTER ONE

THE FLAME-HAIRED WOMAN who answered the door was definitely not his aunt Bertie.

Michael fought the urge to step backward and check the house number intricately worked into the wrought-iron trellis arched over the entryway. He didn't need to look. The graceful circular drive in front, the three-story brick home and every inch of the five-acre grounds were as familiar as his own home in Chicago.

The diminutive woman guarding the door looked ready to slam it in his face, and from her proprietary stance he instantly knew history had repeated itself. *Damn.*

This one might be infinitely more appealing than the last moocher who'd moved in, but he'd make sure she was on her way by nightfall. "I'm here to see Mrs. Wells."

"She's not available."

"I believe she is." He gave the woman a swift, disdainful head-to-toe glance, only to find himself suppressing an unexpected flare of interest. Petite. Delicate features. Wide hazel eyes fringed with dark lashes. He shook off his thoughts and frowned at her.

Apparently Bertie's "housekeepers" had ceased

wearing subdued uniforms in favor of flowing caftans in blinding purple hues, black tights and orange tennis shoes.

Then again, knowing his aunt, a flock of Gypsies could have invaded the old estate.

It wouldn't have been difficult for them to do so. Bertie had been adopting people for years. Impoverished students, the homeless—anyone who told her a heartbreaking story could take advantage of her tender heart. She'd given away untold amounts of money, paid tuitions, helped cover the medical bills of total strangers.

Fortunately she'd accepted Michael's prudent advice regarding the management of her investments, or she would have been out on the streets years ago, just like the drifters she was forever trying to help.

Michael sighed. Saving the women in his life from financial ruin was a full-time job.

The woman before him now cast a disparaging glance at his briefcase. "I'm sure she never buys anything from door-to-door salesmen." With a jangle of colorful bracelets, she started to close the door.

Michael stepped forward and pressed a palm against it. "Hold on, there…"

A deep rumble vibrated through the air with the force of an approaching train. Hot, steamy breath blew against Michael's thigh. Startled, he looked down. And then he smiled.

Poised to attack a most vulnerable part of his anatomy stood a dog the color and size of a rhino. A very unhappy-looking dog, with teeth like sabers and an unholy gleam in its eye. "Baxter, you old fake!"

The dog melted into a massive puddle of ecstasy at his feet. After the requisite ear rub, Michael straightened and held out his hand. "Michael Wells, Bertie's nephew. And you are…?"

The woman frowned. Her gaze focused on his black wavy hair and the widow's peak that the Wells men had inherited for generations past. A dozen old gilt-framed portraits lining the front staircase surely confirmed his identification.

"Have a picture ID?" Apparently she hadn't spent much time studying the strong family resemblance among those portraits.

Michael reached for the billfold in his back pocket and flipped it open, displaying his driver's license.

She studied it, then peered up at him. "I'm Lauren McClellan. Your aunt's…assistant. Heel, Baxter."

After a moment's hesitation she stepped back, allowing the dog and Michael inside, then shut the door and ushered them both into the study just beyond the main entrance.

Baxter led the way, then flopped down in front of the unlit fireplace and lowered his broad head to his outstretched front paws, his eyes fastened on Michael. Now and then his tail thumped against the faded Aubusson rug.

Lauren stood in the open doorway fidgeting with her bracelets. "As I said, Mr. Wells, your aunt isn't here. Can I help you?"

"Probably not." Giving her a brief smile, Michael walked the length of the dimly lit room to the tall windows overlooking the backyard.

Bertie had never been one for the manicured look favored by the neighboring estates, but she'd always grown the most beautiful roses he'd ever seen. Now, a veritable riot of flowers ran rampant in the garden, while the tangle of vines and bushes in the yard appeared to have been untouched by a gardener's hands for years.

Bertie had alluded to higher expenses over the past year. Clearly none of that money had gone into material improvements or upkeep of the property. "How long have you been…helping my aunt?"

She gave him a contemplative look. "A week— since June fifth. Why?"

"Just curious." *With good cause.* He scowled. His beloved aunt had been his substitute mom every summer throughout his childhood, the one person who'd encouraged his dreams. With Uncle Win dead years ago and no one else left in the family with a lick of business sense, he would do his best to protect her.

He turned on his heel, taking in the tall stacks of books, the marble mantel crowded with old photographs, the dark leather furniture.

The comforting, musty library scent brought back memories of stormy summer afternoons when he'd curled up with his latest stack of adventure books in this very room, while the fragrance of rain and roses and fresh-cut grass wafted through the windows. Not one thing in the room had changed since he'd played here as a boy.

But for the memory to be complete, Bertie should

be here with a plate of warm ginger cookies in her hand and that merry twinkle in her eye. Uncle Win had been his Dad's brother, but Michael had always felt much closer to Bertie.

He turned to face Lauren. "Where is she?"

At the edge in his voice, she lifted her gaze and gave a delicate shrug, her silky caftan shimmering into a thousand shades of purple. "I don't know," she murmured, "exactly."

"When she'll return or where she is?"

The woman bit her lip, and Michael found himself studying the soft curve of her mouth. He moved a few steps closer. The fragrance she wore smelled fresh and flowery, evocative of youthful innocence.

"Neither."

"Maybe you could be more specific, Ms. Mc-Clellan?" He pinned her with the look that had made more that one recalcitrant client think twice about suppressing information.

Nonchalantly slipping past him, she sank into a massive wing chair by the fireplace and curled her feet up beneath her. "She's taken off on what she called her 'grand adventure.' She's somewhere in Europe."

"She's *what?*" Michael stared at the woman in stunned disbelief. His eighty-five-year-old aunt was traipsing around *Europe?*

Lauren frowned again, as if debating the wisdom of letting him into the house. "It's strange she didn't tell you."

Michael thought back to his phone call in April. He'd tried to discuss Bertie's investments. As usual, she'd lovingly badgered him—as she'd been doing for years—about coming back to Briar Lake to set up a practice.

This time he'd been ready to accept her invitation.

Still reeling from his law firm's last case, which had resulted in a man's death, he'd taken a swift bitter look at his career and had known it was time for a change. Small-town life and a quiet little practice had never sounded more appealing. When Bertie offered him the carriage house for a law office, he'd accepted.

"Good decision," she'd said in a voice overflowing with joy. "There's so much more to life than what you've had all these years!" And then she'd promptly regaled him with her usual stories about suitable young women in town whom he absolutely had to meet.

Michael settled into the matching chair across from Lauren's and studied her. Clearly his aunt hadn't meant this one. Even Bertie couldn't be this daft.

Unless she was slipping into some sort of senile dementia—and given her abrupt unannounced departure, he wouldn't be surprised.

The thought of her wandering through Europe alone, sent fear slithering down Michael's spine. A familiar burning sensation started in his stomach. "She is on some sort of tour, isn't she?"

Watching him intently, Lauren toyed with one of the dangly silver earrings that nearly brushed her shoulders. "She was."

"*Was?*" The burning sensation in his midsection flared into a full-blown conflagration. Heaven help her, Bertie had been left behind. She'd probably already given her last nickel to a beggar and even now was huddled in some doorway. Michael rapidly calculated the cost of tickets on the first flight to—

"What country is she in? Do you know which city?"

The irritating woman had the audacity to laugh. "I don't think she needs rescuing. She decided to stay in Ireland and look up some old friends, last I heard."

Michael gritted his teeth. "But you don't know precisely where she is or when she'll return."

"Nope."

"I realize you—an employee—don't share my concern," he said through clenched teeth.

"Bertie's been like a second grandmother to me," Lauren shot back. "She and my grandma were lifelong friends." Lauren ran a hand through her bangs. The coppery strands shimmered back into place like silk. "That's why she asked me to take care of this place and her other interests while she was away."

"Really?" The ulcer in Michael's stomach burned hotter.

"You must have heard your aunt mention Frannie."

"Never."

"You didn't come up here much?"

"Every summer. My sister never chose to come, but I did. My parents both had demanding careers, and this was heaven compared to three months of day care and baby-sitters."

"My grandmother had a stroke when she was fifty," Lauren said softly. "She never left her home after that, so you wouldn't have met either of us here. But I would have thought you'd have heard of us. Mrs. Wakefield?''

Michael flinched. How had he forgotten? When he was a boy, his aunt had spoken of the Wakefields often enough—her proud impoverished friend raising a granddaughter on her own, who'd refused Bertie's every offer of assistance. "I see. And you were available for an entire summer because…''

A shadow crossed Lauren's face. "Bertie knew I was…between jobs in Minneapolis.''

And so she trusted you with everything she owns. Well, even if Lauren was basically trustworthy, a person who'd grown up poor—and who was unemployed now—could easily be tempted by the possessions in this grand old house. "Was Bertie okay when you saw her last?''

"Sharp as ever, still walking two miles a day. Though she was always saying how much she missed seeing family.''

Michael caught the subtle accusation and cleared his throat. "I called her as often as I could.'' He didn't need to make excuses. For years he'd put in twelve-hour days at the office. His weekends were spent buried in paperwork he'd brought home. He'd done his best. "Why did she take off so abruptly?''

Before she answered, Lauren casually picked up an envelope lying on the end table by her chair, idly fanned herself with it, then slipped it into her pocket. "She said she wanted one more adventure and couldn't put it off any longer,'' Lauren said finally.

"*Couldn't* put it off?'' Michael sat up straighter. "I thought you said she was fine. How could you let her take off for Europe if she wasn't well?''

"I'm not her keeper, hotshot. She had the money, the independence and the desire." Lauren looked him straight in the eye. "No one makes decisions for Bertie Wells."

"Apparently not." His voice sounded strangled, even to him. Michael took a slow deep breath. "She knew I was coming to start a new law practice here, and offered the carriage house for my office. She insisted that I remodel it however I choose. I'm staying here at the house for the summer while—."

Lauren paled. "But that's not possible. I promised—"

"I'll be happy to settle up with you, so you can be on your way."

"I'm not leaving, Mr. Wells. I'm responsible for this place. She didn't say anything about you coming here."

His initial impression of Lauren melted away. She dressed like an airhead, but there was keen intelligence lurking beneath the purple-silk-and-spandex. And fire, now that her wariness had faded. Michael offered his most wicked smile. "You're saying that I have to wait until she returns? That's not acceptable."

"It will have to do. For all I know—"

"You think I'll throw wild parties? Run off with the family portraits?" He gave her a level look, recalling the envelope she'd neatly pocketed a few minutes earlier. "Maybe abscond with all of her assets?"

"I can't let you do anything here without her permission."

"I'm her heir, Ms. McClellan. A review of her will—"

"She's not *deceased,*" Lauren snapped.

"No, thank goodness. But I believe her intent is clear. She *likes* me."

"And I like the nice kids who come to mow the lawns, but that doesn't mean they're moving in." Her eyes glinting like rapiers, Lauren met his gaze squarely. "You aren't, either, until she says it's okay."

Michael shoved a hand through his hair. How could Bertie have forgotten? He'd loved Briar Lake since childhood, but part of the appeal of moving here had been that he'd be able to spend time with his aunt.

"When did you last hear from her?" he asked.

Lauren tapped one unpolished fingernail on the arm of her chair. "A week ago. She promised to call when she reached her next destination."

"Which was?" Michael asked through clenched teeth.

"Whatever bed-and-breakfast she decided on." Lauren looked pointedly toward the door. "Listen, Mr. Wells, leave your phone number. I'll discuss this with her when I can, and I'll get back to you."

"I'm staying here."

Her eyes widened. "I really don't think—"

Michael rose from his chair. "This place has three floors and six bedrooms. I'm sure we won't be in each other's way."

"You can't!" She was on her feet in an instant, her eyes glittering with anger. And perhaps a touch of fear? "My daughter and I are staying here, which is exactly as Bertie planned."

"I'll get my bags."

"I'll call the police."

She was bluffing—he was sure of it. Until she strode to the massive mahogany desk by the windows and lifted the receiver of the phone. Pausing, she looked at him over her shoulder.

Clad in those outrageous colors, she looked like an avenging clown. Michael bit back an unexpected chuckle. "Call if you wish. But think for a moment. You *know* I'm Bertie's nephew. She may have forgotten to mention my arrival, but she'll certainly be upset if you boot me out of her house."

Lauren hesitated.

"Do I look like a dangerous person?"

She frowned at his three-piece suit. His expensive leather briefcase. His polished shoes.

"Look," he went on, "the Briar Lake Art Festival is in full swing. The town will be overrun with tourists for the whole summer, and every motel room here has been reserved for months—it happens every year. Where else could I stay?"

"I still don't think—"

Good. She was wavering. "As I recall, there's a decent apartment at one end of the carriage house. I can stay there."

Her gaze flicked to Baxter, whose rapt attention had yet to stray from Michael's face. The dog clambered to his feet, ambled across the room, then licked Michael's hand. She dropped the telephone receiver back into the cradle. "You won't start any renovations until we hear from Bertie?"

"Several contractors are scheduled to give estimates," Michael said carefully, "but I won't go further than that."

"When Bertie calls, you'll abide by her wishes?"

She sounded so earnest he could almost imagine she had his aunt's best interests at heart. "Promise."

She looked distinctly relieved.

Don't get your hopes up, sweetheart, Michael thought. *I'll be keeping a close eye on you until I can get you out of this house.*

LAUREN SAT DOWN at the kitchen table and dropped her face into her hands. A dull throbbing ache hammered at her temples.

She'd been happy to come up to Bertie's house at Briar Lake because it had given her a chance, in some small measure, to repay Bertie for all she'd done for Grandma Frannie years ago. Beyond that, a summer at this lovely old resort town had sounded ideal, a cool calm respite from the mess her life had become, a much-needed distraction for her troubled daughter.

Heaven knew, over the past few months she'd hired—and lost—every available after-school baby-sitter within a five-mile radius of their apartment in Minneapolis. Each one of them had quit, saying that Hannah was sulky. Uncooperative. Difficult.

Staying here had meant being able to stay home with ten-year-old Hannah for the summer. Having three solid months to help her work through her hurt and anger before the start of the new school year.

But Michael had spoiled all her plans.

Some remnant of feminine interest had stirred

within her at his dark good looks, his imposing size...or maybe at the obvious love and concern he felt for his aunt. Handsome was nice. *Nurturing* was irresistible, given what her ex-husband had done.

She promptly reined in her errant thoughts. There was no place in her life for a man right now. There never would be, if she had any sense. Marriage to Rick had been lesson enough on that score. Soon she would be able to start teaching again. A decent job, a small house of her own, and Hannah. She didn't need anything else.

Through the open windows she heard Michael's car go up the service lane at the far edge of the lawn and pull to a stop by the carriage house. Set a few dozen feet farther back from the road than the main house and partially hidden by a stand of oaks, the two-story building had the same red brick with white trim. Lauren had to admit it would make a beautiful law office, especially if the man had an eye for antiques, instead of chrome and glass.

Apparently he was planning to move in right away. Which meant she'd have to remove the bird and animal cages from that apartment to make room for him.

How could you do this to me, Bertie?

As if in reply, the old black phone on the counter jangled. Lauren stared at it for a moment, then reached over to pick up the receiver.

"Hi, sweetie. How is everything?" Bertie's cheerful voice sounded distant, scratchy. And altogether too innocent.

Lauren closed her eyes. "Your nephew, Michael, just arrived."

"Really?" Even with a poor connection, her eager tone came through crystal clear.

Lauren spoke more loudly to make sure Bertie heard every word. "He says he's here for the summer and wants to remodel the carriage house."

Bertie chuckled. "That's fine, dear."

"Did you realize he was coming today?"

A burst of static ricocheted in Lauren's ear, nearly masking Bertie's voice. "I...uh...just remembered this morning and thought I'd better call."

Affectionate amusement warring with her frustration, Lauren took a deep breath and mentally said goodbye to the beautiful northern-Wisconsin summer, the sparkling lake just a stone's throw away. She raised her voice. "He'll be able to manage everything now. Hannah and I will head back to Minneapolis."

"No!" Loud crackling came through the line, breaking up Bertie's reply. "...so you must stay," was all Lauren heard.

"What did you say?"

"He can't—"

"I can't hear you," Lauren shouted.

"Please, you promised to stay. Michael's—"

There was a sharp snap, and the line went dead. It wouldn't have taken much to convince Lauren that the elderly woman had deliberately cut the connection.

Shoving away from the table, Lauren strode to the pink, ceramic-tiled countertop stretching the length of the room. A breeze, laden with scent of lilacs, teased the curtains. She stared out the tall window over the sink and imagined herself spending lazy summer evenings on the patio, with a frosty glass of iced tea at her side and a good book in her hands.

It was heaven, compared to the tiny balcony of her apartment with its fine view of the freeway, but she couldn't stay now, not when Bertie's nephew looked at her as if he expected her to run off with the family silver at the first opportunity.

Luckily he hadn't seen the return address of the Hennepin County Court offices on that envelope still tucked safely in her pocket.

With her past, she couldn't afford even a hint of trouble during the next three months. Once his suspicions were aroused, he'd be watching her every move. And heaven only knew what he might accuse her of if he noticed a misplaced object or inadvertent damage of any kind.

Small footsteps climbed the back stairs, then Lauren heard an impatient fumbling at the door. Two thuds indicated the removal of tennis shoes in the entryway.

Hannah trudged into the kitchen in her stocking feet. From her wildly curly red hair, caught in a lopsided ponytail, to her freckled nose, she looked the essence of childhood innocence. Until one looked at her eyes and saw the deep sadness that always lurked there.

It was all so unfair, so damned unfair.

Lauren's heart swelled as she caught her daughter in a hug, not daring to hold her too long, knowing that Hannah would jerk away. "Did you have a good time out in the backyard? Did you play with Daisy or Baxter?"

Standing stiffly within Lauren's embrace, Hannah shrugged.

Another pair of feet thundered up the back stairs. Startled, Hannah turned toward the door.

Michael's broad shoulders filled the doorway. He looked dark and powerful, almost dangerous.

Until he sneezed with explosive force. Twice.

"Mom!" Hannah darted behind Lauren.

Michael sneezed again. "You didn't tell me," he finally managed.

"Tell you?" Lauren asked faintly.

"Birds. You've got birds everywhere out there." He took a slow deep breath and straightened. "And what on earth do you have in those other cages? All of your animals need to be out of that apartment this afternoon, Ms. McClellan. Or sooner."

One wary hand gripping Lauren's shirt, Hannah stepped back into view. "No," she said in a small voice tinged with desperation. "They *live* there."

Lauren curved an arm around Hannah's shoulders and gave her a quick squeeze. After a year of rebellion and long periods of stubborn silence, for Hannah to speak up to this stranger was nothing short of a miracle.

Michael's gaze slid toward the refrigerator, where a jury of five cats sat side by side, staring at him through slitted eyes. "This isn't a zoo. I'm sure my aunt—"

"Actually, they're all Bertie's," Lauren countered smoothly. "She keeps just *some* of them out in the apartment."

"There are more?"

Lauren felt a surprising flicker of sympathy for

this cold stranger who knew so little about his aunt. "Over the past year she started taking in old and abandoned animals, trying to find them homes. Right now she has those five house cats, assorted birds, some guinea pigs, a truly unappealing lizard and a red-toed frog. Oh, and Baxter, but he's a lifer here.''

"And Daisy," Hannah whispered.

Lauren rolled her eyes. "How could I forget?" she whispered back. From the look on Michael's face, he wasn't quite ready to hear about that one.

"Where do they all come from?"

"The day after Bertie left, a shoe box appeared on the front steps. When I opened it, I thought there were three fuzzy bedroom slippers inside until one of them squealed. Turned out to be three long-haired guinea pigs." Lauren held out her hands, palm up. "Bertie takes in whatever appears at her door."

After a stunned pause he sighed. "There must be a local animal shelter. We can take them all there."

Hannah's voice filled with alarm. "No!"

"Don't worry, honey," Lauren said firmly. "We promised we'd take care of Bertie's pets, and that's what we'll do."

"Surely there are zoning regulations—"

"Your aunt has been on the zoning board for decades. She's an institution unto herself around here. There aren't many people who would dare oppose her—especially over a cause like this. She called an hour ago, by the way, and confirmed your claim to the carriage house."

His eyes narrowed. "Why didn't you call me to the phone?"

Lauren gave an exasperated sigh. "I would have, but in less than a minute the connection was broken. She didn't even have time to say where she is right now."

"At least she's alive." Michael sank into a kitchen chair, holding a clenched fist at his flat midsection as if hit by excruciating pain.

Lauren eyed him with concern. "Do you need something?" She opened the refrigerator door and bent to see inside, then looked at him over her shoulder. "Coke? Milk and cookies?"

His dark forbidding features softened into something close to an expression of gratitude. "The latter. Thanks."

Lauren lifted a trio of glasses from the cupboard, nudged the cats away from the refrigerator door with her foot, then pulled out a gallon of milk. After filling the glasses, she pried chocolate-chip cookies from a pan cooling on the counter. Michael watched her, his face still pale.

"I forgot to spray the baking sheet," she said, stacking broken cookies on a plate. She set them and the milk on the kitchen table. "The phone rang and the dog got out and…well, they're good, anyway. If you dunk them."

Michael lifted a glass to his mouth, tipped it back and took a long swallow, his eyes closed.

"Ulcers?"

He ignored her question. "Thanks."

Of course he had ulcers. A man this tense, this serious, might as well have Type A stamped on his forehead.

"Bertie hasn't been thinking clearly about all this. The animals really do have to go."

Lauren bristled, taking perverse satisfaction in opposing a man who apparently didn't encounter much opposition. "That isn't your decision." After a moment's pause she elaborated. "But, of course, I'll bring them all up to the house."

He stifled another sneeze.

Shoving her milk and cookies away, Hannah slumped in her chair. "I could put the birds in my room," she muttered, staring at the floor. "Some of the other cages, too."

The sullen facade was back in place, but at least the child was speaking. *Maybe Bertie's pets will be a first step back.* Lord knew, the counselors hadn't been much help.

Lauren forced a breezy smile. "You see? We'll get it all sorted out. Though maybe you'd like to stay elsewhere?"

"Not a chance." He pinned her with a level look. "I trust this won't interfere with your own…ah… activities?"

From the look he gave her, he placed her just one rung above an escaped con. Exactly what she didn't need—a cold suspicious man underfoot, destroying the peace she'd been desperately needing for months.

Maybe she should have stayed in Minneapolis. She could have tried to cope with Hannah's problems and the frightening changes in her own life there just as well. But she'd given her word to Bertie and had to follow through for her old friend's sake.

Glancing out the window, she realized that the June sunshine no longer looked as bright.

MICHAEL LEANED one arm high on the door frame of the carriage house and peered into the cavernous gloom. This part of the building was a good thirty-by-forty feet and ideal for a reception area, conference room and office, exactly as he remembered. After a good cleaning and a few weeks of remodeling, the place would be perfect. *If* he could find a decent contractor.

Last month he'd called every contractor in the area, and all but three were already booked solid through October.

Dust motes swirled in the dim light filtering through the grimy mullioned windows on three sides. There weren't any animals housed in this part of the building, but generations of discarded furniture, lawn equipment—at least one model of every lawn mower known to man—and untold legions of spiders filled the space.

From behind him came the sound of footsteps. Without turning, he knew it was Lauren.

"Need some help?"

"Got a bulldozer?" He looked over his shoulder.

He'd been a lawyer too many years to ignore his intuition, and something about this woman set off his internal alarm system. A person who wasn't hiding something didn't have that wary defensive edge.

"You wouldn't tear down this beautiful old building!" Lauren moved around him and stepped through the door. With a gasp, she pulled to a halt, then spun slowly around. "I didn't realize it was so...full."

"My thoughts exactly." Michael raised a brow. "Any ideas?"

"You could look for a nice office downtown."

"No."

"Bertie sure must be giving you a good deal. This is going to take an awful lot of work."

"It's rent free, but that isn't why I'm using it."

"Oh?" Lauren said dryly.

"I played out here as a child. It's a beautiful old building, with great potential. I like the sense of history out here."

"History?"

"Apparently this was an underground railroad stop back in the 1850s. My family was too cautious to keep any sort of proof, so it might just be local legend, but I like to believe it's true. People around here were very supportive of slaves heading for Canada."

Lauren laid a hand against the wall and surveyed the room. "Can you imagine the terror of those slaves as they fled?"

"And the determination. They were very brave."

Lauren regarded him with a look of fascination. "What does Bertie think?"

"She believes the legends about this property are fact, and no one will ever convince her otherwise."

He entered the room, climbed over an old mower, then stepped around a vintage Indian motorcycle to open a window. Sunshine and a warm breeze poured in. "An office here will also give me an excuse to check on her every day, after I find a house of my own."

"You're still thinking she's losing her mind?"

"No, I'm *concerned* about her. She's my aunt and she's living alone."

After a moment Lauren turned to face him squarely. "Bertie's lucky to have you. I'm sorry if I've been…difficult. Truce?" She offered her hand.

He dropped his gaze to hers, then reached across the torn seat of the motorcycle to shake her hand. It felt fragile and feminine within his own. Ignoring an unwanted flicker of attraction, he stepped away and hooked his thumbs in his pockets. *Bad sign, Wells. This one isn't your type.*

He cleared his throat and shifted his gaze to the cobweb-festooned ceiling. "I can only imagine what's in the attic."

"I don't know and I'm not looking." Lauren shuddered. "Hannah and I will help you clear this out, though."

A crew of burly stablehands would be hard-pressed to make headway on this mess. But the more time he spent with Lauren, the quicker he could decide whether or not she was up to something. "Thanks for the offer. I don't suppose—"

Behind him, he heard an odd clatter, followed by the sound of tearing cloth.

"Daisy!" A look of horror on her face, Lauren darted forward, her arms waving. "Bad girl!"

Michael looked over his shoulder. And blinked.

He'd stacked his luggage on the other side of an overgrown tangle of rosebushes. Standing atop the bags stood a miniature goat, its forefeet braced on his canvas duffel. Or what had been a duffel. From the size of the canvas swatch gripped between the little monster's teeth, the bag was history.

"Daisy," Lauren wheedled, edging forward and

reaching for the bright pink dog collar fastened around the animal's neck. "How did you get loose?"

Apparently content with both the location and the menu, the goat pinned Lauren with a hostile look and lowered its head.

Lauren took another step.

With a nasal, high-pitched bleat, the goat shook its horn nubbins at her. Despite the damage to his luggage, Michael found himself grinning at the show of defiance.

Just then Daisy raised her head and looked him straight in the eye.

"No!"

Lauren lunged forward.

The goat was faster. Like a fur-covered missile, it launched off the stack of luggage, head lowered. And rammed full force into Michael's right knee.

The knee that had needed two surgeries after an unfortunate slide into home plate during a pickup softball game in college.

Pain shot up his thigh as his knee buckled. An explosion of brilliant colors spun through his head. Dimly aware of Lauren's hands gripping his arm, he sank onto the damp mossy bricks beneath his feet. And prayed his dinner would stay where he'd put it just before arriving in Briar Lake.

The ragged piece of duffel bag still clenched in her mouth, the goat stood twenty feet away, her strange golden eyes sizing him up once more. She gave a shake of her head, apparently satisfied with the damage she'd caused, and sauntered away.

Michael took a deep steadying breath against the throbbing pain. "When I find the owner of that goat, he's going to hear the words 'lawsuit' and 'liability' after the first hello.''

"I'm so sorry!" Lauren's eyes were wide. "I couldn't get to her in time and—"

"Who—" he forced the words through gritted teeth "—owns that thing?"

One hand tentatively poised over his injured leg, Lauren replied, "Bertie."

Michael groaned. "If Bertie—Hey, don't touch!"

"Sorry, just checking." Lauren sat back on her heels. "Do you need an ambulance?"

"*No.* A little ice, some elastic bandaging, and I'll be fine." Michael tentatively flexed his toes, then his foot. Everything south of his knee seemed to be in good working order. "Next time Bertie calls, I want to talk to her. Is that clear?"

Lauren stiffened. "Perfectly." She rose to her feet in one fluid motion.

"And then I can pay whatever she owes you and you can leave."

"She insisted I stay."

Michael felt his temper rising. "I don't think—"

"I believe she thought it would be more convenient for you. Or do you want to tend several hundred houseplants? All her animals? Her birds?" Lauren flashed a wicked smile. "The goat?"

Michael glowered at her. "I could make some arrangements for that goat."

Ignoring him, Lauren crossed the yard toward a chaise lounge, then dragged it back. "Do you want help or not?"

In ten minutes she had him on the lounge with his injured leg wrapped and elevated, an ice bag on his knee, and a frosty glass of lemonade in his hand.

The prescription pain medication she'd found in his shaving kit hadn't kicked in yet, but he was already feeling considerably better.

"Hannah and I will start on the apartment while you rest that knee." Lauren spun on her heel and headed back toward the house, her heavy fall of hair swaying against her back with each militant step. "We'll have the cages out and the place clean by this evening."

Whatever he thought of her motives, she'd been kind, and he'd been a complete heel. "Wait. Please."

Without breaking her stride, Lauren lifted a hand and waved off his entreaty. "Stay off that leg, and I'll take care of everything."

Michael cautiously leaned back, careful not to jostle his injured knee. An unfamiliar sense of remorse curled through him.

In his practice he'd seen an endless stream of clients who were avaricious, who had something to hide. He'd learned to take every statement with a grain of salt. Perhaps he'd become overly suspicious. Just because Lauren seemed edgy didn't mean she planned to do anything wrong. Hell, *any* woman would be alarmed if a strange man appeared on her doorstep and announced his decision to move in.

As the medication took effect and the pain dimmed, he closed his eyes and absorbed the warmth of the gentle northern-Wisconsin sun on his face.

And found himself hoping that Lauren McClellan was as innocent as she appeared.

CHAPTER TWO

THE NEXT MORNING Michael watched the third prospective contractor stride up the brick-paved lane leading to the carriage house.

Built like a bulldog and wearing an expression to match, the man worked his cigarette to the side of his mouth and thrust out a callused paw while still a good three strides away.

"You Wells?" The viselike grip of the man's hand provided convincing evidence of his strength. "Sam. You got a job?"

Wincing as he moved forward on his bad knee, Michael nodded.

Lauren and her daughter had been on the back patio for the better part of an hour, Lauren reading a book and watching as Michael interviewed contractors, Hannah off by herself with Baxter at her side.

Odd little kid. She'd looked away when he'd said good morning to her. She didn't even seem to interact with her mother very much. And for the past ten minutes, she'd even been ignoring Baxter's overtures of friendship, finally deigning to stroke the old dog's head—but only after glancing up at her mom to make sure she wasn't watching. Baxter gave her away, though, wriggling in rapture and thumping his tail against the ground.

Glancing at Lauren, Michael caught her frowning at this latest applicant for the job. She obviously didn't care for him.

But so far, Michael had talked to one contractor who decided he wouldn't take on a job this small, and one whose pupils had appeared oddly dilated, given the bright day. Drugs, Michael had guessed, tactfully ending the interview. Midmorning, and the guy was already high.

Sam, advertised in the phone book as an independent contractor, appeared to be the only decent prospect. If Lauren didn't like him, she could simply steer clear.

Michael nodded toward the carriage house. "I'm looking forward to seeing what can be done here. It has a lot of potential."

As he slowly led the man around the building, Michael pointed out the solid structural qualities. "I don't want the exterior changed," he continued.

When they reached the front, Michael turned and gave Sam an expectant smile. "What do you think?"

Sam dropped his cigarette to the paving bricks and ground it under his foot, then braced both meaty forearms on the door frame and leaned forward to survey the interior. "Wiring?"

"I checked with Bertie's electrician, and he said the building was rewired five years ago. He's scheduled to install phone lines and more electrical outlets."

Sam glared at the jumble of yard equipment and

miscellany that filled the cavernous room. "Plumbing?"

"There is, but I don't know about the condition. I'm temporarily staying in the apartment at the other end of the building, and the plumbing is fine over there."

"You're living out *here?*"

Michael held back a grin at the man's incredulous expression. "One night, so far. Actually it reminds me of some of the places I lived in during college."

Sam eyed Michael's Italian leather shoes, then shifted his gaze to the vintage Jaguar convertible parked by the carriage house and snorted. "Whatever you say."

An hour later they'd systematically gone through Michael's ideas, with Sam jotting measurements and cryptic notes onto his clipboard. Now he stood frowning at the figures, as if they might suddenly try to slither off the page.

"Well?" Michael prodded. "What do you think?"

"I done this kind of job many times. I'll have to draw up some plans and price out materials before I can write a bid."

"How much of a crew would you have working out here?"

Rocking back on his heels, Sam eyed the building. "Probably just me and another guy."

Not very promising. "Could you get it done by mid-August?"

Sam shrugged. "No sweat."

Michael extended his hand. "Call me when you have those figures."

With a quick handshake and a last glance at the Jag, Sam strode down the drive to his battered pickup.

Michael watched him for a moment, then turned toward the carriage house. He'd hoped for a contractor with a good-size crew who could finish the job quickly.

Still, despite his rough edges, Sam had asked knowledgeable questions, had provided good references and, thanks to a cancelation, was available.

At the sound of footsteps Michael turned, expecting to see Sam returning for additional information. Instead, he found Lauren gingerly traversing the brick-paved lane in her bare feet, trailed by a thin older man carrying a briefcase.

Judging from the guy's cautious glance toward Daisy, he'd been here before.

Rays of sunlight filtering through the leaves above sent showers of sparkles through Lauren's hair as she approached, and played across the rich ruby hues of her caftan. Michael found himself wondering just what she wore under those things. Serviceable white? Lacy…

He tore his gaze away and fixed it on the man next to her. He looked to be in his early sixties, wore a well-cut black suit and subdued tie, and his thinning gray hair was cut short. His quiet air of confidence spoke of success.

Lauren stopped in front of him. "Michael Wells, this is Oliver Evans. He's a lawyer here in town— used to be a law partner of Bertie's husband." She nodded at them both as they shook hands, her gaze resting a fraction longer on Evans, then she spun away and headed for the house.

Michael raised a brow. "Here on business?"

"Goodness, no. While walking past I saw all the activity and thought I should stop and say hello. I'm Bertie's second cousin on her father's side. I remember seeing you here when you were just a boy."

The name—Evans—rang a distant bell. Michael searched his memory. As a boy, he'd gone with Uncle Win to the office many times, but this man seemed only vaguely familiar. Of course, back then he would have had dark hair and might have been heavier. "How long were you and Win partners?"

Oliver smiled. "Just during the last five years before his death, though I never worked with him here in Briar Lake. He had heart problems, you know, and had to take it easy. I took over the satellite office in Greenleigh."

Michael briefly explained his plans to remodel the carriage house and start a local law practice in the fall.

"I knew Ms. McClellan was staying here over the summer, but Bertie didn't say a word about your coming. I'm afraid you'll find things around here a little slow for a young attorney like yourself." He rocked back on his heels and pursed his lips, considering. "I do some real estate, trusts, probate, family law...like an old-time country doctor, a bit of everything. Haven't done a criminal case here in twelve years, though. Stable community, you know."

"I'm not interested in criminal law," Michael said easily, "and I'm not worried about making country-club dues. A small general practice is all I expect. I won't provide you with much competition."

"Goodness, I'm not concerned about that." Oliver gave a self-deprecating smile. "I'm hoping to retire this winter, if all goes well. I might move to Arizona. That's where Lila and I always planned to go."

"Lila?" Michael paused tactfully.

A sad smile lifted the corners of Oliver's mouth, but didn't reach his eyes. "My wife passed on ten years ago, and not a day goes by that I don't think about her." He sighed heavily. "I'd better be on my way. I help Bertie with some of her business matters, so let me know if you have any questions, or if there's anything you need. Anything at all."

"Thanks." Michael watched him nod toward Lauren and Hannah, settle his hat on his head, then saunter down the driveway.

At the end of the drive Oliver doffed his hat at a silver-haired woman driving past in a little sports car, eliciting a merry wave from her, then he disappeared down the sidewalk. Apparently Oliver was well liked in the community, from the look of delight on her face.

A dim memory slid through Michael's thoughts—something involving Oliver and Uncle Win years ago. Perhaps a fleeting introduction, or a shared lunch at the Sunflower Café where Win had gone every day?

The place—next to the courthouse—was always packed with a congenial fraternity of courthouse workers, shopkeepers and gray-haired retirees. The waitresses knew everyone by name, and the raucous, down-home banter never stopped.

Michael smiled to himself. In corporate law back in Chicago, high-powered lunches were held at expensive restaurants chosen to impress, where the decor was elegant and the conversation hushed. He'd choose the Sunflower any day.

The moment he'd first driven into Briar Lake, he'd felt the weight of tension lift from his shoulders. He'd made the right decision, coming here.

He was *home* after all these years.

WHAT A DUMB DOG!

A big dumb dog who didn't even understand the word *no*. Who needed a dog like that?

Baxter whined a little, looking up at her with big brown eyes so sad, so filled with understanding, that Hannah felt her heart squeeze. She scowled down at him. ''No!''

But he didn't take his head from her lap. He just sat there in front of her chair on the patio and kept looking up at her as if she was the most wonderful person in the whole world.

Which showed just how dumb he was.

Mom looked up from her book. ''Is Baxter bothering you?'' she called out. ''You can put him in the house, if you want.''

Hannah shrugged and looked away, but when Mom started reading again, she trailed a hand through Baxter's thick black fur. He thumped his tail on the ground, and she knew he wanted to play.

But Hannah hadn't felt like playing in a long, long time. Most of the time she wanted to cry, but only little kids did that, and how would it help? During Christmas vacation in third grade, she'd found out about her dad, and there had been a huge empty place in her chest ever since.

Of course, her dad had never loved her. He was always angry with her, no matter how much she tried to please him. What kind of worthless kid had a dad who didn't love her? Didn't even care enough to *visit* for a whole year and a half.

She tried not to think about him. When she did, her stomach tied itself into knots. Because even while she was hating him, a tiny part of her heart wished he would come back.

Swinging her leg, she thumped her heel hard against her chair in a steady rhythm. *One…two… three. One…two…*

And then, by accident, the toe of her sandal caught Baxter in the ribs. Yelping, he jumped away with a look of reproach in his eyes.

"I'm sorry, boy…" She reached for him, but he backed away, then wheeled around and loped off into the backyard.

"Hannah!"

She already felt bad enough, but the accusation in Mom's voice sent an arrow of guilt straight through her heart. Without answering, Hannah rose and headed for the backyard, calling Baxter's name.

He didn't come, as he usually did. So now he probably hated her, too.

After trudging around the entire backyard without finding him, Hannah stopped at Daisy's chain-link fenced kennel. Meant for a big dog like Baxter, it was large enough to keep the goat contained at night. During the day she was tied to a stake in the yard to graze.

Now, from the other side of the lawn, Daisy lifted her head and bleated piteously when she caught sight of Hannah near her pen.

''I know you just want oats,'' Hannah muttered. She lifted the lid from a clean garbage can by the pen and scooped out a measure of grain.

Daisy's bleats increased in volume. Fighting a smile, Hannah took the grain over to her and shook it into her feed pan, then sat cross-legged on the grass to watch her eat.

The rapid grinding motion of Daisy's jaws made her look like a robot, Hannah thought. She reached out to stroke Daisy's coarse hair.

A cold wet nose bumped at her elbow.

''Baxter?''

The dog dropped his massive head in her lap. She'd hurt him and he'd forgiven her. Just like that. A lump the size of a baseball stuck in her throat as she looked down at the big dumb dog who loved her no matter what.

Not like dads who did bad things and went to jail and forgot they'd ever had a little girl.

Hannah sniffled. Rubbed angrily at her eyes. *I don't cry. I never, ever cry.*

But with Baxter's big warm body cuddled next to her and the way he was looking up at her, the big empty place in her heart didn't seem quite so empty.

Giving in to the tears she'd held back for so long, she wrapped her arms around him and cried into his fur for everything that had gone wrong in her life.

THE CARRIAGE HOUSE apartment wasn't anything like his condo in Chicago. Not even close. But, after four days to adjust, it—almost—felt like home. With one bedroom, large casement windows and a pleasant—if small—living room facing the big house, it was all he needed.

The furniture was comfortable, familiar from his childhood summers. A faded gold-brocade sofa, the massive, impossibly ornate Chippendale bookcase that had once resided in the front parlor, a simple Shaker rocker and an overabundance of end tables. Of course, the décor—cabbage roses on the walls and frothy lace curtains—wasn't what he would have chosen.

Lauren had swept through with lemon furniture polish, a mop and pails of pine-scented disinfectant, and now a local surgeon could perform an open-heart on any flat surface in the place. Not that there were many flat surfaces available, given the liberal scattering of decorative statuary and silk-flower arrangements adorning every nook and cranny.

Needing a breath of fresh air, he tossed back a couple more ibuprofen, grabbed his sandwich and Coke, and stepped into the lush shade outside, careful not to put stress on his injured knee as he limped across the uneven bricks.

Bertie's yard sprawled back almost a city block, with high wood-plank fences on both sides to maintain privacy from the neighboring homes. At the far end an iron fence provided a glimpse of Briar Lake. Dense oaks, maples and fir trees competed for space and sunlight, while overgrown shrubbery ran rampant without any visible design.

Michael smiled to himself, remembering. Somewhere back there was the large goldfish pond he'd loved as a child, though now it probably housed masses of algae. This had been a magical place for a child to explore and dream, a place where he had been Davy Crockett, Paul Bunyan and Spiderman. The scents of damp mossy earth and pine and flowers triggered such—

"Daisy's escaped!" Lauren called from an upstairs window of the house, her voice tinged with alarm. "I can't see her anywhere!"

Michael spun, then sagged against the rough bark of an oak as renewed pain shot up his thigh. Uttering a curse under his breath, he scanned the yard rapidly for any sign of the goat.

A door slammed. Hannah raced into the yard, her long red hair flying like a banner, her pale thin legs flashing through the shadows. "Have you seen her?" she cried. "We're gonna be in soooo much trouble this time…"

She disappeared into the underbrush. A second later she screamed in frustration. "Daisy!"

Michael followed the sound of her voice to a section of fence at the far side. His heart skipped a beat when he found her on the ground. "Are you hurt?"

"No." Hannah crawled partway through a broken section of fence to peer into the neighbor's yard. "Daisy, come back here!"

"Maybe the neighbor can adopt her," Michael said wryly. "I'll bet he likes her a lot better than I do."

"He'll *kill* her!" Hannah sat back on her heels and turned toward him, her green eyes stricken. "If my dad was here *he* would help.'' Her meaning was clear.

Michael looked at her in bemusement. If ever a child had perfected sullen behavior, it was this one. She hadn't said a word to him since the day he'd arrived. Now, with Daisy in jeopardy, she'd come out of her shell. How could he say no?

The jagged hole in the wood-plank fence was low, the ground in front of it torn up and muddy. Apparently Daisy had been working on her escape route for some time. ''You'd fit through there better than I would.''

''And go into the *Millers'* yard?'' Hannah shivered. ''He's horrible. He hates kids worse than he hates goats.''

''What's the chance that Daisy will just keep going?''

She scowled. ''None. She likes his flowers.''

''Daisies?''

''Roses. He has lots and lots of roses.''

And probably tended them with love and called them each by name, from the look on Hannah's face. ''Well, I don't think I can get through that hole.''

Her eyes filled with tears. ''He yelled at me last time. And s-said that he'd have me arrested if I ever came back.''

Michael thought of a few choice words to describe a man who'd frighten a little girl like that. ''Okay, I'll go around, knock on his door and let him know—''

''Wait! Listen!''

From the other side of the fence came the sound of small hooves clattering over cement, then the sound of plants—rather substantial plants—being ripped up by their roots.

From out on the street came the smooth purr of a luxury car turning into the neighbor's drive.

"That's *him*. Pleeease get her," Hannah begged.

"We're a bit late. The damage has already been done."

"Maybe he'll think it was rabbits?"

The little hoofsteps clattered closer. Michael hunkered down at Hannah's side, and they both peered through the fence. An upside-down crimson rose, presumably dangling from Daisy's mouth, wobbled just beyond reach. As he leaned farther down, he could see her small black legs planted amid a bed of variegated hostas that had been haphazardly nibbled and thoroughly trampled.

"I don't think he'll be guessing this was rabbits," Michael said dryly.

"Grab her," Hannah whispered. "She's so close!"

The kid had enough determination for a career as an excellent litigation lawyer. With a heavy sigh, Michael cautiously kneeled in the soft earth, supporting his weight on his good leg, and eased forward. Now he could see Daisy's tiny hairy jaws mechanically chewing on the stem of the rose. And her eyes, closed in blissful appreciation of her stolen meal.

He held his breath.

Reached forward.

And snagged her collar. "Easy girl—"

With a startled staccato bleat loud as any irate taxi driver's horn, Daisy lunged backward, jerking Michael forward into the dirt. Her feet churning up the earth and hostas, she shook her head violently, trying to snag the unexpected predator with her horns, her earsplitting bleats rising in volume.

"Don't! You're hurting her!"

"I'm trying to catch her," Michael managed under his breath. "Easy, Daisy. Come here…"

Of course she didn't come. But she did stop struggling. Her forefeet braced wide, she stared down at Michael as if suddenly considering an interesting new option for trouble.

From the other side of the fence came the sound of hurried footsteps and a roar of anger. The deluge of profanity would have done any redneck proud.

Daisy hesitated, then bolted forward. With her sudden shift of direction she broke free of Michael's grasp, then clambered over him to get through the fence.

"Good decision," he muttered. He gingerly backed up himself and got to his feet as Lauren strode into view through the overgrown shrubbery.

More sounds of rage and disbelief rose from the other side of the fence as the neighbor apparently surveyed Daisy's damage.

"Thanks." Looking up at Michael with new respect, Hannah snagged Daisy's collar with a dog leash and gave her a hug. "You bad, bad girl," she crooned. "You're going to end up in jail."

"We can hope," Michael muttered. "Any chance they might incarcerate her for the summer?"

"At least you're taking this with good grace." Lauren's eyes filled with silent laughter. "I'll bet you haven't had to catch many goats in recent years.''

He seen her angry, he'd seen her stressed out. But until now he hadn't seen that dimple in her cheek or the way humor made those amazing hazel eyes sparkle. ''I definitely think there's something symbolic about her horns and cloven feet.''

''She's got this passion for roses and leather, and if you leave your shoes outside…'' Lauren's voice trailed away as she looked down at Michael's muddy slacks. ''I'm so sorry.''

Footsteps clomped closer and closer on the other side of the fence. A wide section of plywood slapped against the broken area, then someone started furiously nailing it into place.

''That would be Mr. Miller,'' Lauren murmured. The light of humor died in her eyes. ''You'll get to meet him in, oh, maybe five minutes. Unless you want to go back to the carriage house.''

''The man has a right to protect his property.''

She tipped her head in acknowledgment. ''He does. But he's been very difficult over the dog, the cats, the goat, and he terrorizes Hannah. We do our best, but we just seem to aggravate the man more everyday.''

''I'll talk to him.''

''No, it's my problem, and I'll deal with it.''

''As Bertie's nephew, I probably have more responsibility for Bertie's affairs than you do.''

''Actually Bertie gave me—'' From the front of the house came the sound of someone knocking loudly. Lauren sighed. ''That's him. Hannah, you stay back here with Daisy.''

She pivoted and headed for the house, her stride long and steady. For someone so small she certainly showed a lot of determination. So where was Hannah's dad? Were he and Lauren divorced? Separated? Or was he likely to drop by one of these days and whisk his family back to suburbia?

Realizing he was clenching his teeth, Michael forced himself to relax as he followed Lauren around the house to the front, where a tall Ichabod Crane of a guy stood at the door. The florid red of his face stood out in startling contrast to his snow-white head of hair.

"Hi, Mr. Miller," Lauren called out. "Problems?"

He wheeled around to face her. "You know damn well that goat has been in my yard." He shifted his glare to Michael. "And he's the guy who just caught her. Look at his slacks!"

Lauren extended her hands, palms up. "I'm really—"

"Hello, Miller," Michael interjected smoothly. Without thought, he moved closer to Lauren and slid an arm around her shoulders. She was warm and soft and delicate, and he suddenly felt remarkably protective. "I don't believe we've met. I'm Michael Wells, Bertie's nephew."

Miller ignored Michael's offer of a handshake. "I expect full restitution for damages, and I want that goat out of the neighborhood, or I'll be filing a lawsuit. Is that clear?" The man looked as though he was on the verge of a stroke.

"Bertie's goat caused damage to your property,

and for that she is certainly liable. I apologize for the trouble.''

''I'm not interested in apologies,'' Miller snapped. ''That goat has been nothing but trouble. And ever since that kid moved in for the summer, there hasn't been a moment's peace around here. I've had it!''

Lauren's shoulders turned to steel beneath Michael's arm. ''My daughter is only ten years old, and she certainly can't have been much trouble. I—''

Squeezing her gently, Michael gave Miller a level look. ''I'm sure we can settle this. As for the fence line and the goat, we'll need to look at the local statutes.''

''Please…'' Lauren began.

Miller waved off her plea with a wave of his hand. ''I can assure you that the courts will rule in my favor,'' he snapped. ''My hostas have been ruined, my prize hybrid roses have been decimated. And—'' he straightened to his full height and shook his forefinger under Lauren's nose ''—that beast has chased both my wife and I. *Twice*.''

Michael felt an unwanted flicker of empathy. ''Surprising, isn't it, how something so small can pack such a wallop?''

''I'll write up an estimate and have it over here tomorrow,'' Miller snapped. ''You'd better contact Bertie's lawyer.''

''Well…in her absence, I guess that would be me,'' Michael said. ''I hadn't planned to start my law practice here until the fall, but we can handle this in a neighborly way, right?''

Miller's gaze turned cold. ''So you're an attorney, eh?''

''Eight years in Chicago, a partner in the firm, until I decided to move up here.''

One corner of the man's mouth lifted, his eyes narrowed. ''Most people in town call me *Judge* Miller,'' he said, his voice silky. ''Especially the insolent young hotshots who come into my courtroom. I'll have that damage estimate in your hands by tomorrow.''

Michael stared at Miller as he stalked back to his own yard. Any big-city lawyer trying to start a practice within the good-old-boy network of a small town faced a major challenge. Antagonizing the local judge could only make things worse.

Bertie's goat had blasted his knee and had now possibly dealt an even greater blow to his career.

CHAPTER THREE

OLIVER STUDIED his living room. Saturday morning, and everything was in order. His late wife's silver tea service, gleaming in the early morning sun, stood ready on the coffee table. Not a speck of dust remained on the old colonial-style furnishings, no thread of lint marred the serviceable brown carpet. Fresh lace doilies hung wrinkle free over the arms of two chairs arranged with military precision at either side of the fireplace.

He demanded perfection and paid handsomely for it. This time the cleaning lady had earned every penny.

He could have had the room redecorated, even bought a newer home in one of the housing additions on the edge of town. But it seemed right staying in this place, leaving things as they had been when Lila was still alive.

Turning to the oversize portrait above the mantel, he caressed its baroque cream-and-gilt frame. Lila looked down at him as she always had, starched and unsmiling, every silver-blue curl in place. His fingers stilled as he thought back over his life. All he'd hoped for, all he'd lost.

Shaking off the memories, he closed his eyes and

could almost smell the warm tropical breezes of Cancun and feel the sand under his feet.

"A few more months," he whispered. "Just a few more, and our dreams will come true. You would have been happy."

From outside the modest brick rambler came the sound of footsteps and the lilting sounds of women's chatter.

They'd come, as he'd hoped they would. It was so quiet in the house these days, more like a tomb than a home where an old man still had hopes and dreams, and finally had the power to make them happen.

The doorbell rang.

He looked up at his wife's portrait once more. "Your friends are here," he murmured.

And with just the right smile of welcome, he turned to let them in.

HE'D BEEN at Briar Lake for a week now, but Michael still hadn't figured out Lauren McClellan. But, he had to admit, she was damn interesting to watch.

She perched on a kitchen chair, one leg folded beneath her, cradling her coffee mug with both hands. The caftan was emerald this time, a color that accented the pale cream of her skin and made her hazel eyes appear green. With her auburn hair twisted up into some sort of knot on her head, skewered in place by what appeared to be a set of chopsticks, she looked like an elf.

Michael lifted his coffee mug and took a deep swallow. He'd needed a good jolt of caffeine since—"Uh…what *is* this?"

She closed her eyes as she savored a sip from her own mug, then smiled. "I combined raspberry truffle and wild mint. What do you think?"

Michael thought longingly of the giant coffee machines at the convenience store a few miles down the road. Paper cups and two-day-old coffee had sudden appeal. "Very…interesting."

"I thought so, too." She leaned forward, her eyes sparkling. "I've thought of running a quaint little bed-and-breakfast, you know. Someday I'd like to buy an old house and decorate it with antiques. I'd love making pastries and such for the guests."

Michael eyed the half-empty poppy-red casserole dish that sat on the table between them. He'd accepted Lauren's breakfast invitation in the hope that if she got to know him, she'd be more at ease with him. Eating an overwhelming serving of that egg-and-vegetable concoction had been above and beyond the call for a man who never had time for breakfast.

"Thanks," he murmured, setting down his mug. "I should get back outside. Sam plans to start work today and should be here any minute."

"On a Saturday?"

Michael shrugged. "He gave me his estimate late last night and said he was free this morning. The sooner we get started, the better. I need my office ready to go by September first. That gives us ten weeks."

"What are you having done?"

"Sam will divide the space into a reception area, library/conference room and an office. A heating contractor and an electrician will be coming out, as well. And after they're done, the place will need carpeting and wallpaper.''

"That's quite an overhaul." Her brow furrowed.

Michael rose to his feet and looked down at her, his fingers curling in anticipation as he wondered what would happen if he tugged those strange little chopsticks from the bun perched on the top of her head. Would it all stay up there? Cascade to her shoulders?

"The space can be easily converted into a second apartment if I move and Bertie ever wants to rent it out."

From outside came the wheezy sound of an old pickup turning into the drive and the grinding of gears. "Show time," he said lightly. "Thanks again for breakfast."

An hour later Michael leaned against the door frame of his future office and wiped the sweat from his brow with his shirtsleeve. Sam had brought along a surly teenager to help lug Bertie's treasures upstairs to be stored in the building's attic.

Unable to stand by and watch, more than a little concerned about how careful they would be, Michael had pitched in. Finally the downstairs was clear.

"We made good progress," Michael said. "Want some iced tea or a Coke?"

Sam grunted and headed for his truck. "Got my own."

As personalities went, the guy didn't have one, but he worked hard and seemed to know his business. After standing at the open door of his pickup and guzzling something from a thermos, he wiped his mouth with the back of his hand and ambled back to Michael.

"You got some trouble," he announced. "Gonna take more time."

"What?"

"Couldn't see the lower walls when all that junk was still in here. Gotta drywall the whole place."

The perimeter walls looked stained but substantial, until Sam moved forward and nudged a section with his steel-toed boot. A chunk of damp drywall crumbled away.

He tromped across the room. "Maybe some new joists, from the way this floor creaks. Been checked for termites?"

"Within the last year, I think. I'll have to check my aunt's records."

Sam snorted. "Easier just to call an exterminator. There's only one in town. They could look it up."

"Anything else?" Michael asked dryly.

Sam shrugged. "Probably. You sure you want to do this? Tear this building down, and I could put you up a nice steel building in less than a week. See 'em all over the edge of town."

Bertie's beautiful three-story brick home sat fifty feet away. Like a grand society maven who'd hit hard times, it retained its ineffable grandeur, despite the seediness beginning to show in myriad ways. The towering old trees shading the property were older than time. A metal building? "Definitely not."

"Nice colors...or you could get yourself a nice white one. My brother George sells—"

"*No.*"

Sam turned to another wall and poked at it. "Gotta tear all this crap out."

"Fine."

"It'll mean extra days. Add to cost."

"I want it done right. No shortcuts, nothing done halfway. Let me know of any other problems before you go ahead."

With a cursory nod Sam got to work.

Feeling a deep sense of satisfaction, Michael scanned the bare room. Quiet and peaceful, Briar Lake was a beautiful location to begin over. This time, he would be fully responsible for everything that happened.

This time, regrets and that pervasive sense of guilt wouldn't keep him awake at night.

HANNAH CLIMBED to a higher branch of the tree closest to Bertie's house and surveyed the yard below. The heavy curtain of leaves surrounding her made her feel as if she was in a huge tree house. A secret place, where no one would ever find her.

As if anyone really wanted to.

Licking a fingertip, she rubbed her bark-scraped knees. Next time she would wear jeans and bring some books so she could stay up here all day.

Through the lacy network of leaves she saw Michael climb into his car. A pang of loneliness washed through her as she thought about how she and Lisa—her longtime best friend—would have giggled and whispered about him, because he sort of looked like a movie star.

But that was back when her family lived all together. Back when she lived in the same house all the time and had seen Lisa every day.

With a sigh she watched Michael's car pull out of the drive. His car was the size of a go-cart, but Mom said it was worth at least a gazillion dollars and that they should never, ever touch it.

Those words had sent fear slicing through Hannah as memories of Dad and *his* car crowded into her thoughts.

One teensy scratch, made when she was a kindergartner as she took her tricycle out of the garage, and he'd screamed at her until the neighbors started looking out their windows. He was angry all the time and he yelled a lot, but this time he'd hauled her into the garage and spanked her *hard*.

She still remembered every detail, every bit of her fear, as if it had happened yesterday.

Mostly she was glad she hadn't seen him since third grade.

Picking at the bark of the tree, she tried imagining what it would be like to have a *real* dad, like the nice ones on television. Maybe some brothers and sisters, too, so there would always be someone to play with.

Suddenly she heard the sound of kids laughing. Down the road—maybe just a few houses away? The laughter rose to shrieks, followed by a big splash of water. They had a pool!

Sadness welled up inside her, as she looked around her high perch. This tree was okay, but it wasn't much fun without someone to play with. Her T-shirt clung damply to her back. Even in the shade, it was hot and sticky today. Really hot.

A *pool?*

Mom was at the back door calling her name by the time Hannah got back down to the ground. "Honey, have you seen Baxter? He's usually at the door wanting back in as soon as I let him out."

Hannah kicked a toe in the dirt and looked down. "I haven't seen him."

Mom frowned. "Well, can you look for him? But remember to stay on Bertie's land. Maybe he's in the back hunting rabbits."

"Okay," Hannah mumbled.

As soon as her mom went back inside, Hannah ran down the paths leading through the underbrush at the back of the property, and then circled around to the broad sweep of lawn at the front. She found Baxter curled up, sound asleep, under some overgrown lilacs next to the neighbor's fence. When she whispered his name, he didn't even stop snoring.

The sounds of laughter coming from the nearby yard grew louder. Maybe she could just go and take a look. Baxter wasn't going anywhere. Nobody would get hurt if she just looked.

With a glance back at Bertie's house, Hannah started down the bike path edging the road.

Behind a tall fence, kids were playing in the front yard of the second house down. There were two girls and two boys, pretty much her own size, wearing swimsuits and playing tag with water balloons. All of them were dripping wet.

Careful not to step on the colorful flowers planted along the fence, she held on to the bars with both hands and peered through them, her face pressed against the sunwarmed metal. "Hi!"

One of the girls stared at her for a minute, then turned away. "She's just another dumb tourist."

"Maybe she thinks she's at the zoo," chimed the younger one.

The tallest boy spared Hannah a swift glance. "Yeah, but she looks like she oughtta be the one behind the bars." Hooting with laughter, he lobbed the oldest girl a bright blue missile and screamed, "Race you to the pool!"

In a flash of color the kids raced behind the house. The sounds of laughter and splashing water rose from the backyard.

She could imagine the fun they were having. She and Lisa had gone to the public pool near her house a lot. They'd cannonballed into the water, chased each other and collapsed together on the soft grass in a fit of giggles.

The thought of all she was missing made her stomach hurt.

Stepping away from the fence, she looked down at the flowers at her feet. She kicked at one bright red blossom, and then another.

And then she turned for home.

BY FRIDAY, they'd put in four full days of work, and now Michael was trying not to regret his decision to hire Sam. It was   almost noon, and the guy was just arriving for the day, his watery eyes the color of fresh blood.

"Inspector show up?" Sam fumbled with the latch of his toolbox, swore graphically, then banged on the lid with a closed fist.

Michael spoke through clenched teeth. "At 7 a.m.

sharp. Just about the time you were going to be here.''

Squinting at the latch of the toolbox as if trying to solve a great puzzle, Sam gave a noncommittal grunt.

From the doorway came a whisper of movement. Hannah peered inside, her gaze darting away when Michael smiled at her.

Since her one moment of boldness, when she'd persuaded him to rescue the goat last week, she'd reverted to her former self. A tentative shadow, often lurking at the periphery of his vision, then ducking her head and turning away if he called her name.

Slamming his toolbox to the ground, Sam gave it a kick and swore again.

Hannah gasped and pulled back. Her foot caught the wire bail of a bucket. It tipped over with a loud crash, spilling several pounds of nails across the floor.

Sam spun around and shook his fist at her. ''Watch out, dammit!'' he roared.

With a sharp cry she whirled away and disappeared. Seconds later the back door of the house slammed behind her.

A wave of protectiveness and anger surged through Michael on an adrenaline rush. He clenched his fists at his side. ''Pack up your tools, Sam. I'll have a check for you in a few minutes.''

''Huh?''

''You're fired.''

Dull red crept up the man's beefy neck. ''We got a contract.''

''I've already paid for the materials,'' Michael replied coldly. "I'll pay for the work you've done. You can take me to court over the contract."

"I'm being fired because the little princess took off?" He gave Michael a knowing leer. "You and her momma must have a really hot—"

"Shut. Up." Michael enunciated each word, giving him a practiced glare that had made more than one ex-con squirm. "If you want your money now and not next year, get out."

With another oath, Sam grabbed his toolbox and stalked to his pickup. He was behind the wheel and revving the engine by the time Michael came out with the check.

The back door slammed. Both men looked up. Lauren strode across the yard and pulled to a halt next to the pickup.

"Why is my daughter upset?" she demanded, her angry gaze darting from Sam to Michael. "She came out here, and two minutes later she's out on the front steps crying. She won't tell me what happened."

Sam gave a derisive snort. "She didn't hear nothin' she wouldn't have heard—"

Lauren rounded on him, her hands gripping the open window of his truck. "Don't you *ever* frighten my daughter again. Is that clear?"

She looked as though she was ready to launch herself through the open window and rip his throat out with her teeth.

"Uh, Lauren—"

She waved Michael away without turning around. *"Clear?"*

"He's leaving." Michael reached around her to

shove the check through the window and into Sam's hand. "I've given you a little extra so you can go to the landfill with the trash we loaded into the back of your truck."

Michael touched Lauren's shoulder, then slid his arm around her waist to draw her back. Her delicate frame was rock-hard with tension. At first she resisted his touch, then she acquiesced and stepped away from the truck.

Sam peeled out of the drive in a haze of exhaust.

Her shoulders sagged as she watched him disappear down the road. "What an awful man." She sighed, leaning against Michael's side.

She felt so good next to him that he wouldn't have let her go just then, but she suddenly gave him a startled look and moved away, her cheeks pink.

"I…I'm sorry," she whispered. "He upset Hannah, and I just didn't think." She looked at the open door of the carriage house. "There's so much work left to do!"

"You scared off my carpenter," Michael murmured, wanting to lighten her mood…and wishing he still had his arm around her waist.

"Please forgive me. Hannah is…she's been…" Her voice trailed away.

Michael caught the genuine anguish in her eyes. "It's all right. I'd already fired him before you came out."

Relief and gratitude crossed her face. "Because of Hannah?"

"That, and the fact that he was practically embalmed before he got here."

For the past week Michael had seen Lauren at a

distance, no more. If she'd been trying to avoid him, she'd been successful, indeed. Now he found himself wanting to get to know her much better.

She only came up to his shoulders, but she'd been ready to take on a drunk twice her size. Her fire and courage touched him as his ex-fiancée's sophisticated beauty never had, and something in the region of his heart warmed. He wanted to reach out and pull her close for a quick embrace.

And just as quickly he curbed the impulse. *Big mistake, Wells.* Lauren was not the type for a casual affair, and Michael didn't intend to pursue commitment again for a long time to come. If ever. His engagement had been a lesson learned.

At the sound of a car cruising up the circular drive in front of the house, he stepped away from her, distancing himself from the faint lemony scent of her hair and giving himself the space he needed to corral his wayward thoughts. "Expecting anyone?"

She shook her head. "Only if my prayer for a new contractor has already been answered."

Lauren started for the front yard. Michael turned back toward the carriage house.

A woman's horrified shriek stopped him dead in his tracks.

He pivoted and followed Lauren to the front of the house, where a gold Lincoln had parked behind his Jag. An elegantly dressed older woman stood at her open car door, waving an orange chiffon scarf at Daisy.

The goat stood atop the hood of Michael's car like a mountain climber who'd just scaled Mount Everest.

"Bad goat. Bad, bad goat," the woman shouted, waving her scarf faster.

Something brown dangled from the goat's mouth. Her odd yellow eyes and full attention were pinned on the newcomer.

Sizing her up.

"No, Daisy!" Lauren rushed forward and snagged the goat's collar.

Stubbornly bracing her legs as wide as a carpenter's sawhorse, Daisy tilted her head to bring her horn nubbins within battle range. An image of Daisy bashing Lauren in the face flashed through Michael's mind.

"I'll get her," he called out, breaking into a run.

"No, I've got h—"

Daisy jerked backward, then launched forward and leaped off the car like a gazelle, her hooves leaving small dents and deep scratches in the hood. Once on the ground Daisy broke into a disjointed gallop and took off bleating around the corner of the house.

Lauren gave him a stricken look. "I'm so sorry." She glanced at the interior of the convertible, then paled as she took a closer look. She gripped the door with both hands and sagged against the car. "I...I am *so* sorry."

And then she looked up at Michael with raw fear in her eyes.

CHAPTER FOUR

LAUREN'S HEART jammed in her throat, blocking further apologies. She'd promised to take care of the place, the animals and Bertie's affairs for the summer, so this was her responsibility. It was all too easy to imagine Michael's rage over this.

If he chose to sue or press some sort of negligence charges... She closed her eyes. Her blood turned to ice. *Only a couple of months left. Dear God, please don't let this change anything.*

Michael gave the visitor a polite nod, then stood next to Lauren, rested his hands on the door and surveyed the interior of his car. From his whitening knuckles she could well imagine what he was thinking.

The fine leather upholstery was in shreds. The control panel and dash were dented and cracked. If the goat had planned its strategy, it couldn't have done more damage.

Knowing that Michael would surely explode with anger, Lauren steeled herself against the verbal onslaught to come. "Did I say how much Daisy likes leather? Shoes, purses... She likes canvas, too, but not nearly as much—"

"That goat," Michael growled, "has destroyed my car."

"I'm so awfully sorry, believe me. I know I should have had her tied, and I did, but she gets loose somehow no matter what I do and…" Lauren took a deep breath. Hysteria was not a helpful tactic. "I know this was my fault."

The older woman now stood on the other side of the Jag and looked inside. She clucked her tongue. "Bertie and her animals," she said with a shake of her head. "The goat had to be the biggest mistake of all."

Michael looked up at her and offered his hand across the car. "Michael Wells, Bertie's nephew. And this is Lauren McClellan, who is, uh, taking care of the place while Bertie's away."

The woman gave his hand a vigorous shake. "Mildred Walker, a close friend of Bertie's."

Lauren gave the woman a wobbly smile and then turned back to Michael. "I'll pay you for the damages—"

"Relax. We can talk about it later." To Mildred he said, "I'm glad to meet someone who knows my aunt well. Perhaps you can tell me about her behavior over the last year or so. Some of her actions seem…strange."

Mildred's lips twitched. "Strange?"

"When I was a child, she had a dog. Now she has a zoo. And she seems to have taken off for Europe without saying a word to any of her relatives."

With a silvery laugh, Mildred rested one elegant, crimson-tipped hand against the Jag. "Absolutely no one can tell your aunt anything she doesn't want to hear. Not even Oliver…"

"Oliver?" Michael gave her an incredulous look.

"It's not what you think." Mildred's eyes twinkled. "Bertie still talks about your uncle Win as if he were the only man the good Lord ever created." A shadow crossed her face. "She and I are of a circle of friends who've known one another since grade school. The group gets a little smaller as the years pass, but Oliver has been very kind to many of us."

"So Bertie can't be lonely, then. She has her friends. So why the animals?"

"Bertie has to feel *needed.* Last year she started what she termed her 'haven for strays,' but some have proved a bit harder to find homes for than others." Mildred glanced at the ruined leather upholstery. "As you can imagine."

"There's an animal shelter in town."

"Ah, but there's a chance for euthanasia at that place. Bertie feels very strongly about her mission. Much, I might add, to the chagrin of her immediate neighbors."

Michael gave her a wry grin. "I've met Judge Miller."

"Well, I'd best be off," Mildred said briskly. "I promised Bertie I would stop in and offer my help while she was away." She turned toward Lauren. "Is there anything you need, dear?"

A few thousand dollars would be handy right now, Lauren thought. *A couple of plane tickets to somewhere else…* "Everything is fine, thanks."

Michael opened Mildred's car door for her. "Have you heard from her? Does she sound all right?"

"She hasn't called me, but I don't expect her to."

Mildred patted his arm. "Your aunt Bertie is having the time of her life. Don't worry about her."

With a breezy wave, Mildred threw her car into gear, drove around the Jag and headed out of the crescent drive.

Lauren wished she had stayed, because as soon as the Lincoln was out of sight, Michael turned back to survey his car. His smile faded. "First my knee, then my luggage, now my car. I hate to think what that goat will attack next."

Lauren shivered. "I realize this car is worth a fortune."

"It's worth a great deal to me."

"I…I know how every little scratch and ding can be a great aggravation. *Huge* aggravation. I'm so sorry."

Michael gave her a curious look.

"It takes a tremendous investment of time and money to restore such a car," she said.

"I imagine."

"Wh-what?"

"I didn't restore it. I inherited it from my grandfather last year. He hadn't taken it out of storage since 1963."

So until Daisy's attack it had been pristine. Which would surely up the value by thousands of dollars. Lauren stifled a groan. "Why on earth do you drive a car like this? Anything could happen to it!"

"Such as…goats?"

She gave an impatient wave of her hand. "Scratches in a parking lot. Fender benders. Hail damage. Whatever."

"The transmission on my other car blew before I

left to come north. Until driving up here, I'd never driven the Jag farther than a mechanic shop for maintenance."

"Because you don't want to risk your investment."

"Because the blamed thing doesn't have much cargo space. Have you ever tried fitting groceries or a summer's worth of luggage in one of these things?"

Lauren stared at him as some of her misconceptions about him crumbled. She'd assumed he placed tremendous value on the vehicle's macho image and its implication of wealth. Most men would. Rick would certainly have. Her ex's vintage Mustang hadn't been nearly as valuable, but he'd treated it as a favored child, better than he'd treated her and Hannah.

"Let me know what the damage comes to, okay?"

He shook his head.

Lauren tried to keep her voice steady. "Surely you don't think this is worthy of any legal charges."

"Against whom?" He looked at her in surprise. "The goat did this, not you. My own comprehensive should cover what Bertie's homeowner's policy doesn't."

"But it was my fault. Bertie could face higher rates because of this. And your car will be in the shop for ages."

"Can you afford this type of repair bill? I doubt it."

"I mean it. Please—"

"Some of the stitching had broken along the

seams, and a local restoration shop wanted to install a new interior kit. The kit alone was over two grand, and with installation the total would have been double that.''

Lauren gave him a weak smile. "Looks like the stitching problem just got a bit worse."

"I'll talk to my insurance agent, and you just keep that blasted goat confined. Fair?" He ruffled through the ruined shreds of leather beneath his fingertips, a thoughtful expression on his face. "On the other hand, you did run off my carpenter."

"You said he'd already been fired!"

"And you won't let me stay in my own aunt's house."

"You said you were very comfortable in the apartment!"

"Where I'm surrounded by enough lace and frippery to choke a horse. Not, of course, that I'm complaining."

Lauren fell silent.

"I've just thought of a way for you to ease your conscience over this situation."

At his slow smile she stiffened.

"How many hours a day does it take to keep this place up—the animals, the house and so on?"

"A couple hours on the animals, maybe three or four hours total. Why?"

"My contractor is gone, and I have no other options right now. It can't be too hard to do some of this work on my own. Help me a few hours every day for a few weeks, and we'll call it square." He offered her his hand. "Deal?"

She hesitated for only a second, then shook his

hand with a profound sense of relief. A shimmer of awareness rocketed through her nerve endings at the touch of his hand. "D-deal."

"Good! Go get Hannah and tell her we're all going to town. In *your* car."

On her way to find Hannah she realized what she'd just done. After what Rick had put her through, it hadn't been difficult to ignore men who made advances toward her, but there was something about Michael Wells that made her pulse kick into high and her senses heighten. *Work with him every day?* She'd been trying to keep her distance, and this would be sheer disaster.

She turned back to him in desperation. "I've never done any construction. I'll just be in your way. This probably isn't a good idea. Maybe we can advertise for someone—"

Michael held up a hand and gave her a killer grin. "Look at the guy I just fired. He was a drunk with an IQ of five. How hard can it be?"

"ARE YOU SURE you want to tackle this yourself?" The snowy-haired clerk with "Joe" embroidered on the pocket of his denim shirt glanced from Michael to Lauren, then back again. Portly and not much taller than Lauren, he looked like a disapproving Santa Claus. "These supplies are expensive, and you can't return what's been opened."

"We'll be fine." Michael drummed his fingernails on the counter by the cash register, then grinned. "Unless you'd like to volunteer."

Clucking his tongue, the clerk rounded the end of the counter and pawed through the remodeling books and magazines stuffed haphazardly into the wire display rack across the aisle. He collected two, hesitated, then added another one.

"There's a county inspector," he announced darkly, dropping the stack onto the counter in front of Michael. "You need a permit."

"We have one."

"You need the plumbing and electrical inspected before the walls are finished."

"Right."

"Ask him if he knows of any good handymen who could be available," Lauren whispered.

"Some good men up there on the board," the clerk offered, tilting his head toward a bulletin board festooned with business cards, flyers and notices at least three deep. "Can't say as you'll get anyone, though. The good ones are booked way ahead. My advice? Call someone and wait. Or at least try to find some college kid with a little experience."

Michael shook his head. "I need this project done in the next couple months. We'll manage."

"Call now for air and heating bids."

"I called several companies last week." Michael appeared to think a minute. "Anything else?"

Tuning out their conversation, Lauren glanced over to the front door, where Hannah still sat curled up in a lawn chair with her latest volume of R. L. Stein's. She shifted her gaze back to the books on the counter. *Home Remodeling. Carpentry for the Novice Builder. Adding to Your Home or Office.* Easily seven or eight hundred pages of information about which she knew absolutely nothing.

She'd been to lumberyards for nails, shelving

planks, the occasional can of paint. She'd never tried to decipher the sizes and shapes of screws and bolts and washers, or decide what kind, width, length and grade of lumber to buy. She'd bet Michael hadn't, either.

But armed with the list of supplies from Sam's estimate, he had plied the clerk with a thousand questions, then ordered everything on the list and more, adding to the supplies that had already been delivered. Somewhere along the line, the clerk's doubt turned to enthusiasm, no doubt a direct result of the large sale he was making.

Michael retrieved his billfold from a back pocket and flipped a Visa card onto the counter. "None of this can be rocket science, right?"

Santa laughed aloud. "We'll see." As he awaited the credit-card approval, he studied Michael over the rims of his reading glasses. "Bertie's place is on my way home. If you have questions, call and I'll stop by."

"Thanks. I'm sure we will." Michael signed the charge slip, pocketed his wallet and arranged for delivery, then accepted the other man's handshake. "I appreciate your advice."

He stood there, tall and dark, his navy polo shirt stretched across his broad shoulders and tucked into khaki slacks that emphasized his narrow hips and long, long legs. But it wasn't his physical attributes that drew her.

It was the fact that he'd handled the damage to his car with such good grace, even a touch of wry humor. He was proving to be an appealing mix of superhero and mild-mannered reporter, she mused.

Quiet and strong and... well, handsome as sin. Though that didn't matter a bit.

"Meditating?" he asked, his eyes twinkling.

Startled, she looked up at him. She hadn't realized that his transaction was complete and that he was waiting for her.

He flashed a smile at her that nearly welded her feet to the floor.

So you aren't immune, either, she thought as she headed for the door. But mutual interest or not, the last thing she needed right now was a lawyer who might become curious about her past.

FEEDING AND CLEANING UP after five cats, four canaries, six parakeets, two cockatiels, a dog, a goat, an iguana, assorted furry rodents and a red-toed frog took almost two hours if Hannah helped.

Without her help, it generally took half an hour less. But seeing her increasing interaction with the animals, seeing her growing enjoyment, made every moment worthwhile. *She deserves this, after what we've been through.*

Today—the first day of her agreement with Michael—Lauren wasn't in any particular hurry to finish her usual chores.

"Pretty lady," Hannah cooed at the two cockatiels housed in a large birdcage.

Raising their crest feathers high, the birds cocked their heads. "Here, doggie doggie!" announced the gray one. "Cuckoo! Cuckoo!"

The white one marched sideways on its perch. "Brrrrrrrrr. Ding! Ding! Ding!"

Hannah giggled.

"I prefer microwave and cuckoo clock sounds only at the necessary times," Lauren commented wryly, using a wire twist tie to secure the top of a plastic bag filled with soiled cage papers. "No wonder these birds ended up homeless."

Hannah unlatched the cage door and offered the gray her index finger. The bird obediently hopped aboard and then marched up her arm to sit on her left shoulder. Its cagemate followed suit, only to be met with a barrage of flapping wings and squawks. With a little nudge, Hannah guided the second bird to her other shoulder.

Its beak next to her ear, the gray launched another volley of earsplitting cuckoo-clock chimes and then fluffed out its feathers in apparent pride over its recital.

"I wish I could keep you two," Hannah said wistfully, reaching up to scratch the white one behind its crest. In apparent rapture, the bird twisted its head around to offer better access. "I'm gonna miss it up here."

"We both knew this would be just for the summer, honey." Lauren started filling the food cups in the cages with multicolored pellets, a different kind for each type of bird.

"I don't see why we can't stay."

Left unsaid was how dreary their cramped apartment was, how noisy with highway traffic roaring past night and day. Even *that* place was barely affordable, given the moderate amount of money Lauren made at her assortment of part-time jobs. Luckily she'd been able to sublet the place over the summer to an old friend.

In a few months we can start over, an inner voice whispered. *A new job at a school somewhere, a new life.*

Lauren reached out to give Hannah a hug, needing one just as much as her daughter. Both cockatiels shrieked and raised their wings at her approach.

"See, they don't want you to take me away. They're defending me!"

"They're defending their own personal tree," Lauren teased. Guilt nibbled at her every time she saw her daughter's delight at the menagerie.

"Can't we move somewhere close enough so we could visit?"

"We'll see," Lauren hedged, parceling out the last serving of bird pellets. She started removing water bottles for rinsing and refilling, debating over whether to try discussing the past. "If there's ever anything you want to talk over, honey, I'll always be glad to listen. You know that, don't you?"

Hannah turned away, the birds still on her shoulders, and moved to the window. She said nothing.

"It's been a year and a half since the trial, and I know it's been a tough time for you. You've been very brave about it. But...sometimes it feels better to talk things over instead of holding them inside."

Hannah stared silently out at the trees, as if she hadn't heard a word.

"Your father made a mistake, and that's been hard for both of us to understand. But that doesn't mean he's a bad person." Hannah's shoulders stiffened and Lauren added gently, "I do know how you feel."

"No, you don't." Hannah's voice rose with each word. "You don't even care!"

"Talk to me, then. Tell me." Lauren moved forward, wanting to comfort her, but Hannah stepped back, stumbled over a throw rug. The birds squawked and flapped their wings in alarm. "Honey—"

"You don't know anything!" Hannah cried. Choking back a sob, she put the birds back in their cage, then spun away toward the door. Her voice was now a shriek. "Just leave me alone! You never understand!"

Her heart breaking, Lauren watched her leave. Wanting to follow, to make things right, just as she had when Hannah had been little and had come to her with skinned knees and invisible "owies." A kiss and a bandage had always provided a cure in those days.

There wasn't a bandage for this kind of pain. There were no words. She'd used her mothering instincts. Her skills as an experienced teacher. Several counselors had tried to reach Hannah, as well. But these wounds were soul-deep and were going to take time to heal.

From experience Lauren knew Hannah would calm down if left alone. And when she did, that aching silence over the past would continue. Untouchable. Festering. Hidden by a mask of sullen cooperation.

With a deep sigh Lauren turned to the large aquarium along the wall where Albert the iguana resided. A good two feet long and heavily scarred from an apparent attack by someone's cat or dog, he reminded her of a boxer after a few bad rounds.

"It's just you and me, Al," she muttered. "What'll it be today for your first course? Fresh fruit? Veggies?"

He lifted his head and fixed her with an unblinking stare.

"Fruit, you say? Good choice."

When he eagerly clambered over his rock to reach his dish of diced fruit, she gave the creature a sad smile.

What did it say about a mother who apparently communicated better with an iguana than she did with her own daughter?

BY LATE MORNING all the animals and birds had been fed, the various cages cleaned, the houseplants watered, the main-floor carpets vacuumed and the current household bills paid out of Bertie's account.

She had no more excuses. With a sigh she started for the back door. She caught herself fluffing at her hair in the mirror hanging in the back entry hall.

"No way," she muttered, jamming a Twins ball cap on her head. Attractive or not, a man like Michael was not in her future. The trouble he could cause…

She strode the short distance to the carriage house and paused at the open door. Michael was on the other side of the room, tearing out the last of the damaged drywall. Despite her earlier resolutions, she found herself studying him appreciatively.

He wore only a pair of faded jeans that hugged him like the firm skin of a peach, outlining his muscular calves, the long powerful curve of his thighs…and one very, very nice rear. Above narrow hips and waist flared the heavily corded muscle of his upper torso, flesh that rippled and gleamed as he worked.

Feeling like a voyeur, she lingered silently at the doorway. Even if she planned to keep her distance, a woman could definitely enjoy watching such a fine example of prime masculinity at work.

He apparently sensed her presence, because he turned around a second later and gave her a lazy smile. "Ready to work?"

The breadth and power of his chest stole her breath. The lock of disheveled hair, curving over his brow, nearly stole her heart. Where before he had been urbane, polished and coolly unapproachable, now he radiated a level of raw virility that she'd never suspected.

Or maybe it's just that you've been cleaning animal cages for the better part of the day, and anyone would look good, Lauren told herself sharply. *Maybe you need glasses.*

He was smiling at her, she realized dimly. A thirty-two-year-old woman, and she'd been staring at him like an awe-struck teenager. An unfamiliar heat rose in her cheeks. "What should I do?"

His smile widened just a fraction.

"If you don't need help, I've got other things to do in the house." She spoke more sharply than she'd intended, and he had the audacity to chuckle—a deep rumble that sent vibrations clear down to her toes.

"We have a deal. Get a pair of gloves off the box

over there and help me pitch this stuff out the front door. Next we have to tear out the old insulation.''

Most of the drywall was in manageable pieces. For the insulation, they both slipped on masks, gloves and long-sleeved jackets, gathering up armloads of the dusty yellow clouds to haul outside.

By midafternoon she was exhausted. ''With luck the electrician will arrive on time to put in the outlet and the phone jacks,'' Michael said, bracing one hand high on the wall as he surveyed their progress.

''We can't do anything until he does?''

''Don't sound quite so hopeful. I can't believe you aren't having the time of your life out here.''

''Oh, yeah.'' Lauren wiped a trickle of sweat from the back of her neck and blew at the bangs hanging into her eyes. ''At this point I'd probably sell my grandma for a good hot shower.''

He slid her a look of amusement. ''Working out here is that bad?''

''No… You needed the help and I owe you the favor,'' she admitted. ''But if that goat causes any more trouble, I swear that either she goes to some farm or I'm heading back to Minneapolis.''

He laughed, and something sparked between them as their eyes met across the room. ''Tell me about yourself, Lauren McClellan.'' His voice was lower now, darker and more compelling.

She sensed masculine interest, not an interrogation, but still, a touch of uneasiness slithered through her. ''What's there to tell? Um…I'm a mom. Hannah is the best thing in my life. We live in Minneapolis, I work—''

''What about Hannah's dad?''

Now there was a subject to avoid. "Divorced. End of story."

"Hannah mentioned him while we were retrieving Daisy from Miller's yard. Does she get to see him much?"

"What are you—a trial lawyer?" Lauren asked lightly. "No, we haven't seen her dad in a long time. He's moved a few times and I don't even know his address any longer. Needless to say, he's not the responsible type."

"He doesn't support his daughter?"

"Not emotionally, physically or financially. He's totally out of the picture, and that's been devastating to her. She feels…discarded."

Michael swore under his breath. "She doesn't deserve that."

Lauren lifted a brow at the anger in his voice. He would be one who met every responsibility, she guessed, no matter what. "No. He hurt her terribly, and I'll never forgive him for that. But even though she doesn't realize it, sometimes it's better when one loses touch. Rick wasn't always a very nice guy. Now, tell me about yourself. Married? Six kids and a Saint Bernard hidden away in Chicago?"

The steady look he returned suggested that he wasn't finished with the topic of Hannah's father, but one corner of his mouth tipped upward. "No wife, no kids, definitely no Saint Bernard. I was engaged for quite a while, but that ended this spring."

"I'm sorry."

"Don't be." The corner of his mouth quirked a little higher. "I don't think either of *us* was—which shows you just how shallow some people are. Some people are meant for emotional commitments, some aren't.''

''And you don't think you are?'' Giving him an incredulous look, Lauren thought about his gentle treatment of Hannah, his concern for Bertie's welfare. ''If that's the case, you aren't as smart as I thought.''

''After a two-year engagement there ought to be more than just a vague sense of relief,'' he said with a wry smile.

''Then you wasted those years on the wrong person.''

''Until…a few surprises at the end of the relationship, she was all anyone could ask for.'' He pushed away from the wall, then glanced at his watch. ''You can go on up to the house if you'd like. Thanks for the help.''

He snagged a can of soda from a cooler in the center of the room and tossed it to her, then grabbed another, cracked it open and drank deeply, the can held high and his head tilted back.

Lauren watched, mesmerized. Then turned away. With a fast farewell and wave of her hand, she slipped out into the late-afternoon sunshine and escaped to the safety of the house.

The more time she spent with him, the more he fascinated her, and she sensed his interest in her had grown, as well. But she had no place in her life for foolish fantasies, and most definitely had no desire to pursue them.

CHAPTER FIVE

ON MONDAY MORNING Lauren waited until Michael was busy outside, then grabbed her purse and keys, and slipped out the front door to her car, where Hannah was already waiting for her.

Lauren had been at Briar Lake for more than three weeks now. With every passing day she'd dreaded this appointment more.

Hannah slouched down in her seat. "Why do I have to come with you? I'd rather stay home."

"I can't leave you alone, you know that. I just have a quick meeting and then we'll be done."

"Michael's here. I could stay with him," Hannah whined.

But then he'd ask where I'm going. "I promise this won't take long."

With a groan Hannah slumped farther down in her seat. "Bor-ing."

It's not something I look forward to, either. At the end of the drive Lauren looked over her shoulder. She felt a wave of relief as she pulled out onto the highway and headed for town.

She'd caught a glimpse of Michael walking through the trees, heading for the house. He'd given her car a curious look, but he hadn't tried to flag her down. Thank goodness. This was one destination she had to reach on her own. What would he think of her if he knew the truth about her past?

Glancing occasionally in the rearview mirror, she drove downtown to the two-story brick building next to the courthouse and parked in back. The building housed lawyers, county offices and even a deli on the main floor. To a passerby she could be going in for a ham-on-rye or a dog license, but she still felt uncomfortable.

Deferred sentence or not, just the thought of the past made her feel dirty and cheap. How many people back home had believed her innocent? Most of them probably figured she'd gotten off easy, in light of the eight grand Rick had embezzled from the playground fund. They weren't likely ever to forget that he'd deprived children of a safe place to play.

"Come on, honey. This won't take long." Lauren slipped out of the car and stood waiting.

Hannah sighed heavily. "I want to stay in the car."

"You know that isn't safe."

"But—"

"*Now*, Hannah."

Hannah gave in—though at a snail's pace—and followed her into a cramped office on the third floor. They'd been seated in the waiting room for just a few minutes when a short, stocky blond woman in a rumpled gray suit appeared at the inner doorway and beckoned. "You can come in, Mrs. McClellan."

Her heart heavy, Lauren managed a bright smile and kissed Hannah's forehead. "I'll be right inside the next door, honey," she murmured. "You'll be fine. I'll ask the secretary over there to keep an eye on you, okay?''

Her eyes downcast, Hannah nodded. She opened her book and started reading, but Lauren wasn't fooled. She knew Hannah sensed her mother's tension.

Back in Minneapolis, there had been baby-sitters or friends to watch Hannah during these meetings. Here in Briar Lake there wasn't anyone. Lauren rose and motioned to the secretary, who nodded with understanding.

This whole deal was so hard. So very, very hard—all the more because it was so incredibly unfair. Old anger and hurt rose in her throat, threatening to steal her breath.

Never in her life had she wanted to do harm to another human being, but when she allowed herself to think about Rick's lies, her blood raged through her until she felt she'd explode. How could he have done this to her?

Lauren followed the woman down the hallway and into a small cluttered office with "Kay Solomon, Probation Officer" emblazoned on the door. When the woman continued into the room and took a seat behind the desk, Lauren looked at her in surprise, having expected a man. "This is your office?"

At close range the blonde was older than she'd appeared. Early fifties, maybe, with a weary look in her eyes. "I hope you don't have a problem with it, because I'm the only act in town."

"I...I meant no offense, Ms. Solomon." Now she'd insulted the woman who could help her make it through the next couple of months or make her life hell. "You were out of the office when I first came to town, and a guy was in here."

- "Bill covers for me when I can't be here." She settled a pair of reading glasses on her nose and shuffled through a stack of manila files on her desk. Opening one, she peered over it and gave Lauren a long look, then dropped her gaze to the papers inside.

After several minutes she looked up again, her mouth settled in a thin line. "I see that you received a deferred judgment, while your husband served 13 months of a three-to-five for embezzlement and got out in March. Looking forward to getting back together?" The tone of her voice suggested that Lauren's sentencing had been a very good deal, indeed.

Lauren rubbed her damp palms against her denim skirt and fought the tension that swirled through her insides like choppy seas. "*Ex*-husband. He took off for California after his release, and I haven't heard a word from him." She leaned forward in her seat. "We were in the process of a divorce when Rick embezzled that money. I had nothing to do with—"

"My job isn't to retry your case. I just make sure you comply with the terms of your probation." There was no warmth in her eyes. "If you don't, you'll be back in court."

Lauren slumped in her chair and closed her eyes. Until Rick had implicated her in his schemes, this world of probation officers, supervision and the threat of incarceration had been the stuff of television shows, never her reality.

"I did almost twice the required community service back in Minneapolis," Lauren said quietly.

"You probably won't believe me, but I didn't know about the money Rick embezzled until an officer appeared at my door. I cleaned out my own bank accounts and sold my new car to make restitution on half of the amount."

Ms. Solomon's flat look suggested she'd heard excuses and alibis from every person who walked through her door. She flicked the edge of the file with a forefinger. "I understand you are taking care of the Wells place for the summer. Do you have another job lined up for the fall?"

"Not yet. Even fast-food places ask for a criminal check," Lauren said bitterly. "Still, we're able to stay at Bertie's place for the summer, and she's paying me three hundred dollars a month, plus expenses. One of the reasons I agreed to come up here was so my daughter wouldn't have to be in day care all summer. She's had a hard time dealing with what her father did. It got much worse when he never came to see her after he was released in March."

"Your goals once you're off probation?"

Lauren fought to keep her voice steady. "My teaching certificate was suspended because of all this. Rick's lies stole my freedom. My reputation. My career." She found herself standing, her hands braced on the desk in front of her. "But worse, he robbed his own daughter of the security of a nice home in a decent neighborhood. The money to afford nice clothes, all the dance and swimming lessons young girls enjoy."

"Sit *down,* Ms. McClellan."

Lauren slowly sank back into her chair. Inside her

chest, her trembling heart felt as if it had forgotten how to beat.

With a sigh the officer flipped open the file again. "Again, what are your plans after you are released from probation?"

"I…I hope to regain my teaching certificate. I've been fully compliant with everything required of me, so the deferred charges should be dismissed. I hope to find a school board willing to hire me."

"References?"

Lauren managed a small smile. "I had a two-year contract in a good school district and hoped for a five-year contract after that. The students and parents liked me. I got along well with the staff."

"Could you go back?"

Her smile faded. "There can be thirty, forty applicants for teaching positions, even in the small towns. My record will be cleared, but the community is aware of what happened, and that history would be a tremendous barrier. The opinion of the community is a powerful force in education."

"So where will you go?"

"Anyplace I can find a teaching job and support my daughter. Someplace where they haven't heard of me."

"Even when your record is cleared, that incident is going to come up. References, word-of-mouth, whatever," the older woman said gently. "There's a theory that says we're all within six degrees of knowing just about everyone. Someone knows someone else, who has a cousin in a town nearby, whatever. It never seems to be more true than when secrets are involved."

"It's so unfair! I may never escape my past, and I did nothing wrong."

At a tap on the door both women looked up. The secretary cracked the door open and peeked inside. "There's a young lady out here who's worried about her mom. Should I bring her in?"

"No!" Lauren gave the probation officer a beseeching look. "Please. I haven't explained any of this to her because she'll worry about losing me, too. She thinks all this is in the past."

"Tell her that her mom will be out in a few seconds."

With a nod the secretary quietly shut the door.

"Thank you, ma'am." Lauren felt tears well in her eyes. "My daughter is my life. I wouldn't do anything to hurt her."

The older woman stood. "Everything is in order here. I want to see you in a week, and after that we'll probably make it once a month. You can talk to the secretary about the appointment times." She hesitated, then offered her hand. "Don't worry. I think things will work out just fine."

As she accepted the handshake, Lauren allowed herself to believe for just a moment that Kay Solomon was right.

As she waited in line at the bank a few minutes later, Lauren considered Kay's words. She could only guess what Michael—a lawyer—would think if he knew about her past. He'd seemed so suspicious of her at the start, anyway, and if he knew she and her husband had been charged with embezzlement, he might jump on some inadvertent mistake she'd made in handling Bertie's deposits and have her thrown straight in jail.

And if that happened, Hannah—God help her—might end up in her father's custody. The very thought made Lauren's blood run cold.

Shoving a hand nervously through her hair, Lauren glanced over at Hannah, who had curled up with her book in an upholstered chair nearby. *I'm going to keep you safe, sweetheart.*

When Lauren made it to the front of the line, she handed the teller the deposit slip and the checks that had arrived for Bertie, then grabbed them back and read through them one more time. "Can you re-check my figures?"

The young teller, who had helped her a number of times before, gave her an odd look. "I always do. It's my job."

She went through the dividend checks, pausing at the last few. "Wow. Arizona, New York and California. This is way cool. I've never been to any of these places, you know?"

"Polly!" An older clerk in the next cubicle gave her a stern look over the partition.

Rolling her eyes, Polly slid the receipt back to Lauren. "Exactly right, like last time and the time before."

And I just hope and pray it stays that way. Lauren smiled back at her, then stuffed the receipt into her purse as she turned to go. One more day of June, then just two months to go. Surely she could keep everything in good order for that long.

Directly in her path stood a tall muscular man, his

arms folded across his chest and a grim look on his very familiar face.

"You left in a rush," Michael said softly, not moving out of her way. He shifted his gaze to Polly, who was watching with openmouthed curiosity, then lowered his voice. "What have you been up to?"

Speechless, Lauren stared up at him. *Had he followed her to that appointment with Kay Solomon?* Panic rushed through her in a torrent of memories. The night she'd been arrested. The humiliation of her arraignment. The public embarrassment of her trial.

Beyond that was a tidal wave of pure fear that rushed through her as she looked over at her daughter, who was sitting quietly in a chair by the wall reading her book.

"Not here, not now." Lauren lifted her gaze and silently begged him to not make a scene.

He stared down at her, his eyes cold as ice, a muscle flicking along his jaw. "Tonight."

LAUREN HAD BEEN edgy all afternoon—he'd noticed her hands shaking during supper and the distracted answers she'd given Hannah. Good. He'd seen her with that stack of checks at the bank and had heard the clerk marvel at the variety of locations they came from. Bertie had widespread investments— he'd advised her on most of them. What was Lauren doing with Bertie's finances?

It was getting harder and harder to imagine her capable of any wrongdoing, but he needed to follow his head, not his heart.

After supper Lauren and Hannah did the animal

chores, then they curled up together on the sofa and watched one of Hannah's television shows. Bath time and bedtime seemed to be an interminable process. Finally, at ten o'clock Lauren came downstairs and walked into the kitchen, where he was waiting for her at the table.

"You wanted to talk," she said flatly.

"What errands did you run today?"

She dropped her gaze to the floor, then reached up to smooth her hair back and lifted her chin. "Why?"

"Because you're living here and managing my aunt's affairs." Michael winced at his own irritable tone. *Good job, Wells.* He'd planned to skillfully elicit information from her, not have her running for cover in two minutes.

She pulled out a kitchen chair and sat down across from him, eyeing him warily. "What do you want to know?"

"Perhaps you could tell me about the banking you were doing today."

"Banking? You want to question me about Bertie's banking?" Her tense expression relaxed, and a flicker of relief danced in her eyes.

She's relieved? It didn't make sense. He scowled back at her. "My aunt isn't always…careful with her financial concerns."

"I'm not doing anything complex. The bills come, I pay them. When her dividend checks or other monies come in, I deposit them at the bank."

"But she's not here to sign for anything."

Lauren shrugged. "She introduced me to the bank

manager, and then she and I filled out some sort of signature form at the bank.''

''What?'' An image of that stack of checks in Lauren's hand blazed through his thoughts. Followed by much older memories of his father's erratic visits, and the money for another ''great investment'' that he always managed to wheedle from Michael's mother. Temptation could take many forms.

''Talk to your aunt next time she calls.'' Lauren gave another nonchalant lift of her shoulder and stood. ''If she wants you to take over, that's fine with me. I'm heading upstairs.''

He watched her leave, his thoughts reeling. What had Bertie been thinking? She should have known better. After all, she'd fallen prey to con artists and people with hard luck stories who had run off with a good share of her money. And now she'd handed over complete control of her assets to someone who wasn't even a relative.

Despite his earlier doubts, he'd come to see Lauren as a responsible dependable person—a person he was starting to care for very much. But he'd dealt with the dark side of the human soul throughout his career and knew temptation could lure the most unlikely people. He'd seen it repeatedly in his clients.

He'd seen it in his own father.

From now on, he would definitely be keeping a closer eye on Lauren McClellan.

AT THE SOUND of footsteps Michael looked up from *Carpentry for the Novice Builder* to see Lauren and her daughter walking up the lane. Lauren's auburn hair glinted in the late-morning sunlight, as if strewn with sequins.

Settling back in the lawn chair, he took a swallow of frosty iced tea as he tried to envision Gloria sauntering through the quiet streets of Briar Lake. He couldn't. Cool and aloof, wearing a severely tailored black suit with her champagne-blond hair twisted into a tight knot, she'd once presented a commanding sophisticated presence both in and out of the courtroom.

It was hard imagining her untwisting that hair and taking off the power suit for the balding senior partner she'd snagged weeks after giving back Michael's engagement ring. But now she had exactly what she'd always wanted—money, prestige and a lifetime membership to the most exclusive country club in Chicago.

He knew he should feel regret and emptiness, but he felt only a subtle sense of relief. It was unnerving to know that he'd proved just as shallow as she had. What kind of guy reached the end of a two-year engagement and didn't even care? A guy who didn't have the genetics for love and commitment, if such things even existed anymore.

But Lauren...now there was someone with fire in her blood. Michael chuckled, remembering her anger at Sam. Her panic over Daisy's propensity for trouble. Her initial determination to prevent him from setting so much as a foot on Bertie's property.

She'd said almost nothing about her past, and Michael now found himself wondering about her background. Had she been happy? Why had her husband left her, and why didn't the jerk pay child support?

Michael tossed the book aside and went to the back door of the house. He knocked twice, then let himself in.

He found them in the kitchen, slathering butter on unevenly sliced chunks of bread. An automatic bread-maker sat on the counter, its lid open and the aroma of fresh bread filling the air.

Lauren nodded in greeting, her expression cool. No surprise, given that he'd questioned her integrity last night. She'd had plenty of time to think about the meaning behind his words.

"Lunch?" He gave Hannah a hopeful smile.

She ignored him.

"We're having peanut-butter-and-banana sandwiches, Hannah's favorite," Lauren said. "Want one?"

He tried to imagine the combination and couldn't, but at least she was speaking to him. "Uh…sure."

She continued slathering peanut butter onto the slices of bread lying on a plate in front of her. After a moment her expression softened. "I'll bet you'd rather have the new smoked deli ham and Swiss cheese in the fridge. We splurged on our way home," she added, with a self-conscious lift of a shoulder.

"What you're having is fine." He tried to remember when he'd last had peanut butter. Camping, maybe. Up in the Boundary Waters during college. "Afterward, maybe I can treat you two to ice cream downtown?"

Hannah still didn't respond.

"And here I thought you might be the kind of girl who would just love going to Taylor's," he said, giving her an incredulous look. "Guess I was wrong."

Her head bobbed up and the mask of reserve slipped just a notch. "Taylor's?"

"If we can use your mom's car."

"Mom?" Hannah gave her mother a pleading look.

Lauren handed him the sandwich she'd made, then started making another. "You aren't working on the carriage house today?"

Michael took a bite, then suddenly found himself unable to answer clearly. "Got milk?" he managed.

A corner of Lauren's mouth lifted as she poured him a glass of milk from the gallon jug on the counter.

"I had some business to take care of this morning, but I hope to get in a few hours this afternoon. Are you free?"

"Feed us at Taylor's and we'll follow you anywhere." After a split-second pause a faint blush rose in her cheeks. "Well, not really. But yes…we'd love to go."

Michael found himself feeling completely charmed by her awkward embarrassment over so little.

In the light of day his concerns over Bertie's banking chores seemed illogical. No one who wore her heart on her sleeve like Lauren McClellan could be capable of trying to fleece an elderly lady, who'd been like a grandmother to her.

"Look," he began. "About last night…"

"It's all right." Lauren shifted her gaze to Hannah, then back to meet his, gently warning him to say no more. "I understand your concerns completely." She smiled at him. "Let's get done here so we can make that trip to Taylor's, okay?"

After wolfing down his own sandwich and half of Hannah's, he helped them straighten up the kitchen, then they all went out to Lauren's old Escort and headed for town.

There was a parking spot right in front of Taylor's. Hannah hadn't said a word on the way there, but she was out of the car and inside the building before Michael had his seat belt unbuckled.

"I can tell she doesn't care for this place at all," he said wryly, taking the key out of the ignition. "I haven't seen her show that much enthusiasm for anything since I arrived."

"Her moods come and go. But you're right, she does love Taylor's."

Michael's elbow brushed Lauren's, and she drew in a sharp breath. They both stilled. "Sorry," he said quietly.

She waved off his apology without looking at him, then concentrated on releasing her seat belt, her movements jerky. With a final tug the belt gave way.

Watching her, he found himself imagining how it might feel to sift his fingers through her glorious hair or to touch the soft warm nape of her neck. "I regret being so blunt last night."

"What?" Her gaze flew to his.

Her wonderfully changeable hazel eyes looked more green today, the gold flecks sparkling like sunlight dancing across Briar Lake. He struggled to find his last train of thought.

"I'm protective of the women in my life—perhaps too much, at times.'' He gave a self-deprecating laugh. ''Or so they tell me.''

''*All* your women?'' she said dryly, raising a brow.

''My mother. Bertie. My sister.''

''Sounds like quite a challenge.'' Giving him a breezy smile, she opened her door and started to launch herself out of the car.

He caught her wrist and gently pulled her back, not quite knowing why he did.

But though his mind was running in slow motion, his body knew exactly what to do with the woman just a heartbeat away.

He found himself stroking the wrist he'd just caught. Slowly, feeling a sense of pure male satisfaction at the pulse leaping beneath his fingertips.

There wasn't much room with the blasted steering wheel in the way.

It was broad daylight.

Pedestrians were passing by just inches in front of the car's bumper. None of that mattered. He slid a hand up beneath that wild hair and cupped the back of her head, then drew her close for a quick hard kiss.

Nothing long and lingering, no savoring of her soft skin beneath his hands. He instinctively knew that this was all he could have, yet he couldn't have stopped himself if the earth had exploded beneath his feet.

At first she melted into the kiss. Then she drew back, her eyes wide, her hand fumbling for the door handle. ''I-I'm sorry. This isn't possible.''

In a flash she slipped out of the car and disappeared into Taylor's.

The kiss had been a reckless, undeniable impulse. But he'd just found out something he wouldn't have guessed about Lauren McClellan. She might profess a lack of interest, but he now knew otherwise.

Because she had kissed him back.

TAYLOR'S WAS the quintessential ice-cream parlor of days gone by, with a long soda-fountain counter and wrought-iron tables set out front. It took a good ten minutes of waiting in line to order their sundaes— and Lauren didn't look at him once. High color stained her cheekbones, though whether from anger or embarrassment he couldn't tell.

Out on the sidewalk they found an empty table under the dense shade of a Norway maple.

Lauren watched Hannah as the girl wolfed down her chocolate-and-almond sundae. Michael was touched to see how pleased Lauren was at her daughter's enjoyment. He recalled Lauren mentioning how much Hannah had been hurt by her father's absence. Obviously these moments of happiness were few and far between.

But now Michael knew how to make them *both* happy. Ice cream.

"You sure are adventuresome," Lauren murmured, eyeing Michael's dish of vanilla. Her own dish held mint chocolate-chip ice cream and marshmallow-crème topping with enough mixed nuts to simulate a rock slide.

"Nostalgic. I used to come here when I was a

kid, and I've never found another place that could rival Taylor's for vanilla."

Her expression warmed and a glimmer of a dimple appeared in one cheek. "Somehow, I can't see you pursuing a very lengthy quest."

"Most of my adult life, in every major city."

Hannah savored another spoonful of her own, then looked hopefully at her mom's dish. "Can I?"

Lauren slid the dish across the table. "Only if I can try yours."

They both looked at Michael's dish, which looked singularly bland, then simultaneously shook their heads and spoke at once. "Nahhh."

They burst into laughter at their perfect timing. Michael stared at the transformation in Hannah. She really was a beautiful child, when she allowed herself to smile.

After taking a small taste of Hannah's sundae, Lauren nodded her approval and set down her spoon. "So why didn't you come back here years ago, Michael? To live, I mean. Beautiful little town, great ice cream—what else is there?"

Michael thought back over his career—the twelve-hour days and the weekends spent at the office, the missed dinners. The days, weeks and months that had sped by. "Maybe I should have," he mused.

"Did you have a solo practice in Chicago?"

"A good-size firm. Twenty partners and around sixty associates."

That seemed to catch Hannah's attention. "Did you meet lots of bad guys?"

Thinking of the heavy, almost funereal luxury of

those offices back in Chicago, with their dense carpets, teak woodwork, and tasteful oils on the walls, Michael had to smile. "Corporate accounts, mostly. No one wearing biker shirts and tattoos. No guns. We didn't handle criminal law."

Hannah's face fell.

Michael chuckled. "You're right—it wasn't very exciting." He thought for a moment, wanting to see her smile again. "In fact, you probably have more exciting things in your life than I do."

Hannah stiffened. Her panicked gaze flew to her mother's, then dropped to her lap.

Good one, Wells. God only knows what she might have gone through with her dad. In a minute you'll have her in tears. "I mean, I'll bet not many kids get to spend a summer like this one. How cool could anything be?"

She didn't look up, but one shoulder lifted in a shrug.

Michael summoned his most melodramatic tone. "I never, in all my life, had so many animals to play with as you do. All I ever had was a hamster and two goldfish. Here you have…let's see. Five cats. A dog the size of Texas. Two exceptionally noisy cockatiels, both of whom are having an identity crisis."

Lauren clearly tried—and failed—to stifle a laugh. "Identity crisis? How can you tell?"

"Hannah, what do those birds think they are, anyway? Appliances?"

The child lifted her chin, but didn't meet his gaze. A smile wobbled at the edges of her mouth. "They make sounds like a microwave and a cuckoo clock."

"See? They're completely confused. And what other animals do you have this summer?" Michael paused, pretending to be deep in thought. "A killer goat that likes you, but hates me *and* my car. Three mismatched bedroom slippers that squeal."

"The guinea pigs?" Hannah's shoulder visibly relaxed. Her eyes danced.

"And a lobster with red feet."

That startled a laugh from her. "It's a red-toed *frog*."

"Well, I was close." Michael lifted his gaze to meet Lauren's and caught a wave of such pure gratitude that his heart skipped a beat.

Thank you, she mouthed.

Tipping his head in silent acknowledgment, Michael leaned an elbow on the table and rested his chin on his hand. "I'd love to hear about which animal is your favorite, and why."

Hannah began haltingly. Obviously responding to the encouraging murmurs and direct kindly eye contact that had helped Michael with many a client through the years, she warmed to the topic and talked about the birds, and Baxter and how sweet Daisy could be.

Finally, Lauren broke in gently, "Maybe you should finish that ice cream, honey. And then we can be on our way."

From the corner of his eye he noticed a couple sitting at a table inside the shop. The urbane, well-dressed gentleman with neatly cut graying hair was facing away from the window. "I think that's your friend Oliver." He nodded toward the glass storefront, and Lauren looked up.

''Is that the woman who stopped by…Mildred?'' Lauren squinted against the glare on the large window. ''No, wait. This woman is much older. Maybe she's one of his clients.''

The woman reached across the table and patted his arm, then Oliver gently took her elbow and helped her to stand. As he walked her out of the shop, he glanced up, caught Lauren's gaze and waved.

The woman touched his arm, then started down the sidewalk. Oliver sidestepped through the tables and headed for Lauren.

''Good day,'' he said, offering them all a smile. ''Enjoying our perfect June weather?''

Michael nodded. ''Join us?''

Oliver hesitated, then sat down in the fourth chair at the narrow table, his slim briefcase in his lap. ''How are you faring out at Bertie's place? Have you heard from her?''

''Not for some time.'' Lauren set aside her empty dish. ''She said she wouldn't be calling very often, but Hannah got a postcard from her yesterday. She wrote that she's having the time of her life and that Ireland is everything she remembered. She also mentioned something about seeing an old friend.''

''And everything is going well with your practice?'' Oliver shifted his gaze to Michael. ''All on schedule?''

''I plan to be ready to start by September first, even if the building isn't ready.''

''I've been meaning to stop by again. If you have any questions or concerns, just let me know.''

He reached into the inner breast pocket of his suit

coat and withdrew a business card and pen. After writing on the back of the card, he gave it to Lauren. "My home phone and address are here, as well as the office. Don't hesitate to call me for any reason at all."

"Er…thanks," she murmured. "I appreciate your offer."

"I'd better be on my way and let you young folks enjoy your afternoon. Good day, Lauren, and to you, young lady." With a nod to Hannah and Michael, he rose and slid his chair back to the table. "I'll make sure to stop by the house more frequently."

Lauren's eyes widened. "Oh, no, you really don't…"

But he was gone.

She sagged back into her chair. "Do you suppose Bertie really wanted all these people keeping an eye on things?" she asked dryly. "First him, then Mildred… At this rate, I'll have the whole town on the doorstep every day."

"It sounds as though he feels quite an obligation."

"Five or six years ago we were up here, and my husband had a long visit with him out on Bertie's front lawn." Lauren frowned. "They hit it off quite well, but I'm sure Bertie said later that she used someone else as her lawyer."

"She could have dealt with any number of attorneys since my uncle's death. Didn't she tell you before she left?"

Lauren thought for a minute, then shook her head. "The information would be in her files, though, if we ever need to find out."

Michael leaned back in his chair and watched Oliver walk down the sidewalk, then disappear into a crowd of tourists.

Oliver was personable, clearly well liked in the community, and his concern for Bertie's interests was understandable. But the intuition that had always served Michael well was giving him a nudge right now.

Why did he get the feeling that there was more to Oliver Evans than met the eye?

CHAPTER SIX

I DON'T NEED THIS, Lauren told herself as she drove her old Escort back to Bertie's house, trying to ignore her heightened awareness of the man sitting just a foot or so away.

But Michael Wells was a very hard man to ignore.

Not because of what he said—he'd barely said a word to her since they'd climbed in the car—but because of the effort he'd made to draw Hannah out. With a few deft questions, he'd gotten her started on the personalities of Bertie's animals. Now—truly a miracle—she was chattering away, precluding any necessity for small talk from Lauren.

A good thing, because Lauren didn't know what to say. *You're a heck of a good kisser, but don't ever do that again?* That one swift kiss had turned her heart upside down and sent Fourth of July sparklers clear down to her toes.

And now he sat so close she could sense the warmth of him, could detect the faint masculine scents of aftershave and soap. When he laughed at Hannah's amusing stories, Lauren felt the deep baritone vibration against her skin.

Not, of course, that she should be paying any attention. As agreed, she would help him work on his remodeling project, but there would be no more kisses.

Her blood warmed.

No more unexpected touches.

Her toes started to tingle, reminding her just how devastating his kiss had been. What in heaven's name would it be like to kiss him for real—with candlelight and soft music, the two of them alone?

Her toes would likely go up in flames. *I know it sounds strange, doc, but all I did was kiss him back....*

As Lauren turned into the shady crescent drive at Bertie's place, Hannah unbuckled her seat belt and leaned over the backseat.

"Mom?" Her voice rose in alarm. "Is that *smoke?*"

Off to the right of the house, wisps of smoke wafted skyward through the trees. An acrid smell filled the air.

"Oh, my Lord," Lauren breathed. "The carriage house?"

Hannah grabbed at Lauren's shoulder. "I think Baxter's in there!"

Michael twisted around to face her. "Are you sure?"

"W-we were playing in the back room before lunch. And...and it was like we had a secret fort, and—"

Lauren pulled the car to a rough stop in front of Bertie's house, then raced inside with Hannah in tow to call 911. Michael launched himself out of the car and shot across the lawn.

By the time Lauren and Hannah caught up, he'd

already reached the carriage house and was darting inside.

Smoke poured out of an open second-story window. A dark haze filled the first level.

Fear flooded Lauren's senses as she listened for the sound of barking. For Michael's footsteps. She could hear only the sharp crackle of the flames, and then an explosion—an aerosol can?—from somewhere inside.

Seconds ticked by. Each lasted a lifetime.

Lauren knelt down and looked Hannah in the eye. "Are you sure, honey, *absolutely* sure you left Baxter in there? If Michael's in there searching and can't find him—"

Tears streamed down Hannah's face. "I know he's in the storeroom. I shouldn't have left him there, but I never thought there'd be a fire!"

"I know, sweetheart, I know." Lauren wrapped her arms around her daughter and held her close.

From the smoky interior of the building came the sounds of rapid footsteps. Coughing. A split second later, Michael appeared, doubled over a large form held in his arms.

"Baxter!" Hannah broke free and rushed forward.

Michael strode past her and stopped only when he reached the patio. There, he knelt down and released the dog.

"Is he okay?" Hannah sobbed, her hands at her mouth. "Did he get burned?"

Baxter struggled to his feet, looking dazed. "He's okay," Michael replied, "but he was afraid, and I had to carry him. The door was closed, so the smoke hadn't gotten to him yet.'' Michael put a hand on Hannah's shoulder. ''Now do me a favor. Take Baxter with you and go into the house. Stay there and watch over him, okay? Don't let him get outside, no matter what. Can you do that?''

Hannah rubbed her tears away and nodded fiercely.

''Good girl!'' Michael ran back to the carriage house.

Her heart hammering against her ribs, Lauren stared after him. *He's gone back inside.*

She grabbed Hannah's hand. ''When you're in the house, I want you to stay there where it's safe. Don't come back out. Promise?''

Hannah nodded, her eyes wide in her pale face. ''What if we hadn't come home?'' she whispered. ''What if Bertie's animals still lived out there?''

''They're all safe. Everything will be fine. Now, hurry!'' Lauren watched until Hannah and Baxter disappeared into the house, then she headed back toward the burning carriage house.

''Michael? Where are you?'' The heat and smoke took her breath away as she reached the door he'd entered. *''Michael!''*

He stumbled out and thrust a laptop computer and briefcase into her hands. ''There are a few things upstairs I need to get,'' he called over his shoulder as he raced back in.

''No, don't!'' she shouted.

But he was already gone. A wave of fear washed through her as she followed, then hovered at the door leading to the stairs.

The distant discordant wail of sirens rose and fell, drawing closer.

"Michael?" Embers showered from the window above the door. Jumping back, she hugged the laptop to her chest, her hands trembling and eyes burning. The smoke was heavier now. She gagged, choked on it as she tried to move closer. Where were the fire trucks? The EMTs?

Time stood still as she tried to see through the smoke. Wanting to rush in after him. Knowing that without oxygen and protective gear, she'd never have a chance. *Where was he?*

Horns blared. The sirens reached an earsplitting level. Two fire trucks pulled into the drive, disgorging a dozen or more yellow-coated firefighters. One of them ran up to her and hauled her away from the building.

She fought against his iron grip. "There's a man in there—you've got to get him out!"

Another firefighter whirled back toward the truck and in seconds reappeared with an oxygen tank on his back and a face mask already in place. He loomed closer to her, like some alien creature. "Do you know where he might be?"

"He ran upstairs after something."

Firefighters unreeled hoses. Shouted orders at each other. Then swarmed the building, blasting it with sweeping arcs of water. From somewhere inside came a rush of steam. The roar of flames. Explosions. More aerosol cans? Old ammunition?

The billowing smoke changed from black to charcoal, then pale gray. Acrid smells of wet cinders and smoke and melting asphalt shingles filled the air.

A shout rose above the din. "We've got him!"

Someone pulled at her arm. "Are you sure no one else is in there, ma'am?"

Shaking her head, Lauren twisted free and rushed forward. "Michael!"

A firefighter led him out the door, then gently took a large box from his arms. "He wouldn't let go of it," the man called out to her. "It damned sure better be something of value."

An EMT appeared and took Michael to a rescue van parked behind the second fire truck.

Following, Lauren looked around in dazed amazement. Police officers, EMTs, firefighters and emergency vehicles filled the backyard. Beyond them, on the grass beside the mainhouse, stood a crowd of gawking strangers. Where had all these people come from?

She quickly crossed the yard to the house and set Michael's laptop and briefcase inside the back door. Hannah appeared in the entryway, her face streaked with tears.

"Is Michael all right?"

Lauren gave her a quick hug. "A bit smoky, but he's fine. Stay in here, okay? It's really crowded out there."

Planting a quick kiss on her daughter's forehead, Lauren went back outside to Michael.

He was sagged against the back bumper of the rescue truck, his hands braced on his knees. Soot streaked his face and had blackened his ivory polo shirt. He wheezed and coughed, his shoulders shaking.

An EMT was checking his blood pressure, pulse

and respiration. "Here you go, sir," he said, fitting an oxygen mask over Michael's face. "Just breathe easy."

Lauren laid a hand on his shoulder. "Shouldn't he be taken to a hospital?"

The EMT squatted down in front of Michael and examined him for burns. "Looks like you were lucky. We'll run you to the hospital so they can check you over. How do you feel?"

"I'm fine." Wrenching the mask away, Michael broke into a coughing spasm. "I'm not going anywhere."

"Sir, smoke inhalation seriously impairs judgment—probably one reason you took such a chance back there. I really think you should—"

"No." His face pale beneath the streaks of soot, Michael stood. "If I start feeling worse, I'll take myself in." He scanned the scene at the carriage house, where firefighters were now milling about, collecting equipment, reeling up hoses. "I'd like to talk to someone in command."

A lanky firefighter nodded at him. "That's Chief Reynolds. I'll get him for you."

Suppressing the urge to wrap him in blankets and haul him to the hospital whether he liked it or not, Lauren stepped back as a burly man approached.

"Chief Reynolds," the man boomed, extended a hand to Michael. "A shame, seeing this happen at Bertie's place. And you are...?"

After a round of brief introductions, Michael lowered his voice. "Any idea as to the cause?"

Reynolds gave him a measuring look. "Do you own this part of the property?"

"No, but Bertie gave me a semipermanent lease."

The older man raised a brow. "Semi?"

"Bertie gave me a lease that's permanent as long as I want it."

"Building insured?"

Michael broke into a series of hacking coughs. "Under her homeowner's policy. I haven't moved much of anything up here, yet."

Reynolds shifted his gaze to Lauren. "What sort of condition was the building in?"

A chill of uneasiness slithered through her stomach. "The small apartment at the far right was fine. The rest of the interior was being remodeled. How bad is it inside?"

"Some interior damage, but nothing structural. Where have you two been for the last couple hours?"

Michael's jaw tightened. "At Taylor's. The building was on fire when we returned."

"Was gasoline stored in there?"

"Just for the lawn mowers, nothing more than that. We took it out before we started remodeling."

"Did anyone spill gasoline in there today?"

"No." Michael straightened. "You think it was arson?"

"Gasoline seems to have been the accelerant, but the fire started in just one place. Usually there's more than one starting point with arson." The chief frowned. "Know of anyone with motivation to do that?"

"We'd just begun working on the building!" Lauren cried. "Why on earth would anyone want to destroy it?"

The chief didn't take his gaze from Michael's face. "Revenge, malice, vandalism…insurance."

"None of which would apply to either of us here. I can't think of anyone…" Michael's voice trailed off. "I did fire a contractor recently, but I don't think he's crazy enough to do this."

While Michael and the fire chief conversed, Lauren slipped away and peered through windows and doors to survey the damage.

In the large area destined for Michael's office, sodden refuse from the fire lay about the floor in smoldering heaps. At the far end, a haze of smoke still filled the apartment, though she couldn't see any damage through the windows.

Fear slid through her at the thought of someone trespassing and purposely setting fire to the building. What if he—or she—had come in the dead of night, trapping Michael in the flames?

She wrapped her arms tightly around her waist, trying to still her shaking hands. Maybe that person was here right now, milling around with the other onlookers. Appreciating the results of his handiwork. Didn't arsonists do that sort of thing?

"Don't go in there, ma'am," a male voice called out. A young volunteer firefighter ambled up to her with a comforting smile.

Numb, she lifted her chin and looked at him. *Still such a baby,* she thought. *I'll bet he doesn't even shave.* "How bad is the damage?"

He led her back to the other end of the building and pointed through the door to the center support pole. "That's the worst, right there. The alligator charring shows intense heat—where the fire burned hottest.''

"It's so hard to imagine someone doing this on purpose.'' Lauren gave him a sad smile. "The remodeling had to be done by the beginning of September.''

"The carpenters shouldn't find this too big a job.'' The young man stepped forward and scanned the interior. "Replace the center beam, add some new supports... The walls weren't finished yet, anyway. There's a lot of smoke damage upstairs, but not any major structural damage. What's this place going to be?''

"An office, but Mr. Wells hasn't been able to find a good contractor. By the time he came to town, everyone was booked well into the fall.''

The young man pursed his lips. "He doesn't have anyone hired?''

Lauren shook her head, unable to take her eyes from the smoke-filled apartment.

With the aplomb of a born salesmen, he thrust out a hand. "Brad Olson. Construction Tech I, II and III, Briar Lake High. I'm home for the summer, then I'm going into construction management at the community college in Greenleigh. Think he'd like some help?''

Startled, she looked at him from head to foot. The kid looked young, but he met her eye to eye and had the firm handshake of a man. "You've actually done construction?''

"Every summer since I was fifteen, with my uncle. And I helped build a three-thousand-square-foot house during my high school building-trades class.

My dad is Mark Olson. We're in the Briar Lake phone book.''

Lauren managed a grin. ''I'll put in a good word for you.''

She turned to look at Michael, who still stood talking to the fire chief, then shifted her gaze to the house. Hannah stood at the back door, her eyes huge in her pale face as she stared at the firefighters climbing aboard the trucks.

With a quick farewell to Brad, Lauren skirted the people still milling about and headed for the house.

''Are you sure Michael's okay?'' were Hannah's first words.

''He's fine, and there isn't much damage to the building.'' Giving her daughter a hug, Lauren whispered a silent prayer of thanks. ''It could have been much, much worse.''

''Where will he stay now? With us? And what about his office?'' Hannah stepped back and looked out the door. ''Are you sure he's okay? He's still over by that rescue truck.''

Chuckling at the barrage of questions, Lauren tapped Hannah on the nose. ''Don't worry. He breathed in some smoke and that makes him cough. As for the rest, I don't know.''

''He can have my bedroom and I can move into one of the smaller rooms down the hall.'' Hannah worried at a fingernail with her front teeth. ''I don't mind, honest.''

''We'll see.'' Lauren turned away to fill the teakettle with water, then set it on the stove.

Where would he stay? Fire hadn't destroyed the apartment, but there was significant water damage, and the overpowering smell of smoke wouldn't clear for a long time to come. It was only right that Michael move into Bertie's house.

MICHAEL COUGHED HEAVILY, wincing at the pain in his throat. Hannah and Lauren sat on the other side of the kitchen table in Bertie's cavernous kitchen, wearing identical frowns of concern.

"You should go to the hospital." Lauren rose. "I'll drive. Can you get my purse, honey?"

"No. I'm fine." Michael tried to suppress the next cough and failed. He took a slow swallow of the hot lemon-and-honey tea Lauren had set before him. "Just...sit down. I'm not going anywhere."

"I bet he's afraid of the hospital."

"Yep, I think so, too." Lauren peered at him from under her heavy fringe of bangs. "But if we went with him, he—"

"*No.* But I appreciate your concern." He suddenly felt more tired than he had in weeks. "I'd better get out there and start going through that apartment. There's considerable water damage, I'm sure."

"It's unlivable. The walls and floors are soaked. The smell of smoke will never come out of the drapes and carpets."

The summer had shown such promise. A few months of remodeling, the start of a new career. Luckily, as he'd told the fire chief, he hadn't brought many of his things with him on this trip north. The lack of cargo space in the Jag had proved an unexpected stroke of luck.

"You should take the main-floor bedroom," Lauren continued, her eyes on her own cup of tea. "It's one of the largest and would be more private. You'd have your own bath facilities."

He thought about frequently encountering Lauren in her bare feet, a robe…maybe less. Until this summer he'd always been in complete control of himself, but he sure hadn't been able to control that impulse to kiss her in front of Taylor's. Living under the same roof would increase the opportunities—and temptations—a hundredfold.

He closed his eyes and imagined the frustration. "I don't think—"

"Since Hannah has most of Bertie's pets upstairs, you won't be bothered."

Uncomfortable, Michael lifted a shoulder. "It isn't that…"

He willed her to look up, to read the meaning in his eyes.

She studied the loose bangles at her wrist.

He cleared his throat. "There might be some other place."

"You know the whole town is booked solid for the summer months in advance. Not," she added quickly, "that I'm trying to railroad you into staying here. But Bertie is your aunt, for heaven's sake. You belong here."

"Well…"

She leaned forward and lowered her voice so that only he could hear. "If it was indeed arson, who's to say that the guy won't strike again? We'll feel safer if you're here."

Another fit of coughing took him unawares. Lauren didn't look particularly worried over the prospect of an arsonist, but the thought made his own blood chill. If Lauren and her daughter were alone in the house...

"Fine," he said at last.

"Good." She gave him a satisfied smile. "We'll help you get your things in. I just have one question, though. Why in the world did you go into that building a third time? You could have died in there!"

"Just...a few things."

"Things?"

He shrugged and didn't answer. She was right. But while he and Sam had been moving some furniture to the second floor, he'd seen some of Bertie's treasures up there. Old photo albums that had somehow found their way into storage. A box of old dolls he knew had been hers as a child. And nowhere on earth could there be a more sentimental woman than Bertie Wells. The impulse had been foolish, but he'd managed to get most of the stuff jammed into the one box he'd carried outside.

Lauren shifted her schoolmarm look to her daughter's face. "Don't ever, ever go back into a burning building, honey. Nothing is worth your life."

Hannah nodded, then looked up at Michael with something akin to hero worship. "But he did save Baxter."

"Thank goodness for that. But don't ever risk your life, even for a pet you love. *Promise.*"

Hannah nodded, her expression somber.

"By the way, Michael, I found you a new employee."

"A *what?*"

"An employee. He's got carpentry experience, energy and is eager to get to work."

"You hired him?"

"Nope, but you will." She flashed Michael a smile of such magnitude he felt his skin flush. "Unless all that smoke disrupted your common sense. In which case, I'll hire him for you myself. As a favor. But you have to pay him."

Michael stared at her in bemusement. She'd seemed so flamboyant that first day, a riot of colors from head to foot. Another one of Bertie's endless offbeat, hard-luck cases come to stay. He'd learned to read people well during his career in law, but with Lauren he'd completely missed the boat. She was far more intriguing than he'd thought.

"So you're saying I don't have a choice?" he asked dryly.

"Right."

"And this guy is going to be perfect for the job?"

"Of course!"

When he lifted his cup in mock salute, her warm laughter danced across his skin and then headed straight for his heart.

CHAPTER SEVEN

HANNAH STARED at the open cage door and then at the open casement window. Just this morning she'd lowered a rope and basket from her window, pretending she was Rapunzel captive in a high lonely tower.

She hadn't meant to leave the window screen off.

Worse, she'd forgotten to latch the door on the cockatiels' cage. If Mom found out, she'd never, ever let her have any pets after they left Briar Lake.

Baxter wandered in and plopped down at her feet as if he knew how bad she felt. Looking down at his sorrowful expression, she felt tears burn in her eyes. It was bad enough not having anyone to play with the whole summer, but the cockatiels had been so much fun. What if a cat got them? Or they flew a thousand miles away?

Cranking open the windows as wide as they could go, she rested her waist on the sill and leaned out, searching the high branches.

"Pretty bird, pretty bird," she cooed, hoping that one of them might answer as they often did, with a strange imitation of the microwave, or cuckoo clock, or vacuum cleaner. "Pretty bird!"

Maybe she could find them if she climbed up in

the trees. Filling a pocket with bird treats, she darted down the stairs.

She was halfway out the back door when the phone rang.

Michael had left for town on some errand, and Mom wasn't answering.

Hannah had just started in on her "Wells' house, Hannah speaking" when the man on the other end said words her mom would never, ever let her say.

She started to replace the receiver on the cradle. Then she heard the words *damn birds*. She jerked it back up to her ear. "Did you say birds?"

After a stunned silence, the caller cleared his throat. "I didn't realize I was talking to a child."

"My mom doesn't like those words, either," Hannah retorted.

"I've got two of Bertie's birds outside my window making an infernal racket. After listening to them for the last two hours, I'm tempted to shoot them."

"Oh, no—please don't! Who...who is this?"

He heaved a sigh. "Judge Miller, next door."

"Please, wait. I'll be over right away." Hannah dropped the phone onto the counter, then dashed out the front door, down the crescent driveway and into Miller's front yard.

She was already at his front door before she realized what she'd done: she was in enemy territory, and Mom didn't even know she'd gone.

Miller was standing on his front steps, his face as red and hair as white as ever—a really scary combination. His face grim, he pointed to the tree branches above his head. And there, almost too high to see, sat the two cockatiels.

Hannah swallowed. Unlike the trees in Bertie's yard, none of these had lower branches. She'd have to shinny up a good six feet to reach the first branch, and even from that point on, the spacing between tree limbs was long and erratic.

Worrying her lower lip with her teeth, she scanned the area for something to stand on, spied a lawn chair, and dragged it next to the tree.

"What are you doing?"

She stood on the chair. "Trying to get the birds."

"No—I won't allow it."

She bent her knees, then took her best leap upward. *Not even close.* She slipped backward, the rough bark of the tree scraping her knees and calves.

"Young lady, you get down from there!"

The chair wobbled beneath her feet. Her skin burned. Glancing over her shoulder, she could see the judge turning an alarming shade of red. "Do you have a ladder?" she asked.

"Certainly not. Those da—Those birds must be forty feet up," he sputtered.

"I can't get them if I can't get up the tree."

He began to pace the front porch. "What about birdseed? Do you have something they like?"

"Just this." She reached into the pocket of her shorts and pulled out the bird treats. "They like these a lot. I put some on my windowsill, hoping they would come back."

The judge snorted. "Good luck."

"Maybe you could put some on *your* sill, and you could catch them."

"I don't like birds. I've never had birds. I have *no* desire to catch these."

Hannah gave him a curious look. "They don't bite, you know."

"I'm not *afraid* of birds. I don't *like* them."

He frowned at her, and Hannah imagined him in his big black judge robe, telling people they were going to prison forever and ever. Maybe even to the electric chair. He probably enjoyed his job a whole lot.

From up in the tree came an ear-piercing whistle, following by a perfect imitation of a cuckoo clock. As far as that bird was concerned, the time was always twelve noon.

The judge looked upward, then fixed Hannah with a stern glare. "Go get your mother or that nephew of Bertie's," he said through clenched teeth. "Find a way to get these birds out of my trees. You hear?"

"I could climb out one of your upstairs windows. The branches are pretty close."

"And have you fall and break your neck?"

"A ladder—"

"Even if you got close, the darn things would just fly somewhere else."

And then they might get hurt, or eaten by a cat, or shot at by someone just as mean as the judge. *Just one more try.* Flexing into a deep knee bend, Hannah launched herself upward, grabbed at the rough bark and gripped tight with her knees.

The judge gasped and started down his front steps toward her.

Hannah reached up and caught the rough edge

where a branch had been sawed off. Shinnied higher, ignoring the burning pain in her legs.

Miller reached the tree and grabbed for her leg, but she clawed her way just out of range.

"Get down!" he thundered. "Now!"

She dragged herself higher, her toes feeling for purchase in the bark. "I'm…almost…there."

"Young lady!"

"I'll get them for you. Honest." She was high enough to see over the fence into Bertie's yard. Almost high enough to reach that lower branch.

Now she was high enough for Mom to see, too.

"Hannah!"

Uh-oh. Now Mom would be over here any minute, wanting to know what was going on. Biting back a sob, Hannah managed to hook an arm over the lowest branch and haul herself up. With her mom staring at her from across the fence and Judge Miller glaring at her from below, the idea no longer seemed like such a good one. The next branch up was well beyond her reach.

The ground was a *long* way down.

Hannah straddled the branch and leaned against the harsh bark of the tree, trying to ignore the stinging scrapes on her legs and arms. A warm tear trickled down her cheek, burning as it crossed a scratch. Looking up, she couldn't even see those dumb birds anymore and knew she'd been foolish even to try catching them. *Nothing ever turns out right.*

"Young lady, I want you down out of this tree!" Miller's face was still red, but she could hear a note of worry in his voice.

"You wanted me to catch them."

"No, I want Bertie's nephew to get them," he sputtered. "And right now I want you down from there and on your way home before you break your neck."

Trying to ignore the queasy feeling in her stomach and the dampness of her palms, Hannah cautiously shifted her position inch by inch until, with a death grip on the branch, she could straddle the trunk and start easing down.

It would have worked. But just then she looked down and saw some kids standing out on the sidewalk in openmouthed fascination. They were the kids she'd seen playing in a neighbor's yard.

Hannah leaned forward to get a better look. As she shifted her weight, the scrapes and scratches on the inside of her legs connected with the harsh tree bark.

With a cry of pain she flinched. Her hands slipped.

And suddenly the ground was rushing up to meet her.

"Oof!" Dazed, she looked up at the branch she'd been on. It was at least a mile away. Her ankle hurt like crazy. Her elbow and her butt, too.

Judge Miller squatted down and reached out to touch her leg, then hesitated. "Are you all right?"

His voice was gruff, but she could see the worry in his eyes. Footsteps approached at a run. *Mom,* she thought with a sinking heart.

"I'm sorry," Hannah whispered. She looked toward the driveway. Sure enough, Mom was on her way.

But worst of all, those kids were still watching.

They were laughing and pointing at her. The taller boy flapped his elbows up and down, squawking like a chicken.

They all turned to go, but Hannah caught wisps of conversation as they left.

"What was she doing in *Miller's* tree? Dumb kid…"

"…did she think she could fly?"

"…talk about stupid!"

Their laughter felt like physical blows.

Her cheeks burning with humiliation, Hannah closed her eyes and wished she'd died on impact.

THREE DAYS AFTER THE FIRE the heavy smell of wet charred wood still hung in the air. Lauren finished scooping Daisy's feed pellets into a pan and checked her water bucket, then gave the little goat a quick rub behind her ears.

Daisy, as if aware of the gravity of her attack on Michael's car, had been on good behavior for an entire week, but it was only a matter of time before she found a new way to escape.

If and when Michael's car was finished, Lauren fervently hoped he would lock it in the garage or store it elsewhere. Preferably in the next state.

She looked up and saw Hannah moping on the patio, with Baxter at her side. "Want to help me?"

Hannah looked up, scowled and went into the house, slamming the door behind her.

It had been those kids, Lauren knew. She'd heard their taunts and cruel laughter. She'd wanted to run after them, haul them back and make them apologize, but how would that help? Resentment—added to their callous attitudes—wouldn't be the basis for kindness, much less the start of any friendships.

So now Hannah—a bandage on her sore ankle, some minor scrapes and bruises, and another, much deeper wound in her heart—had rebuffed every one of Lauren's efforts to discuss what had happened. Another time, Lauren might have gone after her and called her on her rude behavior. But those wounds were too fresh, and there was too much hurt and anger in her eyes.

Someday soon we're going to have our own home, sweetie, Lauren promised silently. *Then you'll be in one place for good, and you can make lots of nice friends.*

The sound of hammering in the carriage house stopped. Michael came to the door and grinned at her. "Ready?"

With a last check of Daisy's chain, Lauren ran a hand through her bangs and joined him inside the the carriage house.

The young volunteer fireman Brad Olson had proved as good as his word. Michael had hired him after a brief interview, and the kid had shown up every day on time. He'd gathered a crew of friends that first day after the fire, and they'd helped clear out all the smoke-damaged materials on both floors of the building. The next day they'd come back to help replace the main support beams.

Yesterday, Michael, Brad and Lauren had torn up the flooring and had replaced a number of the floor joists. Lauren was grateful for the extra help, and also grateful for the boy's presence.

Not a day went by that she didn't feel a spark of

unwanted awareness when she met Michael over coffee at breakfast or when she worked with him, side by side. If anything, he became more distant with each passing day, so that hint of chemistry apparently didn't go both ways. Having an extra person around made the situation more comfortable.

Lauren stood in the center of the room and looked around. "Only a few more joists to go," she announced. "Then what?"

Michael gave her a wry look. "Ask our contractor here."

"Subflooring." Brad looked up from his nail gun and gave her a broad smile. "You sure look good, Mrs. McClellan."

"Oh, yeah. A real trendsetter in old tennis shoes, cutoffs and a grubby T-shirt." He waggled an eyebrow, and Lauren couldn't help but laugh. "I'd hate to see how many hearts you break in the next few years, Brad. You have way too much charm."

Buckling on his tool belt, Michael shot her a grin. Lauren felt her heart skip a beat, then race a little to catch up.

In those faded jeans, with that tool belt riding low on his narrow hips and a worn T-shirt molded to the heavy muscling of his chest, he looked like one of those all-too-appealing guys on the cover of a romance novel. Until now, she'd figured guys like that didn't really exist.

Wrong.

Lauren turned away on the pretext of finding her hammer. At the touch of a hand on her shoulder she froze.

"Here," Michael said, his voice low. "You'll be needing these."

He handed her a pair of leather gloves. "Thanks," she mumbled, jerking them on without looking up at him. From the periphery of her vision she noticed Brad's fascinated expression.

She stepped quickly away from Michael. "Well, Brad, tell me what to do."

He laughed. "About what?"

"Brad!"

With a shrug he pointed the business end of his hammer toward the stack of lumber just outside the door. "We'll get this floor done today."

The morning sped by. After a quick lunch they went back to work. By late afternoon Lauren was exhausted. Michael looked as though he was ready to go another eight hours.

Peeling off his gloves, he rested a hip on one of the sawhorses and glanced around the interior of the building. "It sure gives a guy a sense of satisfaction to see this kind of progress."

"You've caught on real quick." Brad unplugged the nail gun and set it aside, then started gathering in the extension cord. "Bet you'd like building a house. When you start with bare ground and end up with a home, you feel like you've really accomplished something." He glanced over his shoulder at Lauren and winked. "Maybe someday you two will decide to build your own."

"I doubt I'll ever do more than put up a shelf in my apartment," she retorted, carefully ignoring his implication. "But Michael might have other plans for his future."

Brad just smiled.

LAUREN LOOKED DOWN at the two cats at her feet. The calico and the gray had spent the better part of an hour sitting side by side, their noses inches away from the door of the refrigerator, staring up at the handle with expressions of patient devotion. They might have been a pair of furry bookends, except for the twitching ends of their tails.

Now they'd positioned themselves by her chair and were trying the same rapt expression on her. This time it was working.

With a sigh she rose from the collection of bills on the table and rummaged through the cupboard under the sink for the bag of dry cat food. "This is what you're after, right? If only those darn cockatiels would come in for *their* meal."

She'd heard the birds in the trees all day, but hadn't caught a glimpse of either one. At this rate, they could be on the loose forever.

The two cats followed her to the row of dishes by the back door, their tails high and straight as broom handles.

"I suppose you two would like to feast alone, but where are your friends?" She bent down to divvy out equal portions of food, then straightened. "Kitty, kitty, kitty!"

The other three cats appeared and made a beeline for the dishes. At the sound of a knock on the door, Lauren tossed the empty bag on the counter and went to the front entryway.

Through the panes of glass in the door she saw Oliver standing on the flagstone steps, his briefcase in one hand and his umbrella tucked under the other arm.

Suppressing a sigh, she forced a welcoming smile as she unlatched the screen door. There wasn't anything outwardly unpleasant about the man. He just seemed to feel his help was needed, as if he thought she wasn't capable of managing while Bertie was away.

"Good day," he murmured, doffing his hat. "May I come in?"

Ushering him into the entryway, she nodded toward the front room. "Can I get you something? A cup of coffee?"

He gave her a self-deprecating smile. "Oh, no, my dear. I've just stopped on my way home for lunch. I always walk, you know. Good for the heart. Aren't Michael and your daughter here? Usually I see them outside."

He shows up uninvited, and he's nosy. She silently chastised herself for the thought. A widower, he was probably a lonely guy and missed being able to visit with Bertie. "Michael is running after some supplies, and Hannah's upstairs."

Once he settled himself on the brocade couch in the front room, she took a seat in one of the stiffly formal chairs placed at either side. "Is there something I can help you with?"

"Goodness, no. That's why I stopped. To see if you had any concerns. Quite a big place to care for, I know." He waved a hand, encompassing the old house and extensive grounds beyond. "So much responsibility."

Well, she'd heard that before. He'd told her at least five times.

"It's delightful being here," Lauren countered. "We're doing just fine." She thought for a moment, then lifted a shoulder. "Except for the fire, of course."

Oliver sat forward, his brow furrowed. "Does Bertie know yet? Have you located the insurance documents? Filed any claims?"

"No...she hasn't called recently, and I couldn't guess where she is right now. I did call the insurance company, though, about the fire damage and, er, the Jaguar."

"You had the phone numbers handy? The policy information?"

"Bertie left numbers for every conceivable situation." Lauren gave him a patient smile. "Michael has already taken his car in for several estimates, and the adjuster came out right away after the fire."

"Good, good." Visibly more relaxed, Oliver sank back into the couch. "I wouldn't want Bertie to have any such worries while so far away. You must promise to contact me regarding anything else that comes up."

"Like I said, except for the fire, there hasn't been anything out of the ordinary." He frowned at her, and Lauren fought the urge to squirm in her chair. "Bertie explained everything well. So far, everything is fine."

After a pause, Oliver lifted a wrist and glanced at his watch, then gave her a tight smile. "Well, then, I'd better be off. I haven't yet been home for my lunch, and I've got to get back in time for some afternoon appointments.''

It wasn't until he was long gone that she noticed his umbrella, placed neatly at the side of the couch.

Picking it up, she sighed, then placed it in the umbrella stand at the front door. He could return for it, or she could drop it off at his house. The latter would be a far better choice. She wouldn't even have to knock. She could just set it inside his screen door.

He was the picture of a nice, rather stuffy old uncle, but his persistent eagerness to help, which had been merely bothersome before, now filled her with a sense of unease.

Oliver was a lawyer. He would have connections at the courthouse. A chance meeting with someone there, a casual word about Bertie's summer house-sitter...

Lauren's legal history was public record, but wasn't common knowledge away from her home-town. When people found out, they invariably thought the worst of her. And now—so close to the end of her probation—she just couldn't afford to have anyone's false expectations lead to trouble.

What if Oliver was checking up on her because he'd found out about her past?

CHAPTER EIGHT

THEY FINISHED the floor joists by five o'clock. Brad declined Lauren's invitation to stay for supper, saying that he had Big Plans with someone named Tina, and took off with his pickup tires squealing and a big grin on his face.

By six, Lauren had showered, changed into white cotton shorts and a loose gauzy top, and started supper. She didn't look up from measuring a cup of milk as Michael came in the back door, but all her senses announced that he was there.

"You'll eat with us, won't you? It's silly for you to go to town when you could have supper here." She looked up, awaiting his answer, and once again felt that silly school-girl reaction at seeing him. She was thirty-two, for heaven's sake!

Since leaving the carriage house she'd reassured herself by deciding that the tool belt slung around his hips had given him that edgy sort of James Dean masculine appeal.

Well, the tool belt was gone, and he hadn't lost one bit of the appeal.

Shoving a hand through his hair, he glanced at the pots and pans on the stove and gave her a tired grin. "Do I have time to clean up?"

"Uh…sure. Maybe fifteen minutes?"

"No problem." He toed off his old sneakers, then headed across the kitchen for the hallway to his bedroom. "But if I don't show up, knock on the door. I may fall asleep in the shower."

He didn't move like someone bone-tired. He moved with the athletic grace and power of someone who was used to spending hours doing hard physical labor.

She turned back to stir the beef and macaroni casserole simmering on the stove. Instead of the creamy pasta concoction, she saw Michael standing in the shower with steamy water sluicing over those muscles, down the broad expanse of his chest and back, down the deep indentation between his shoulder blades.

He'd been in the house for three days now. Politely greeting Lauren and her daughter at breakfast, making his own sandwiches at lunch, leaving for town the last two evenings and disappearing into his room when he returned. They were barely more than strangers who happened to share the same space. So where had these errant thoughts come from?

At the ding of a timer she grabbed a couple of pot holders and pulled a pan of corn muffins out of the oven. The fabric, dampened by a spill of her iced tea, conducted the heat in a flash.

She dropped the hot muffin tin on the counter with a clatter, then turned on the kitchen faucet and plunged her fingers under the rush of cold water.

Think too much about Michael Wells, and you'll really get burned, she reminded herself ruefully. A man like him could never be seriously interested in a woman with a past like hers. And she would never,

ever add to Hannah's insecurity by conducting a casual affair.

A tentative knock sounded at the front door. Oliver, she thought, back already for that darned umbrella. "Hannah! Can you get the front door?" Lauren called out, hoping her voice carried to the library.

She heard a pair of feet shuffle to the front door. The massive oak door creaked open. But it wasn't Oliver's precise tenor that drifted into the kitchen. Instead, Lauren heard a woman's voice. Setting a stack of plates back down on the counter, she headed for the front entryway.

Hannah stood frozen and mute, with one white-knuckled hand on the doorknob and red flames of humiliation in her cheeks. From her rigid stance, Lauren knew she would turn and flee any second.

Out on the front steps stood a tall, elegant young blonde dressed in tennis whites, with a girl about Hannah's age—one of the kids who had taunted Hannah a few days earlier.

Between them, tethered on a dog leash, stood Daisy.

The woman smiled down at Hannah, then lifted her gaze. "Hi, I'm Sue Mason from down the street, and this is my daughter, Ashley. I believe we have Bertie's goat." She lifted the end of the leash with a smile of amusement. "She seems to like our roses."

At least she's smiling. "I'm so sorry for the trouble she's caused. Thanks for bringing her home."

Hannah shot Lauren a look of pure misery and

took a step back. Only Lauren's hand at her back kept her from running.

Sue gave Hannah a sympathetic smile. "I hear that the neighbor kids haven't been very nice to you, and they all know better than that." She rested a firm hand on her daughter's shoulder. "I think Ashley wants to tell you something."

Ashley hung her head and scuffed a toe against the cement landing. "And I'm sorry we laughed at you." She took a tortured breath. "It was really mean."

Her words came out in a rush, as if she'd recited them all the way over. When she finally found the courage to look up, her face was as pink as Hannah's, and her eyes were filled with embarrassment.

After a long pause Hannah nodded.

Knowing how hard it was for her daughter to give that small measure of response, Lauren's heart lifted. "Could you two girls take Daisy to her pen?"

Sue held out the leash to Hannah, who shook her head. "Ashley can lead her, if she wants." The girl reached out eagerly.

As soon as the girls disappeared around the corner, Lauren gave a sigh of relief. "Thank you. This means more than I can express. Would you like to come in?"

Sue shook her head. "It's suppertime, and we have to get back. I'll just follow the girls." From somewhere up in the trees came the sound of a cuckoo clock chiming twelve noon. Sue halted and stared up at the dense foliage overhead. "What on earth…?"

"Just another of our escapees," Lauren said

dryly, stepping out onto the porch and following Sue across the lawn. "Two of Bertie's cockatiels are now living in that tree, and I can't do a thing about it."

Sue shot her a sympathetic look. "Challenging summer?"

"At times…a bit. Hannah says it's her fault the birds escaped and she feels awful about it. I really wanted this summer to be wonderful for her. But she's a bit lonely."

"Maybe she can come over and play someday soon?"

Ahead, the girls walked stiffly on either side of Daisy, neither one speaking. Then Ashley shot a tentative look at Hannah and said something to her. After a long hesitation Hannah replied.

Lauren sighed with relief. "It's a start. You don't know how much I've hoped that Hannah would find a friend for the summer."

"It looks as if they'll get along now. I swear I'll never understand why kids can be so rude to newcomers."

"Well, I appreciate your coming over." Lauren watched Ashley stroke Daisy's rough coat. "Thanks again for bringing the goat back—I swear she's the Houdini of Briar Lake. If she did any damage, I'll call the insurance rep. He's getting used to hearing from me this summer."

Sue lifted a shoulder. "Good grief, no. Daisy pruned a few bushes, and I never get around to that, anyway. The roses were my ex-husband's idea, not mine." She gave a sultry laugh. "Actually I think it's rather appropriate that a goat gnawed them off."

They stopped at the edge of the patio and watched the girls secure Daisy inside the chain-link dog run, then Sue called to her daughter.

"I hope we'll get to see you again soon," Lauren said softly as the girls approached.

With a graceful wave Sue smiled and shepherded Ashley toward the driveway. Hannah stood by Lauren and watched them leave.

"So, what do you think? Are you two going to be friends?"

"Maybe…"

"She seems like a nice little girl."

"She likes Daisy a lot and she said I could maybe come over sometime." A wobbly grin appeared on Hannah's face. "Could I?"

"Oh, Hannah, of course you can. And if you like her, she's welcome here anytime. Now scoot back into the house and wash your hands, and you can help me put lunch on the table, okay?"

LAUREN HAD JUST PUT the casserole on the counter when Michael strolled into the kitchen, his damp hair gleaming like polished ebony and his skin a bronze contrast to the crisp white of his polo shirt. When he drew closer, she caught the clean scents of shampoo and soap.

"All set?" he asked, a dimple deepening in one cheek.

Grabbing a basket of muffins and a bottle of honey, she nodded toward the table, where she'd already set out crisp lettuce salads in wooden bowls.

Michael carried the casserole over, and in a few minutes they were seated.

"Thanks for supper," he murmured politely, eyeing the casserole. "It looks…delicious."

Lauren handed it to him with a sigh. "I didn't have time to add anything to it, so I'm afraid it's not very interesting."

His expression brightened. "I'm sure it's excellent."

"Oh, by the way…" Lauren reached over to the counter and snagged a postcard lying there, then handed it to him. "This came to us today. From Bertie, with a postmark from Switzerland."

Michael glanced at the mountain scene on the front, then scanned the looping scrawl on the back. "The time of my life…a wonderful old friend you must meet…" He looked up at Lauren. "What friend? Someone on the tour?"

She shrugged. "Bertie mentioned this person on the first card she sent. I have no idea."

"And then she says she hopes we're *really*—she underlined it twice—enjoying our summer together." He raised a brow. "Do you think…"

"Yes, I certainly do. She didn't forget your arrival—she planned to be gone just in time. We were set up."

Hannah fidgeted in her seat. "I met a new girl today," she announced to Michael, her eyes sparkling. Then she turned to Lauren. "Did you know her mom is a teacher, too? Only, she teaches high school, not grade school. So she has the summer off, too. And Ashley likes that because her mom can be home a lot. Isn't that cool?"

Michael took a swallow of iced tea, then set his glass down. "That's super, Hannah." He slid his gaze to Lauren and gave her a measuring look. "So that's why you're free this summer. I thought you were unemployed, but you didn't say that you're a teacher."

Lauren nodded, then gave Hannah a quick glance, mentally urging her to stay quiet. "How is the casserole, everyone?"

"Good. So where do you teach?"

Lauren shrugged casually. "Actually I'm not contracted right now. We moved a few times while I was married, and I've been out of teaching for a while."

"Have you applied at the Briar Lake schools?"

Sticky subject. Until her suspended sentence was over in September, there wouldn't be any point in applying. Her application would hit the wastebasket in record time. "I'm thinking about subbing in the Minneapolis area for a while, maybe looking for a school in the western suburbs. We'd be near friends—"

"*What* friends? Mom, come on!" Hannah was at full attention now. "I want to stay! I love Briar Lake! And we could see Bertie's animals, and now I even have a friend."

"Hannah, we've talked about his." Lauren glanced at the clock above the stove. "Now, let's get finished so we can go for a walk into town, okay?"

"But, Mom—"

"*Hannah.*" The steel in Lauren's voice finally registered.

Michael gave her a curious look.

Like a blessed reprieve, the phone started ringing.

"I'll get that." Lauren stood abruptly and crossed the kitchen. The caller asked for Michael, so she held out the phone. "It's the fire chief. Do you want to take this in the study?"

He nodded and disappeared down the hallway. By the time he returned, Lauren and Hannah had finished eating.

Lauren shivered at his grim expression when he returned. "Hannah, could you go feed Baxter and Daisy while I do the dishes?"

Flashing a quick smile, Hannah took off.

"She loves doing dishes almost as much as I do," Lauren said. "I figured she'd be better off not hearing what you had to say." She took a chair across from Michael as he sat down to finish his meal. "Do they know who set the fire?"

"They interviewed Sam and talked to all the neighbors. Sam had an alibi and the neighbors don't remember seeing any cars pull in while we were gone."

"Though, with these large old estates and long driveways, who would notice?" She closed her eyes, and once again she could feel the heat and see the pulsing flames leap against the walls. He could have been killed in that burning building.

"True. They even checked for fingerprints on the gas can found in back of the building, but didn't find anything at all—not even mine, and I'm sure I moved that can when we were clearing out the junk in the carriage house."

"So someone wiped the prints off?"

"Possibly. Or maybe one of us was wearing

gloves and smeared away any prints that were there.''

''Is that it, then? They aren't going to check any further?''

''Without any likely suspects, they don't have anything else to go on for now. The chief is saying that maybe it wasn't arson. Maybe it was just...an accidental fire.''

Michael stood and took his plate to the sink. ''This'll take just a minute or two if I help.''

''But how did the fire start?'' Lauren persisted.

''Maybe it was some young kids out looking for trouble. We may never know, unless something else happens around here.'' Michael shrugged as he scraped and rinsed a plate. ''For now, that's the end of the story.''

''I just have this feeling that there's more to this.''

''Without evidence, there's no way to prove anything.''

When he reached for a dishcloth and wiped off the table, she leaned against the counter and hooked one hand on her hip. ''Somehow, you hadn't struck me as the domestic type,'' she teased. ''I'll bet you grew up with maids and a cook and had someone cleaning the house, too.''

''A life of privilege?''

''In spades.''

He laughed at that. ''Not exactly.''

She thought of the somber family portraits lining the staircase. Bertie's relatives, and his. The average family had photographs, not oils, and didn't have them showcased in ornate gilt frames. ''You've never told me much about yourself. You spent your summers here, right?''

''Always.'' He found a roll of foil in a drawer and tore off a piece, then covered the casserole and put it in the refrigerator.

''What about your family?'' she prompted. ''Where are they?''

''I have a divorced sister—she's an accountant and lives in Baton Rouge with her two children.'' His expression softened. ''Those two rascals keep her busy. Bertie's gallivanting who-knows-where. And my mother is in St. Louis.''

''Your dad...passed away?''

''No,'' he said flatly, shaking bits of salad greens out of the salad bowls. ''But he and I were never close.''

She'd touched a chord there. ''So why did you go into law?''

With deft movements he rinsed the last dish and slid it into the dishwasher, then shut the door with a controlled movement that belied the sudden tension in his jaw. ''My father.''

''He was a lawyer?''

''Yeah.'' With a glance around the kitchen, Michael strode to the back door. ''And someone had to make sure that he'd never be able to hurt our family again.''

SHE FOUND HIM standing at the edge of the patio, looking toward the carriage house.

''Hannah and I are going for a walk,'' she called out.

He didn't turn around.

"Did I ask too many questions?"

"No. I don't know why I even brought that up—it isn't anything I ever think about anymore."

He turned and sauntered up to her with a twinkle in his eye, then his gaze dropped to her hands. "Expecting rain?"

She glanced down at the umbrella she held and laughed. "Oliver left it here. I'm returning it before he decides to come after it."

From up in the trees came the odd all too-familiar sound of a cuckoo clock. Bertie's vagabond cockatiels.

Hannah stood looking upward, her hands on her hips. When she gave one of the tree trunks a calculating look, Lauren cleared her throat. "No, honey."

"But Mom—"

"We've had one too many tree-climbing escapades already. One of these days those birds will come down for a visit and we'll nab 'em then."

"But it was my fault. They could get hurt—"

"No, Hannah. I'd rather have you in one piece than a dozen captured cockatiels. Go find Baxter and tie him up so he doesn't follow us, okay? We'll leave him home this time, in case we stop anywhere."

With a last disgruntled look skyward Hannah disappeared into the backyard. In a few moments she returned with Baxter and snapped on his chain. The dog's expression—from sad eyes to drooping tail—telegraphed his feeling of betrayal at being left behind.

"We're all set, then," Lauren murmured. The afternoon heat had melted away, leaving a warm silken breeze that ruffled through the leaves and teased at the loose hair curled at her nape. All peaceful sensations, peaceful images.

Except for the man standing too close to her.

"May I join you?"

She hesitated for just a heartbeat. "Of course."

They strolled along the walking path next to the highway, past elegant old estates and some that were in more disrepair that Bertie's, with sagging iron fences and overgrown vegetation. Hannah walked behind them, stopping every few strides to gather dandelions and violets.

"The upkeep on these places has to be enormous," Lauren said, surveying the peeling paint and ragged shingles on one particularly disreputable three-story at the edge of town. "Wouldn't this have been beautiful in its day?"

"Some of these old places were converted to sorority and frat houses while the college was still open. Today they're either apartments or vacant."

Hannah bounded ahead, leaving Michael and Lauren to walk side by side. Now they were passing neat bungalows, white Cape Cods, the occasional modest two-story.

At Elm Street she gestured to the left. "Oliver's house should be down a block or so, according to the phone book."

The house was a neat little brick house with white trim, grass mowed short as a marine's haircut and two trees planted on either side of the cement sidewalk leading to his front door. Red petunias marched up the narrow flower beds flanking the walk.

"I'll bet this house is spotless inside," Lauren murmured as she rang the bell.

Hannah and Michael waited on the walk. "Maybe he isn't home," Hannah said hopefully. "If you just put the umbrella on his steps, we can leave."

The door swung open a moment later and Oliver appeared. He'd taken off his suit coat, but still wore his brown slacks, a crisply pressed white shirt and tie snugged all the way up.

"Hi," Lauren proffered the umbrella. "You forgot this at our house."

He stared at her blankly for a second, then smiled and stepped back to usher her inside. "Well, thank you. Do come in for a moment, won't you?"

Looking over her shoulder at Michael, she mouthed the word *no*. "We were just on our way, and really—"

"Sure, why not?" Michael strode forward with Hannah in his wake and gave Oliver a single handshake. With his hand at the small of Lauren's back, he swept her along inside.

The interior was just as she'd thought—bachelor barren, spotless, not a knickknack in sight. A neat stack of mail on an end table next to the sofa was the only temporary item in the room. The precisely placed doilies over the arms and backs of the two upholstered chairs did not offer an invitation to sit down.

She tried to imagine Oliver sitting anywhere in the room in his robe and slippers, and couldn't.

The large framed photograph of a stern, gray-haired woman over the fireplace caught her eye. "Your wife?"

Oliver nodded. "Gone ten years now, but it's like she's still here with me."

No wonder, with that picture dominating the room. "Lovely woman."

He pursed his lips and looked up at the photograph. "Yes, my dear, she was."

Hannah edged in front of Lauren and looked around. "Oooh, kitty, kitty!" she crooned, darting toward the sofa. "Look, Mom, isn't she pretty?"

A startled cat gave a high-pitched meow and leaped from its hiding place under the coffee table and to the sofa, then bounded onto the end table, scattering Oliver's mail across the slippery waxed surface.

"Young lady!" Oliver snapped. "Leave the cat be!" He dropped to his knees and began scooping up the envelopes strewn across the floor.

Lauren leaned down and gathered a few that had landed near her feet, but he snatched them quickly back.

"I...I'm sorry," Hannah whispered. "I only wanted to pet her." She looked ready to burst into tears.

Lauren dropped her hands onto Hannah's shoulders. "It's okay, honey. No harm done."

Oliver's sharp glance said otherwise.

Michael leaned over to collect two business envelopes that had landed near his shoes. "Guess we should be heading on," he said mildly. "I'm sure Mr. Evans is busy." He handed back the envelopes. "We'll have to get together sometime, Evans."

Apparently back in control, Oliver cleared his throat. "Could I offer you some coffee, perhaps? Tea?"

Hannah gave her a beseeching glance that Lauren deciphered without any problem. "Thanks, but I think we should be on our way. It'll be dark soon. Another time?"

"Interesting guy," Lauren murmured under her breath once they were back outside. "He sure seemed tense."

Michael gave a noncommittal shrug. "He's lived alone for a long time and is probably set in his ways. Maybe company—especially kids—in his home makes him nervous."

She thought for a minute as she watched Hannah skip on ahead, then stoop to pick some dandelions. "Well, I still don't think he should have jumped on Hannah."

"You're right," Michael said cryptically, reaching for her hand as if it was something he'd done every day for years.

Her hand warm within his, Lauren just smiled and nodded her head in response. She couldn't keep her mind on Oliver Wells. Not while Michael's long strong fingers curled around hers. Not while his clean masculine scent teased at her senses and his deep baritone sent shivers of awareness through her.

The horizon was awash in deep pinks and lilacs, with thin charcoal streamers tossed across the sky like a tangle of a child's hair ribbons, as they started down the street. The air felt balmy. Perfect.

A deep sense of contentment filled Lauren's heart as she walked beside him, holding his hand...wishing that this evening would never end.

CHAPTER NINE

"I DON'T SUPPOSE you know what day this is," Michael said over coffee the next morning.

Hannah gave him a somber look. "July the Fourth."

He studied her face over the rim of his cup. "Do you like fireworks?"

"They have them *here?*"

"Honey, every town has fireworks," Lauren said over her shoulder as she flipped a batch of chocolate-chip pancakes.

"But this town isn't very big."

Michael chuckled. "Just wait. We start celebrating at noon, and the town is still rocking at midnight."

"Really?"

He made a show of looking at his watch, surprised at how much he wanted to please the girl. "You and your mom be ready at eleven and we'll go downtown to pick out the best seats in the house."

Hannah was ready an hour early, dogging Michael's heels, asking nonstop questions. "You always came here on July the Fourth?"

"You bet. I spent all my summers here, from first grade through high school." He grabbed a couple of old quilts from the linen closet. "Do you have a fanny pack? You'll need one for the parade."

He laughed at her surprised look and refused to elaborate. Instead, he urged her to find one and get her mother, so they could head for downtown.

With a shout of delight she took off, her braids flying. Soon she reappeared with a bright pink fanny pack buckled around her waist and her bemused mother in tow.

God, Lauren looked good, he thought.

Once she'd started helping him out in the carriage house, she'd abandoned those voluminous caftans for cutoffs and baggy T-shirts, but today was his first good look at the rest of her.

Her trim peach slacks fit as if custom-tailored, while the matching sleeveless top skimmed surprisingly full breasts and narrow waist, revealing a gorgeous figure.

He looked a little higher and found her staring back at him, her eyes filled with doubt. "Is something wrong? Should I change clothes?"

"Lord, no," he managed, noticing the deep blush on her cheeks. "You look wonderful."

She wavered for a second, then wheeled around and started for the stairs. "I'm changing."

"Mom, no. We'll be late!" Hannah cried, dashing after her. "Please!"

Lauren sighed and turned back. She took one of the quilts, followed Hannah and Michael outside, and locked the front door behind them. Hannah danced on ahead like an anxious filly at the starting gate.

When they reached Main Street, early arrivals had

already staked out curbside seats with lawn chairs and folded blankets. Children chased one another through the crowd. Moms fished cans of pop from coolers, quieted babies and called to other moms across the street.

At the intersections, deputies and parade officials wearing *Briar Lake Rocks!* ball caps wrestled traffic barriers into position to close off the main thoroughfare.

A frazzled-looking woman with three kids in tow gave Lauren a curious look, then waded through the crowd to her side. "Aren't you the gal living at Bertie Wells's place for the summer?"

Lauren nodded.

"We had those birds of Bertie's in our trees for the last day or two, just thought you'd want to know. They've flown off somewhere else, though."

"I'm sorry. If they show up again, please give me a call, and I'll try to catch them."

No less than three more people gave her bird-sighting reports as she followed Michael toward his secret destination.

After the fourth one, she gave Michael a weak grin. "At least these people aren't all as hostile as Judge Miller. We'd have a riot out here if they were."

When they reached a shady slope rising above the sidewalk, Michael shook out one quilt, then took the second one from Lauren and spread it on top of the first. "Ringside seats, ladies. We're high enough to see well, and the parade route turns here. Hannah will have good hunting."

After Lauren promised to drop Ashley at home, Sue had left an hour earlier saying that she had a bad headache.

Lauren knew how she felt. It had to be at least ninety degrees in the shade. The raucous carnival music, the noise of the crowd and the roar of carnival engines were pounding through her head in a relentless jungle beat. "Anyone ready for home?"

Michael had been trailing them through the midway since Sue had left, saying little. Now he gave the girls a thoughtful look. "You two need to rest up for the fireworks tonight or you'll fall asleep before they even start."

Both girls looked grimy and more than a little exhausted. By the time they'd dropped Ashley at home and reached Bertie's house, Lauren was ready for a good hot shower and supper—preferably catered. The air-conditioning in the house felt like absolute heaven. Hannah promptly collapsed on the sofa.

Michael glanced at the clock above the stove. "The fireworks will start around nine-thirty, and afterward there's a street dance with a live band. Do you think Hannah's too tired to stay up late? I know Ashley's mom plans to take her."

"I don't know—"

From the living room came a shriek of delight. "Yes!"

"I guess so," Lauren amended. "But she has to be home and in bed at midnight, no later."

Michael nodded. "I'll order pizza, so neither of us have to cook." He disappeared down the hall to his room.

Should be a wonderful evening, Lauren thought wistfully, watching him leave. Hannah would experience the excitement of a small town on a Fourth of July night with her friend. Michael and Sue would probably realize that they were a match made in heaven.

And Lauren could wonder about where her life had gone wrong.

THE COOL DAMP EVENING AIR made Lauren shiver as she sank onto the grass along the shore of the small lake south of town.

Crowds had gathered in the darkness until the entire south shore of the lake was rimmed with folding chairs and blankets. Kids lit sparklers and swung them in arcs and figure eights, laughing with delight.

Hannah and Ashley had already exhausted their supply of sparklers and now sat cross-legged on the grass, squealing their excitement at each new explosion overhead.

Michael and Sue stood a dozen feet away. Sue murmured something to him and he laughed.

Hannah and Ashley turned around to look at them.

"He's so cool," Ashley whispered, her voice dreamy. "I think my mom really likes him."

Hannah stiffened. "Well, my mom liked him first."

The girls fell silent, watching Michael. "I don't think that matters," Ashley said finally. "It's whoever likes who the best, not who was first."

Catching the escalating tenor of their conversation, Lauren moved between them. Their friendship was too new to withstand much conflict—and the subject was more than a little embarrassing.

With a rapid *thump-thump-thump* three fireworks volleys shot into the sky, then blossomed into glittering balls of crimson and diamond sparkles. "Look girls, it's starting! Watch the sky!"

Reflected in the still water of Briar Lake, the fireworks lit the sky in a rapid-fire display of brilliant colors. Cascades of sparkles showered toward the lake like falling stars. The loudest explosions vibrated the ground beneath them.

All too soon it was over in a blinding grand-finale display. "It's soooo beautiful," Hannah breathed in awe.

Ashley rose to her hands and knees and crawled next to Lauren. "I invited Hannah for an overnight. Is that okay?"

Startled, Lauren looked at Hannah.

"Please?" her daughter begged. "I never get to do overnights. Ever."

Sue held out her hands, palms up. "It's fine, really. I owe you for watching the girls this afternoon. We've got some new toothbrushes on hand, and Ashley has extra pajamas. Hannah wouldn't even have to stop at home first."

"You'll be good, Hannah? Not stay up all night?"

Hannah crossed her heart. "Promise!"

"We'll listen to the band a while before we head home." Sue gave Michael's arm a playful nudge. "I'd like just one dance before I go."

Lauren looped an arm around each girl's shoulder and started back to Main Street, feeling more like an outsider than ever. Even before marrying Rick she'd never been good at flirting, and now she didn't have a clue how to even begin.

It's for the best, she reminded herself for the tenth time in as many minutes. *She's local, she's lovely, and I never had a chance with him, anyway.*

But the truth didn't ease the pain in her heart.

MICHAEL TOOK another swallow of Coke and watched the crowd filling Main Street. Not one of the band members was under fifty and most of them were bald, but they weren't half-bad. Their amplification system was outstanding.

The ground shook as they launched into one old Elvis Presley hit after another, drawing out the middle-aged crowd, then rollicked into a fast version of the "Beer Barrel Polka" that sent everyone into the street.

Kids danced with kids, preteen girls swung each other around. A few white-haired couples spun through the street at alarming speed and with amazing skill. Hannah and Ashley were now at the curb, flushed and breathless.

He danced with Sue twice. She was lovely, witty, with soft doe eyes and a body that could have graced the cover of a fashion magazine. She was a sweet woman, and as persistent as a bad cold. He wished she'd go home.

It didn't look as though she planned to do so anytime soon. He gently uncurled her fingers from his arm and nodded toward the girls. "I think they're both beyond exhaustion, and I really should find

Lauren. She was here just a minute ago saying good-night to Hannah.''

"I guess you're right. We'll be off, then."

"Do you need us to walk you home?"

"My car is parked just a block away, so we'll be fine." She gave him a wistful look. "It's been a long time since I had so much fun. Thanks."

Despite her protests, Michael walked her and the girls safely back to her car. Hannah held back when Sue and Ashley got in.

"Can I tell you something?" Hannah whispered. She tugged at Michael's hand and led him a few steps away from the car. Her courage seemed to fail then, for she fell silent and dropped her gaze to the sidewalk.

"Are you worried about staying overnight with Ashley? You can still change your mind."

"Oh, no. It's not that." She shot a glance at Sue's car. "It's just that I thought…well…" She blushed scarlet. "Ashley's mom is nice and everything, but I think she's sort of old."

Stifling a smile, Michael tipped his head. "Old?"

Hannah's blush deepened. "I just thought you should know all the cool stuff about *my* mom. In case you didn't know. Like, that she's a super teacher, and she won lots of awards in college for playing the piano. And she's a really good cook. She's honest and nice to everyone. And she's *really* pretty."

Earlier, Ashley had edged close to him and offered a similar description of her own mother. Evidently the two little matchmakers had become rivals, champions for their moms.

And he'd bet neither mom knew it.

Hannah's earnest appraisal and worry for her mother's welfare touched his heart. "Your mom is a very special lady," he agreed solemnly. "You can be very proud of her."

Back at the car Sue slid from behind the wheel and stood at her open door. "Hannah, are you still coming with us? Is everything all right?"

"Coming." Hannah fidgeted from one foot to the other. "I gotta go. I just wanted you to know."

Michael reached out and ruffled her bangs. "Thanks, kid. You have a good time tonight, okay?"

After Hannah joined her friend, Michael wound through the crowd looking for Lauren. He found her a block away from the band, perched on the top step of the courthouse. Framed by the massive pillars of the entryway, she looked even smaller and more delicate than usual. A half smile curved her lips as she watched the festivities below. She didn't see him until he was at the bottom step.

"Having a good time?" she asked softly.

He bounded up the steps and sat next to her. "I was worried about you."

"Worried?" she looked startled. "Whatever for?"

"I couldn't find you."

She laughed a little at that. "I knew the girls were about to leave. I kissed Hannah good-night and then came up here to enjoy the band."

At the far end of the block, the band set aside their instruments and stretched, then wandered into the crowd for a break.

Someone turned on a CD player, and the lonesome, achingly beautiful notes of Patsy Cline's "Crazy" rose into the velvet night. The younger families were mostly gone now, leaving grown-ups to slow-dance beneath the street lamps.

Lauren had seemed relieved at Sue's arrival at the carnival midway, eager to leave the two of them behind. She'd made herself nearly invisible at the fireworks and the dance tonight, making it clear that she wanted to keep her distance.

But now the music coursed through him, and he had to have just this dance, if nothing more.

"Please," he said, his voice low.

She looked up at him in surprise. "What?"

"Dance with me." He took her hand, pulled her to her feet, and then drew her back into the cavernous shadows.

"Here?"

His eyes twinkled. "I have it on good authority that you are the perfect woman."

"What?"

"Your daughter. Tonight she made sure I knew about some of your finer attributes. And I think she's right on every count."

A rosy blush colored Lauren's cheekbones. "This is so embarrassing. I think Hannah and Ashley might be competing for you. Did Ashley—"

"She did. But I liked Hannah's list better."

Lauren groaned. "I'll talk to her."

"Don't." Sliding his arms around her back, he silently pulled her close, until her head rested against his chest.

The deep pulsing rhythm of the music was even

stronger here, reverberating within the soaring cement walls and pillars until it felt like a shared heartbeat between them. He tipped his head, inhaling the fresh lemon scent of her hair, savoring the feel of her soft pliant body against his own.

They danced in the darkness until it was no longer enough. Michael raised a hand and tipped her face up to look into her smoky hazel eyes. He hesitated just long enough to be assured of her acquiescence, and then he lowered his head and kissed her.

If the pulse of the music had taken over his heartbeat before, it was no match for the explosive shock of kissing Lauren McClellan. When her lips parted beneath his, his blood turned hot. Pounded through his veins. He tentatively lowered his hands, cupped her bottom and held her closer.

Somehow he'd backed her against the wall. He kissed her with the intensity of a long-lost lover, with the desperation of one who'd never hoped for a moment like this. Time stood still. The night and the music and the cold surface of the courthouse wall vanished, leaving only them in the velvet darkness.

"It's time to go home." His voice a low growl, he framed her face gently with his hands.

She looked into his eyes as if seeking the answers to unspoken questions, and then smiled, as if she'd found what she needed to know. "Then let's go," she said simply.

The song had finished. Michael followed her down the steps and then draped an arm around her shoulders and held her close as they walked down Main Street.

They'd just reached the corner when she stopped so abruptly he nearly lost his balance. He looked at her in surprise.

Lauren's face paled. Her eyes widened with horror.

A stocky middle-aged blonde stood talking to an older man not ten feet ahead. At Lauren's sudden halt the woman looked over at her and frowned, as if trying to place her identity. "Uh...hello—"

But just that fast, Lauren disappeared into the shadows.

CHAPTER TEN

MICHAEL STRUGGLED to catch up to Lauren, who was already half a block away. Having to navigate around the crowd leaving the dance slowed him down, but he could see her moving at a rapid walk, darting around people, as if she was trying to escape.

Why had she been frightened? Some overwhelming, primitive force sent adrenaline surging through him, made him want to charge into battle, to be her defender against any foe. But those people back at the dance had hardly seemed threatening.

The middle-aged blonde had looked up, shrugged, when Lauren had turned away. Her companion had given them just a fleeting glance and then continued his conversation.

"Want to tell me what's wrong?" Michael ventured, finally catching up to her.

"Nothing."

"Were they serial killers? Bank robbers?"

She kept walking.

"Local drug dealers?"

She waved off his question.

"Bill collectors?"

Finally she pulled to a halt. Her face still ghostly pale in the soft moonlight, she cast an uneasy glance back toward town and then said exactly what he expected.

"I didn't know them."

"You ran like hell from total strangers?"

"I wasn't running."

"And I did the four-minute mile to catch up." Michael reached for her hand, but she backed up, wary as a deer.

"I'm sorry." After a moment she offered a tremulous smile. "I should have slowed down, you being older and all."

He looked down at her and narrowed his gaze, willing to play along just to keep her talking. "Exactly how old do you think I am?"

"Very. At least…thirty-five?"

"Thirty-six."

"You have four years on me, then." A dimple flashed in one cheek, but there was no hint of humor in her eyes. "Yep, I should have slowed down."

"Tell me," he asked, his voice low, "are you in any trouble?"

She gave a startled laugh. "Me?"

"I'm a lawyer. I spend a lot of time reading people, and I'd bet my diploma that something's wrong."

"Not at all." She wrapped her arms around her middle as if chilled.

He watched her, letting silence fall between them, hoping she'd be uncomfortable enough to fill it, just as most people did.

Her gaze skittered away and settled on the string of street lamps trailing out into the darkness. Like loosely strung pearls, the distance between each one increased until the illumination ended at the edge of town. Beyond that, maybe another quarter mile, lay Bertie's house.

"Nice night," she said finally. She laughed self-consciously, as if finding her own comment hopelessly inane.

"Walk with me."

She hesitated, then fell into step beside him. When he caught her hand in his, she didn't pull away. After a few moments he released his hand and curved an arm around her waist without breaking stride. "If I had a jacket, I'd give it to you," he said. "You're shivering."

"Cool night," she whispered.

But it wasn't. Her beautiful eyes were hauntingly dark in the moonlight, full of silent pain when she looked up at him. He suddenly wished she trusted him enough to confide in him.

Yet with all his interrogation skills, with all his years of experience at delving into hearts and minds in search of truth, he didn't know what to say.

They walked the streets in silence, through wisps of night mist that smelled of moss and damp earth and lilacs, until they reached Bertie's front door. She fumbled for the key. He took it from her shaking fingers, unlocked the door and ushered her in.

She stood silently in the entryway, not making a move to turn on the lights. "I'm sorry for racing off," she said finally. "I'm sure you realize there was nothing sinister about those people. They just…reminded me of things I want to forget."

"I can't help you if I don't know what's wrong," he said softly.

Looking down at the floor, she shook her head. "It's not that simple."

Need for her still thrummed through his veins. Not just desire, but an inexplicable unfamiliar need to protect her and keep her safe at all costs.

The overwhelming heat generated between them back at the dance had shattered the moment Lauren saw the woman with the blond hair. It was for the best. They shouldn't go farther than that one devastating kiss. But something about her made him feel he could do anything, be anything…and even think about a future and commitment.

Which was impossible. He barely knew her. And though logic and single-minded perseverance had helped him achieve every one of his career goals, he'd been a complete failure at relationships.

He moved forward and embraced her, tucking her head beneath his chin, resolutely offering his friendship if nothing else.

"Good night, Lauren," he whispered into her hair. A sense of emptiness spread through him. "Sleep tight."

When he stepped away, she looked up at him with stricken eyes. Then she turned and fled up the stairs.

Watching her, he wondered when he'd made his greatest mistake today—when he'd kissed her, or when he'd let her go.

BY FOUR O'CLOCK in the morning Michael gave up on sleep, pulled on a pair of briefs and a robe, and wandered into the kitchen and then into the study to find something to read.

He'd lain awake imagining what might have been

if Lauren hadn't been spooked by the people she'd seen last night.

The answering machine on the desk blinked steadily.

He crossed the room and hit the button, then picked up a pencil and pad and jotted notes. The vet called—Baxter was due for his vaccinations. The cleaners wondered when someone would be picking up the drapes.

And then Bertie's faraway voice, faint with distance and a poor connection, echoed through the room.

"Hi, Michael. I assume you'll hear this message, or Lauren will tell you. I need you to check on some two-year deposit certificates that came due at my bank in Briar Lake this week. The bank will automatically renew them at the current rate if nothing is done. Can you check on the rate? See if there's something else I should do? I completely forgot. Check my files, lower left drawer of the desk. Lauren has power of attorney, so she can handle the paperwork when you decide."

Michael's hand stilled. He stared at the machine as that familiar burning sensation in his gut flickered, then flamed. *Power of attorney.*

Giving Lauren the tasks of paying monthly bills and depositing dividend checks during the summer was logical. Giving her full access to Bertie's substantial wealth was entirely another thing.

And Lauren hadn't said a word.

When he'd seen her at the bank, she'd blithely mentioned signing some papers, but he'd assumed that had just allowed her access to Bertie's household account. His mind raced, fueled by far too many years in criminal law.

Perhaps she'd been stringing him along, waiting for the right moment to seize Bertie's assets and disappear. The woman in town could have been her conspirator, or an investigator tracking her from some situation in the past.

A cold feeling swept through him at the possibilities, but even as they flew through his mind, he could see her laughing with Hannah. Struggling with the damned goat. He could feel her soft warm body next to his and taste her mouth on his.

He'd felt her integrity and strength, and now he was almost afraid to examine just how deeply she'd settled in his heart. He couldn't have been so wrong about Lauren McClellan.

Yet…Bertie's welfare was at stake.

Her files would reveal a lot of answers. After going through them, he would go to the bank. No matter what feelings he had for Lauren, he would search until he knew the truth. Because whatever he believed in his heart about her, he'd just been reminded of an important lesson.

Before going into corporate law he'd been a defense attorney, and he'd dealt with the worst of humanity. A grandmother who poisoned her grandchildren. Fathers who murdered their children. He knew all too well that the kindest face could mask the blackest heart.

He grimly thought back to his father. He'd been charming and handsome, and it had been charisma more than talent that had rocketed his career to success. There'd always been one more scheme, one more investment opportunity, and he'd cajoled Michael's mother into cooperating until the last cent of her inheritance was gone. She'd loved him too much to question his actions, much less say no, and she'd ended up broke and alone. Michael had never forgotten that lesson on the dangers of following one's emotions.

Lauren McClellan would not be disappearing into the night with anything that didn't belong to her. Not Bertie's money, and definitely not with his heart.

MICHAEL LOCKED the door of the study and came out only for brief breaks. He mentally cataloged the stacks of files and papers on the desk and floor every time he left to make sure nothing was disturbed in his absence. If Lauren had something to hide, she'd slip in when he wasn't around.

She was at the stove stirring something in a big pot when he walked into the kitchen at noon. She glanced at him, a faint pink blush rising in her cheeks, then turned away. Embarrassment about last night, or something else?

"Haven't seen you all day, stranger," she said, not meeting his eyes. "Are we working on the carriage house today?"

"Probably not. Bertie left a message on the answering machine. She wants me to go through her…investments, and help her decide what do with them."

"I'm glad she asked you and not me," Lauren said easily, settling a lid over the pot and turning down the temperature. "I wouldn't want that responsibility."

She didn't *look* unduly worried about the prospect of Michael delving into Bertie's finances.

"It will probably take all day to go through everything, so you don't have to stick around if you have something else to do."

"We'll head for the beach, then." She inclined her head toward Hannah, who was busy setting the table. "She just got home from her overnight at Ashley's."

"Did you have fun?" Michael asked.

Hannah's eyes sparkled. "We got to stay up late, and we didn't get up till ten. Then we had blueberry waffles with ice cream on top."

"She's probably not too hungry for lunch," Lauren said dryly. "Would you like to eat with us? We're having homemade vegetable soup. Hannah found an overgrown vegetable garden in back. Apparently Bertie planted it this spring and then decided not to follow through."

Another worry. Bertie hadn't let him know she was leaving the country, hadn't remembered the due date on her deposit certificates, and now, heaven help her, she had forgotten an entire garden in her backyard. The sooner she returned from Europe, the better. Maybe with the right medications, the right doctor…

"Well?" Lauren gave him an expectant look.

"Uh…yes. Lunch would be great. How often have you seen my aunt over the years?

"Mmmm…maybe just a few times since college, but we exchange letters four or five times a year."

"Have you seen changes in her? Forgetfulness? Confusion?"

Lauren laughed. "Are you still worrying about her? Believe me, if you and I are as sharp as she is when we hit even sixty, we'll be doing well. She's amazing. From the looks of her, she'll be gallivanting around when she's 103. Now let's eat, okay?"

Lost in thought, he barely tasted the soup. Ten minutes later, he was back in the study with the door locked. Lauren was probably right about Bertie. That issue aside for the moment, he started analyzing Lauren's lack of response regarding his afternoon project.

She'd seemed practically relieved that he would be occupied for the day and had taken Hannah to the beach right after the dishes were done. Either she hadn't embezzled any money or had covered her tracks very well. Or maybe she had yet to make her move.

His laptop set up on the desk, he carefully inventoried the records Bertie kept on her stocks. Bonds. Mutual funds. Next he started on her bank statements for the past five years to look for patterns of withdrawals and destinations of the money.

The process gave him a headache as soon as he realized that in those five years Bertie had never once balanced her checkbook. Often the checks weren't even recorded in her checkbook registers and just appeared in the bank statements and in the stacks of canceled checks. The recipients of some of the checks were nearly indecipherable due to her looping impatient scrawl.

It was a miracle that he hadn't found more than

a few overdraft notices in all that time. Then again, anyone who kept at least ten grand in her checking account wasn't likely to overdraw very often. By evening he'd reached the current year.

And then he found exactly what he'd hoped he wouldn't. A dozen two- and three-thousand dollar withdrawals out of her savings account within the past six months, most within the past three. And the bank statements for the past few months were missing. From the dates shown on the other statements, the next one was due to arrive in two weeks. What would that reveal?

With a sinking heart he began making a list of his next actions. Now he needed to find out exactly how long Lauren had been ''helping'' his aunt, when she'd obtained her power-of-attorney status and the identity of the mysterious blonde at the dance last night.

By the time Bertie got back to town, he would have the answers he needed, but he wouldn't worry her with the details until then.

Drumming his fingernails on the desk, Michael stared out the tall windows at the purple-and-blood-red wash of color in the evening sky and wondered if it echoed the bruises in his heart. When had he come to care so much for Lauren, and why did it all have to go wrong?

It was time to ask Oliver a few questions.

OLIVER SWITCHED on the light in his study and locked the door behind him. No one was in his house, but only a foolish man took chances. Oliver was not a foolish man.

With reverent care he fitted the small key into the slot and lifted the lid of the velvet-lined box. Inside lay five black velvet pouches. And within them, his investments. Untraceable. Secure. Not a fortune, but enough for one lonely old man.

Sometimes he enjoyed spilling the contents out onto a square of black velvet placed under a bright light, so he could see the fiery brilliance of each diamond and touch his future.

The phone jangled. His heart skipped a beat when he heard the voice on the line.

"I've found some…irregularities in Bertie's accounts, Oliver. Before I go any further with this, I thought I'd check with you."

Oliver closed his eyes. His pulse pounding in his temples, his wrists. *Not now.* "I don't know that I can be much help. I'm not Bertie's attorney, you know."

"I did find your name on a few documents."

"There were a few times she came to me, just small matters. I helped her out as a favor to a dear old friend."

"Do you know how long Lauren McClellan has been associated with my aunt?"

"They've known each other since Lauren was a child. Her grandmother was one of Bertie's closest friends."

"In a business sense. Recently."

Oliver stroked the velvet box. It calmed him, as it always did. Helped him think. "I couldn't say— probably well before Lauren actually came to town for the summer. Bertie seemed very confident that Lauren would handle everything."

"Did you ever write any business contracts between the two of them?"

"I didn't, but Winthrop had a number of associates over the years, and they were all very fond of both him and Bertie. She could have called on any one of her late husband's friends. Given her haphazard record-keeping, you probably won't find any documentation." He cleared his throat delicately. "If you…think anything is amiss, I wouldn't want Bertie to know until she returned. It would be terrible to worry her too much while she's out of the country, don't you think?"

"That's true."

Above Oliver's desk hung his framed college diploma. He glanced up at his reflection in the glass and wondered when the man looking back at him had grown so old. With a weary sigh he hung up the phone.

Michael had just given him the perfect answer to his dilemma, and enough time to make it happen.

Oliver picked up the phone once more and began to dial. It was time to call in a favor.

CHAPTER ELEVEN

LAUREN PACED the kitchen floor, glanced at the clock, then paced some more. Michael had been oddly cold and distant yesterday, and she'd felt bereft. It had been a clear wake-up call.

She needed to tell him the truth about herself. It hung over her like a storm cloud, tempering what she said and did. Fear of discovery had been eating at her. Heaven knew, she'd tried to tell him about her deferred sentence and Rick's incarceration before, but somehow the words always lodged in her throat. Hannah was so happy this summer, and Michael had been a wonderful influence on her. What if he couldn't accept Lauren's past?

Still, he deserved the truth. This morning he had borrowed her car to go check on the progress being made on his Jaguar's repairs, but when he came back, she was going to tell him everything.

When she heard him come up the back steps, her stomach started dancing, and her pulse kicked into high gear.

You can do this. It won't be so bad. He'll listen and he'll understand. And then maybe there will be a chance for this relationship to go farther.

He gave her a swift assessing look as he walked

into the kitchen. His eyes narrowed. "You look a little nervous."

"Me?" Her heart skipped a beat. "Just restless, I guess. Did they say when your car will be done?"

"The interior kit was shipped from some company in California last week. After it arrives, it depends on the shop schedule. Could be this month, maybe next."

Lauren looked up at him from beneath her lashes, trying to gauge his mood. "I'm still really sorry about what Daisy did. She hasn't escaped since then, thank goodness."

"I'd say that one incident was enough. The insurance agent laughed so hard he nearly passed out, and then he tried to deny the claim." A flicker of amusement glinted in Michael's eyes, then disappeared. "But there was an upside to it all—your help with the carriage house."

"I really haven't done all that much."

"You've been a real trooper." He sighed heavily, his eyes filled with sadness and doubt. "I know you've been doing Bertie's banking while she's gone. Is there anything you'd like to tell me?"

At the Fourth of July dance he'd kissed her as if he'd been starving for her, yet he didn't even trust her. That hurt more than she could believe. "I pay her bills and deposit her checks. What else is there?"

"You never mentioned having power of attorney."

"I told you she had me sign papers so I could handle her business. Bertie wanted me to be able to handle anything that came up until she got back to the States."

"You said that you'd signed a bank document so you could make deposits and write checks. That's not the same."

Lauren sank into a chair, her thoughts sliding back to another time. The questions, the accusations. Lawyers who twisted what she said and only looked for guilt. How could she have forgotten that Michael's career was spent doing the same thing?

"Are you are accusing me of something?"

"No, I'm just stating facts and looking for some answers. I found some…discrepancies in Bertie's accounts, and I've been trying to sort them out for her. Perhaps you can help."

"Discrepancies? Are you wondering if I did something on purpose?" She'd once been falsely accused of a crime in a court of law, and by people on the streets of that town. None of it had hurt as much as these words of doubt from a man who'd touched her heart. "I think of her like a second grandma, Michael. I didn't ask for any legal powers, but she insisted. But believe whatever you wish, because people usually do."

"Do you want to elaborate on that?"

"It wouldn't matter, would it?" She rose abruptly, tears stinging her eyelids. If he was so suspicious about the simple power-of-attorney situation, she could only guess at what he'd think about her legal history.

He gave her a long pensive look. "I just said I was trying to sort things out, Lauren. I didn't accuse you of anything."

"The message was clear enough. You think I *wanted* to be Bertie's power of attorney, and now you've found that her accounts don't add up."

"No, I—"

"Go ahead. Hunt through her records. You won't find proof of something that never happened."

"I think you're overreacting here."

Over-reacting? A few minutes ago she'd been on the verge of trusting him with knowledge about her past. Hoping that with the truth out in the open, there might be a chance for their relationship to deepen.

Now she knew that if any money was missing, he would assume her guilty and have her arrested. She could face the loss of her probation, and worst of all, Hannah could fall into the hands of her father.

No matter what the outcome of this situation with Bertie's accounts, his lack of faith had just threatened Hannah's safety. And that Lauren could not forgive.

Michael reached for her arm, but she turned and walked away.

THE FOLLOWING WEEK was one of the slowest Lauren could remember. Rain fell four days out of the seven, and the temperatures soared, bringing on record humidity, even for mid-July.

Hannah alternately sulked and whined about the weather, wishing she could be outside. Several people called, reporting that they had seen the cockatiels, but invariably the birds were gone by the time Lauren and Hannah arrived.

And every moment Lauren worried about Bertie's

financial records, feeling both hurt and regret at Michael's veiled suspicion.

He went through all the files again, but could find no proof that anyone other than Bertie had made withdrawals. Of course, he'd added, with Bertie's haphazard bookkeeping, one couldn't be sure of anything.

Small comfort, Lauren had thought. Since then, she and Michael had formed a wary truce. Two adults sharing a house. Polite coexistence and nothing more.

Clearly aware of that undercurrent of emotion, Hannah became tense and cranky, but refused to talk about her feelings. Lauren knew that her daughter still harbored hope for a future with Michael as part of her family. It could never happen.

Lauren followed through on her promise to help him with the carriage house by showing up every day, but it took several days for a crew to install the heating and cooling system, and then Michael and Brad started working on the walls. Lauren ended up taking Hannah and Ashley to the municipal pool or to the beach whenever the sun shone.

Another seven weeks and the summer would be over. The tension of living in the same house would be over, too. After that she'd never see Michael Wells again. A good thing, she reminded herself firmly. Definitely a good thing.

Lost in her thoughts as she fed the parakeets, the jangle of the phone startled her.

"I'll get it!" Hannah yelled from the kitchen.

The sound of feet thundering up the stairs came almost immediately. "It's some people in town.

They say Bertie's cockatiels are in their tree and to come right away! They, uh, don't sound very happy about it.''

During the past week she and Hannah had posted notices all over town about the lost birds. There'd been two more sightings since the Fourth of July, and a couple of crank calls, but the birds were still flitting about town, sharing their odd sound effects with all their unwilling—and annoyed—hosts. ''Did you get the address and phone number?''

Hannah triumphantly held up a slip of paper. ''I'll bet we get 'em this time!''

They made it to the house on Sycamore Avenue in minutes. A balding man in a white T-shirt and suspendered pants marched out of the house as soon as they parked.

''In the backyard,'' he growled, dispensing with any effort at the usual pleasantries. ''I've never liked those damn cuckoo clocks, and I've been listening to one all morning in my apple tree. If I'd had a gun, I would have shot those birds an hour ago.''

''That's what everyone tells me,'' Lauren said reasonably. ''I understand.''

He appeared somewhat mollified. ''I've got a couple of fishing nets, if you think it would help. With good long handles.''

She looked at Hannah. ''Nothing else has worked. What do you think?''

''Maybe. If the net was in front of them and I climbed the tree? If we get one, I'll bet the other will be a lot easier to catch.''

''Sounds good to me.''

The man brought the nets from his basement and held them up for inspection. "This do?"

Lauren managed her first real smile in days. "With those long handles and your height, we might just get them this time. Let's hope!"

They all moved quietly to the backyard and surveyed the tree. The birds were sitting side by side on an outer branch midway up, apparently dozing.

"First time they've been quiet for hours," he muttered, glaring up at the tree.

Lauren moved a lawn chair into position, stood on it and held her net as high as she could. She could reach within inches of the birds. If they swooped downward, she had a chance. If they didn't... She tried not to imagine the ongoing phone calls, the angry people in town.

The man followed her example, and his reach was even better. Hannah started climbing the tree.

Lauren held her breath. "Careful!" she mouthed when one of Hannah's feet slipped.

High enough now, Hannah eased out along a branch just above the birds. Reached out slowly. The branches rustled beneath her hands. The birds awoke. They craned their heads around to look at her, then they peered down at Lauren. In a flash, Hannah nabbed the gray.

Amid piercing squawks and wildly beating wings, the other took flight and careened off a branch, then blundered down into Lauren's net. She quickly dropped to the ground and reached inside to protect its flapping wings with a gentle grasp.

Within minutes both vagabonds were in the cage

Lauren had been keeping in the backseat of her car for the past few weeks.

"The streets of Briar Lake will be quiet once again," she muttered, draping a cloth over the cage. "And I'm not going to miss all those irate phone calls a bit. Not," she added quickly, looking at the old man beside her, "that I blame anyone for being irate. I'm so thankful you called."

"Just keep the damn things at home."

"Hannah?" Lauren crossed her arms and gave her a stern look.

"I'm really sorry. They'll never get loose again, cross my heart!"

Lauren fervently hoped her daughter was right.

THE AWKWARD SILENCE between Michael and Lauren faded to cool civility by the following week. He'd been unfailingly polite and thoughtful, and had been especially kind to Hannah, who now seemed to hang on his every word.

No matter how his doubt had hurt, Lauren couldn't fault the man for being concerned about his aunt's welfare. His strong sense of honor and responsibility had been clear from the start. And, truth be told, she probably had overreacted to his questions. But given her history, it was hard not to expect the worst.

"Brad and I are painting today," Michael said over coffee at breakfast on Wednesday morning. "Would you and Hannah like to help?"

Hannah beamed at him. "Oh, yes!"

At the thought of Hannah's exuberance combined with a few gallons of paint, Lauren frowned. "You wouldn't be too worried about neatness here, would you?''

"Spills don't matter because the carpets don't go down until next week. Hannah could start in the storeroom.'' His eyes twinkling, he lowered his voice so only Lauren could hear. "She'd have fun, and I can touch up the walls later.''

Hannah shadowed him all day and talked about him at night. In just one summer Michael had shown her that all men weren't like her dad.

"Thank you,'' Lauren murmured. "You've been very kind to Hannah.''

"I wish…'' His eyes deep with regret, he reached out to lay a hand on her arm. "I wish I could take back what I said to you after I went through Bertie's records. Just because there's a mistake somewhere doesn't mean that you had anything to do with it. Sometimes I seem to possess a remarkable lack of tact.''

"I understand.'' She tried to smile. Someday there might be someone who would be able to give her his unequivocal trust, but Michael would not be that man. "Shall we get to work?''

In an hour they were unwrapping new paint rollers. Michael gave Hannah a small brush and an ice-cream pail with a few inches of paint in it.

"Thanks, kid,'' he said, tapping her nose. "I hardly recognize you with all that pretty hair under a scarf, but you're still cute.''

As he walked away, the look of adoration in Hannah's eyes nearly broke Lauren's heart. The end of summer was going to be hard in many ways.

She looked over her shoulder. Brad was out of

sight, but Michael had gone back to painting near the front door. In a tattered T-shirt with the sleeves torn away and those faded blue jeans, he still looked like a million bucks.

But there was no point in admiring his body or imagining anything more. With a sigh she turned back to the storeroom wall.

Hannah grinned up at her. She'd painted the outline of a cartoon superhero on the wall, complete with improbably bulging biceps and a toothpick waist.

"Hannah!"

Hannah made a face back at her. "I'll just paint over it."

"Do it before we get fired for goofing off." Lauren laughed and studied the picture for a moment. "Is this anyone you know?"

"Michael," she said shyly.

Hannah's obvious hero worship of Michael touched Lauren's heart. "I think he needs bigger feet."

Hannah dabbed on longer feet, then leaned back to admire her work. "Yep, I think this is him." She giggled.

A shadow fell across the floor. Lauren looked up to see Michael, his hands braced on either side of the door. "Just had to see what was so funny about my storeroom," he said, studying Hannah's artwork. "Interesting paint job. This guy looks pretty tough."

Blushing, Hannah silently dipped her brush back in the paint bucket and obliterated every square inch of the figure on the wall with rapid strokes.

He looked over Hannah's head at Lauren and

raised a brow. She shook her head. Obviously mother and daughter had been sharing a secret neither was ready to divulge.

"Thanks for doing such a good job in here. You two are a great help."

When he was back out in the other room, Lauren reached over and curved an arm around Hannah's shoulders. "Do you want to talk about anything?" she murmured.

Hannah kept her gaze fastened on the wall and continued working. "No."

"You know you can always talk to me about anything that's bothering you."

"I'm not a baby. I don't need a dad," Hannah muttered. "Just…sometimes it would be kinda nice, you know? Maybe if we had one, you wouldn't have to worry so much about everything."

"You do have a father, Hannah," Lauren said carefully. "I know he isn't here, but—"

"*No.*" Hannah's voice was low and fierce. "I don't. Real ones love you no matter what. They don't lie and steal and end up in jail."

"Oh, honey—"

"My dad could have come to see me in March when he got out. He didn't even care enough to come find me, not even to s-see how much I'd grown up." Hannah angrily rubbed at her eyes with the back of her wrist.

Lauren put her roller back in the tray and gave Hannah a hug. "If I could change that, I would. But you know what? Everything will be fine. Soon we'll have a nice little house of our own, and I'll be a teacher again. We'll stay in one place so you can make lots and lots of friends. I promise.''

Hannah stared down at the paint splatters on the floor. ''Ashley thinks Michael likes *her* mom, but I think he likes you best. Maybe you could get married, and we could all stay here.''

Lauren gave a startled laugh. ''Things aren't always that easy. Adults take a lot of time finding the right person. Even then, it doesn't always work out.'' Giving her daughter a swift kiss on the forehead, she pointed to the wall. ''Now let's get done here so we can go to the pool later, okay?''

By noon the storeroom and reception areas were painted, and Michael and Brad had nearly finished the office. Hannah was tired and had headed back to her bedroom with a book.

Lauren stood in the center of the reception area and studied their progress as she peeled off her gloves. The large windows and high ceilings, coupled with the oyster-white walls, gave the area an airy spacious look.

''It's too bad you'll have to be lining these walls with a ton of law books,'' she called out.

Michael stepped out of the office, a paint roller in his hand. ''I'll have some, but dusty old law books aren't necessary anymore. We have everything on disk.''

''Then this place ought to look really nice.''

He grinned at her—his first genuine smile since their confrontation a week ago. With a paint smear on his cheek and that dark hair tipping over his forehead, he looked as pleased and proud as a young boy.

She couldn't help but smile back. "What about the furniture? Wall decorations?"

"I was just going to ask if you and Hannah would like to go to St. Paul with me to do some shopping. It's just a few hours away."

Now *there* was a bad idea. Being trapped in a car with Michael for an entire day was a *very* bad idea.

She'd long since squashed any romantic notions about him, but the man emanated a sensual heat that her body seemed incapable of resisting.

"I'll take you two to dinner. Your choice."

"I don't think so. The animal chores, you know. The place in general." She gave a helpless shrug. "But thanks."

"If we leave in the morning, we'll be back by early evening."

"No."

He sighed. "Come with me, and we'll have time to talk in the car. I'd like to have you and Hannah along. Please?"

It was the last *please* that did her in. The old warmth had stolen back into his eyes.

Brad had stepped out of the office but had clearly heard every word. Behind Michael's back he gave her a two-thumbs-up and nodded his head vigorously.

She sent Brad a dark look, then shifted her gaze to Michael. "Okay. But one negative comment and you'll be hiking all the way back."

She wondered if they would even make it past the city limits.

CHAPTER TWELVE

BRIMMING WITH EXCITEMENT, Hannah helped with the animal chores the next morning, while Lauren made a quick phone call in the privacy of her bedroom.

Kay Solomon answered on the second ring.

"I want to go to St. Paul for the day. Is that okay?" Lauren twisted the phone cord around her fingers, holding her breath. How would she ever explain being unable to leave town if Kay said no? The terms of her deferred status were very clear—she could only leave town with the knowledge and permission of her probation officer.

"Job hunting?"

"Not yet. Michael Wells wants my daughter and me to go with him. He's looking for office furnishings."

"That guy you were with at the dance? *Not bad.*"

"It's not like that at all. We're just…company for him, I guess. Nothing more."

Kay's throaty chuckle came through loud and clear. "Tell that to someone else, but not me. I saw you two dancing in front of the courthouse."

Heat rose in Lauren's cheeks. "I want to apologize for ignoring you after the dance. Seeing you took me by surprise. I was afraid…well…"

"...that I'd shout, 'Hey, Lauren, how's your probation coming along?'"

"It's hard, worrying about people finding out and what they'll think. People love gossip, and especially love to think the worst."

"Your judgment is public record, but no one up here is likely to ever start researching your past without good cause," Kay responded, a smile still in her voice. "And I don't plan to be announcing it."

"I'm really sorry if I've offended you." Lauren bit her lip, feeling as if she'd betrayed a friend. "I should have known better."

"Understandable concern, really. As for St. Paul—you have permission to go. And, honey, good luck. That man looks mighty fine."

Mighty fine certainly described the brand-new, customized van waiting outside the house when they were all ready to leave.

"Wow!" Hannah breathed. "A color TV, a VCR...oh, and earphones! This is great. Is it yours?"

Michael looked at her in the rearview mirror as he started the engine. "It's just rented for the day. I'm not sure how much use we have for those extra features, though. What do you think?"

"Cool!"

To Lauren he said, "My car is ready to pick up, but it would have been a tight fit for all of us, and yours doesn't need all the extra mileage. Can you hand Hannah the package by your feet? I stopped for a couple of movies."

Twisting in her plush captain's seat, Lauren

helped Hannah start the television and VCR, then helped her adjust the headphones.

Within moments they were out in open country and Briar Lake was far behind. Michael glanced in the rearview mirror at Hannah again, then smiled. "For all she knows we could be in Siberia," he said, slipping a Loreena McKennitt CD into the stereo and turning the volume low. He settled back in his seat. "Everything okay?"

"Perfect." Lauren studied his strong profile and curbed the temptation to sweep back that recalcitrant lock of hair that always fell over his forehead. "I'm still not sure why you wanted us to come along, though."

He shrugged. "I figured you and Hannah could use a break, and having you two along makes the trip more enjoyable."

"I'm not sure you realize how much you mean to Hannah, but I want to thank you again for being so nice to her."

"She's a great kid."

"I mean it. She's never really had a good man in her life, and until this summer I didn't realize how much she needs that. One of these days…"

Michael's hands tightened on the steering wheel. "What, you'll marry some guy just so she can have a dad?"

"No, never that. But maybe I should think about moving closer to relatives, so she can have more contact with her uncles and cousins."

"I thought your only relative was a grand-mother."

"She raised me, but I have a couple of uncles in Oregon and California, and some cousins out East."

"That far?"

"Well, it's not like we would have to walk there," she said dryly.

Michael fell silent, his eyes on the road ahead. Jewellike lakes sped past; stands of pines and hardwoods interspersed with rolling meadows. Every hill brought new, postcard-perfect panoramas of dairy cattle on hillsides, towns tucked into valleys, white steepled churches.

An early-morning rain, now clearing into dazzling sunshine, turned every color vivid and fresh. Sparkling whites. Impossible emeralds. Hip-roofed barns the brightest ruby-red.

Hannah, engrossed in *Star Wars,* hadn't yet thought to start her when-will-we-get-there? routine. Lauren sighed with contentment. Why had she even hesitated to come along?

Michael glanced at her. "Still awake?"

She tipped her sunglasses down and looked over at him. "This country is so beautiful I'd hate to miss it."

"I wanted a chance to talk to you." He nodded toward the backseat, where Hannah remained enthralled by the movie. "This might be the best chance I'll get for a while."

"You're probably right. Hannah has always been a night owl, and she gets up with the birds in the morning. I swear she runs on batteries." Lauren caught sight of a white clapboard church on a distant hill. Its steeple towered above the trees. "Isn't that just beautiful? Such a shame that the newer ones are so modern. I wonder if—''

''Lauren.'' His voice was low, a quiet command. ''I don't believe you had anything to do with Bertie's missing money.''

She gave a short laugh. ''Why did you come to that conclusion? I don't look like an ex-con?''

''I just don't think you're capable of something like that.''

''So now I'm not smart enough?''

''Lauren.'' With an exasperated sigh he shifted his weight in his seat, then continued in a lower voice, ''When I discovered that you had access to Bertie's finances this summer and then found those discrepancies in her accounts, I jumped to conclusions.'' He reached out and took her hand in his. ''I'm sorry.''

She gave him a wary look, then managed a smile.

''I'd like the three of us to have a good time today. What do you think? Truce?''

His hand was warm and hard, and her own felt delicate within his grasp. Protected. Maybe—just for today—she could pretend she had neither a past to hide nor a future to fear. ''Truce.''

They drove on in companionable silence for several miles, then he began a conversation. ''We've shared that house for some time now, yet there's so much I don't know about you.''

''Ditto. You first.''

He laughed at that. ''What do you want to know?''

''Are you looking forward to starting a solo practice?''

"Absolutely."

His answer came so swift and hard that she stared at him in surprise. "From the looks of your car and your wardrobe, you did pretty darn well back in Chicago."

"Almost too well. I had the right address, the right car, the right fiancée, the right country club. I was a partner in a successful firm. What more could there be?" With a humorless laugh, he reached for the thermostat. "Cool enough?"

She nodded. "So why did you leave paradise?"

At least a mile sped past before he answered. "I believe in the law. I believe in justice and honor." A muscle jerked in his jaw. "As a partner, one doesn't control the firm as a whole."

"Your partners were incompetent?"

"No."

"Dishonest?"

He hesitated. "No."

She'd bet otherwise, looking at the fine lines of tension bracketing his mouth and the small muscle that still flicked in his jaw. "Tell me about your career."

He relaxed. "I started out as a public defender, then I went into corporate law."

"Why did you switch?"

"As a public defender I dealt with murderers, rapists, child abusers. Professionally I had to do my best, and I was good at my job, so a lot of my clients went back out on the streets." He gave a heavy sigh. "I reached a point where I couldn't live with that responsibility."

"What about corporate law?"

"My clients wore suits, instead of tattoos and leather. But some of them were just as guilty. And I got tired of the long hours spent protecting their bank accounts. I'd rather work with individuals than corporations."

"Then Briar Lake ought to be ideal."

A corner of his mouth lifted. "Yes. On my own, I'll have the kind of life I want to lead, without the incredible pressure for billable hours. My old partners billed for time if they thought about a case while they were taking a shower." He shook his head slowly. "I can give clients quality representation for an honest price, and if my name is associated with a case, I'll have control over how it's handled."

Lauren smiled at him. "You sound like the kind of lawyer the rest of us hope to find."

"I just wish I'd made my decision a couple years sooner."

"Why?"

He stayed silent for several moments. "We represented a pharmaceutical company in a product liability case involving a high incidence of birth defects. When one of our partners found obscure early research on the drug indicating risk, the company quietly demanded that she bury the information so it wouldn't be used in court." Michael fell silent, his face etched with deep regret. "She did, our firm won the case, and two days later a grieving father killed himself on the courthouse steps. The letter he wrote before his suicide was the most gut-wrenching thing I've ever read."

"Were you on the team defending the company?"

"No."

"Yet you feel responsible?"

"I was a partner in the firm."

"How could you possibly know all the details of every case it handled?"

"This time I should have," he bit out. "If I'd been a little less trusting, a tragedy might have been prevented." Michael gave a deep sigh. "But that company accounted for over fifty percent of that partner's annual billings. She decided their business was more valuable than ethics."

"That's awful. But I don't see how you—"

"Now there are new lawsuits pending, and the reputation of the firm has been tarnished. That partner was disbarred."

"You can't change what happened."

A corner of his mouth tipped into a wry smile. "Thanks for trying."

"To console you? I'm not. It's just that you can't take the blame for a partner's actions."

"She wasn't just another partner," he said heavily. "She was my fiancée."

Lauren took a sharp breath. "Maybe there was some explanation—"

"She was my *fiancée,* for God's sake. I believed in her. If I'd known what was going on, maybe I could have changed things before it was too late. I'll never forgive her or myself for that."

"I...I'm so sorry," Lauren whispered as her own dark secrets flashed through her mind.

Now she knew exactly how Michael would react

when she told him about her past. For him, honesty was absolute, and he'd already been betrayed by a woman he'd loved.

THEY STOPPED in Stillwater for an early lunch. Cars jammed the main thoroughfare. Tourists crowded the sidewalks and filled the shops. Just by chance they found a parking place within a few blocks of an Italian restaurant.

"And I thought Briar Lake was busy," Lauren murmured when they found an empty booth inside.

"It's a popular town in summer. I used to have a boat near here, on the St. Croix. This was my favorite place to eat back then."

Hannah looked up from her children's menu. "You have a boat? Really?"

Laying his menu aside, he shook his head. "I sold it a few years ago because I never had time to use it."

"And now that you're moving to Briar Lake?"

His smile was pure satisfaction. "I expect to have time to do everything I haven't done in years. Get a dog. Travel more. Buy a sailboat. I'm planning on nine-to-five work days and having a life."

"What kind of dog?" Hannah piped up.

"A golden retriever...or maybe some homeless mutt from an animal shelter. Maybe both."

Hannah's expression turned wistful. "Will you have kids, too?"

"Be careful or Hannah will volunteer," Lauren teased. "That all sounds like a lot of fun."

Over plates of spaghetti and manicotti Lauren looked up and caught Michael watching her, his expression pensive. She eyed her forkful of spaghetti. "What, I'm not eating this right? I'll admit to a few batches landing in my lap, but—"

"No. I was just wondering what you planned to do in the future. Where you wanted to be in five years, that sort of thing."

"Either I want to find a good career or I want to win the lottery. Maybe both," she said lightly, winding more spaghetti around her fork.

He leaned over and dabbed at Hannah's chin with her napkin. "Italian food sure can be tricky to eat. How's your lunch?"

A pink blush stole across the girl's cheeks and she lowered her eyes. "Great. It's really great." She pushed a meatball around her plate, then corralled it against a heap of spaghetti. "I wish we got to do things like this a lot."

"You like going out to eat?"

Her gaze shifted to a family seated in the corner, with a toddler smashing crackers on his highchair tray and an older girl coloring on a placemat. The father bent over his daughter's artwork and gave her a hug.

A look of pure longing filled Hannah's eyes. "I...just like being together, like a family."

Lauren covered one of Hannah's hands with her own. "You and I *are* a family, sweetheart," she said quietly. "The very best, for always and forever."

Lauren always listened to Hannah's prayers when she tucked her in at night, but she'd also overheard her daughter's extra prayers, whispered long after the lights were out.

Lauren knew what Hannah wanted. She wanted a

dad who would love her with all his heart. One who would spend time with her. Lauren had seen the wistful look on her daughter's face whenever she saw families playing together at the park.

Over the past weeks her prayers had changed from simply wanting a dad to wishing Michael could be her new father.

And that was one wish Lauren couldn't grant.

In twenty minutes they were back on the road, heading east. Hannah chattered about Bertie's animals and her friend, Ashley, then fell silent as the skyline of St. Paul appeared on the horizon and the freeway traffic grew heavy.

Michael took an exit, made a number of turns down narrow city streets and finally pulled up to a towering old brick building near the river. A small brass sign over a side door read *Sawyer Antiques.*

Lauren looked around in surprise. "I thought you were hunting for office furniture."

He turned off the engine and pocketed the keys. "I am."

"Somehow I'd expected a big state-of-the-art building by one of the suburban malls." She glanced over her shoulder toward the backseat, where Hannah was now watching a cartoon. "Maybe we're better off out here. The combination of antiques and young children makes me a little nervous."

"Bring her in. She'll like this place," Michael said. "You two have to help me decide what to get, then afterward we'll find someplace good for an early supper."

Lauren unbuckled her seat belt, then helped Hannah turn off the TV and VCR.

The building was more than just a store. It was an immense warehouse packed with antiques of all description. A jumble of furniture. Paintings. Cases of old jewelry and glassware. Old books were stacked twenty high on tables scattered throughout the area and crammed into towering bookshelves against one wall. Period costumes gathered dust on headless mannequins. In the dim light it looked more like a museum storeroom than a place of business.

At Hannah's gasp of delight Lauren caught one of her hands within her own. "Stay with me. And whatever you do, don't touch anything!"

From somewhere in the back came an elderly man. Gaunt and stooped, with wire-rim glasses perched at the end of his hooked nose, he looked as though he were one of the antiques on display.

"Daniel." Michael shook the man's gnarled hand, then introduced Hannah and Lauren. "This time I need office furniture. Do you still have the pieces we discussed?"

The old man motioned for them to follow him to a far corner of the warehouse. He flipped a switch along the wall, illuminating dozens of desks, tables and bookcases.

"What do you think—will this do? It came from an estate sale in Summit Hill. Fella was a well-known judge in his day." A broad smile crinkled Daniel's face into a mass of lines as he motioned to several large pieces at the back. He looked down at Hannah, then waved dismissively. "You don't have to hold on to her, ma'am. This furniture has been around a good 150 years and will outlast us all. She'll be fine back here."

Hannah squealed with delight as she darted forward. "Wow! Is that ever cool! Look at all the drawers!

The pieces he'd pointed out were massive. Two large bookcases with glass doors and spiral-carved trim. A heavy library table. A matching monstrous barrister's desk with at least a dozen cubbyholes and drawers.

"This is absolutely beautiful," Lauren breathed, running a hand over the silky-smooth surface of the library table. "Is this cherry?"

Daniel nodded in approval. "Correct. It's darkened with age, of course. Look here." He bent down to swing back a heavy piece of trim on the desk to reveal a bank of small drawers. "It has false-bottomed drawers and secret compartments throughout. I probably haven't found them all."

While Hannah searched for hidden doors in the desk, Michael inspected the condition of each piece. "The history of this furniture seems to give it life, don't you think?" he mused.

Lauren watched him in rapt amazement. "For some reason I figured you for chrome and steel. Something powerful, distant. Sort of cold."

"Thanks." He came around the back of a bookcase and gave her a dry smile. "Was that a personality assessment or a furniture description?"

Daniel chuckled. "She definitely hasn't seen your home." He leaned closer to inspect the grain of the library table. "These pieces will be a fine investment. They'll only become more valuable as time goes on.''

"They aren't meant to be an investment, but I'll keep that in mind. So, ladies, what do you think? Would this work in my office back in Briar Lake?"

"Oh, yes! I love it!" Hannah exclaimed. "Just think what you could hide in all those drawers!''

"I'm glad you like it." Michael grinned back at her, then looked at Lauren. "Well, what do you think?''

"Absolutely perfect. It's all beautiful.''

She watched the two men confer over prices and delivery options, still feeling a little shell-shocked. He was a deep, complex man and she had a feeling it could take years to delve through all his layers. But at the core he was a strong man with a rock-solid sense of honor, one who would protect and love his family well.

And with every passing day, she fell in love with him just a little more.

THERE WAS SOMETHING…intimate about driving in the darkness back to Briar Lake. The headlights cut a bright swath of illumination through the night, but the van's interior was lit only by the soft glow of the instrument panel. Hannah had fallen asleep in back soon after they'd left St. Paul. Lauren was curled up in her seat, her feet tucked beneath her, staring at the road ahead.

In the dim light her red hair looked deep auburn, those changeable hazel eyes a dark brown. She hadn't spoken in a long time. "Tell me about your marriage," he murmured in a low voice. "Were you happy?"

She gave him a startled look. "What?"

"I'm not asking for intimate details. I was just wondering if you were happy."

She glanced over her shoulder at Hannah. "He gave me my daughter," she said simply. "And she's my life."

"Have you heard from him lately?"

"No. As far as I know, he's still in California. We haven't seen him in several years."

"*Years?* What about Hannah?" From the cool tone in her voice Michael knew she wanted to drop the subject, but she'd avoided the topic once before and he had to know more. "Visitation? Shared custody?"

"He didn't ask. Of course, I should have guessed that he wasn't planning on child support, either."

"That isn't his choice." Anger rose in Michael's chest. "Hannah deserves better than that."

"Yeah, well...he made some fairly serious threats the last time I saw him. It's better having him out of our lives than to have the money."

"The courts would protect you." Michael's anger grew. "There's a federal law against fleeing a state to avoid child support."

"Knowing Rick, he's probably been through three jobs in the past three months and doesn't have a dime. Sometimes—" Lauren turned to face Michael, a pensive look in her eye "—I wonder how I could have married a man who could change so much. Did I see qualities in him that never existed? Was there something wrong with *me?*"

Michael draped his arm across the back of her seat and ran his fingers through her long hair, then massaged the back of her neck, half expecting her to pull away. Instead, she leaned into his touch. Her thick curly hair felt like silk. Beneath his fingertips, the skin at her nape was warm and impossibly soft.

If they'd been parked somewhere, he would have given in to the overwhelming urge to envelop her in an embrace. If they'd been alone in the car, he would have pulled to the side of the road. Hearing about her past made him want to give her comfort, support. But that was hardly an option with a child in the backseat.

He shook his head, trying to pick up his last train of thought. His mind went blank.

He'd hoped to reestablish rapport today. Hell, he missed her company. The sound of her laughter and having her close enough that he could breathe in the soft scent of her.

"I want to apologize," he said finally. "It seems that my first instinct is to doubt and my second is to protect. More than once I've been unfair to you."

That got her attention. She turned to face him.

Michael shoved a hand through his hair. "I'm a lawyer, and none of this is coming out right," he said ruefully. "You'd think I could do better."

"I think I'll like this, anyway." Her eyes twinkled in the darkness. "Apologies are always good."

"I once mentioned that I needed to watch out for my mother and sister, as well as Bertie. They're fine women and I'm proud of them, but I can't count the times I've bailed them out of financial disasters.

They give too much, try to help too much, and not one of them has a lick of financial sense.''

"So you're always riding to the rescue?"

"In one way or another—which is why I've been so concerned about Bertie's finances while she's gone. Frankly, a lot of money seems to be missing and I can't figure out where it went. But it isn't just her—my mother nearly had to claim bankruptcy last year, because she got so far in debt with her credit cards. And my father—'' Michael caught himself.

"What?" She was looking at him now, her eyes gentle and expectant.

"He wasn't much better."

She waited for him to continue. Maybe it was the quiet darkness in the car or the late hour. Maybe it was the woman beside him. He never talked about his father, but now he found himself dredging up the old memories.

He gave a bitter laugh. "My father made as many fortunes as he lost on the stock market and ended up broke. He always said I'd never amount to anything because I was too much like my mother's side of the family—lacking in the vision and daring it takes to make millions.''

"Sounds like he was reckless, not visionary and daring." Lauren paused. "And you became a great success. Did he ever admit he was wrong?''

"By then it was too late."

"I'm so sorry."

"Oh, he's not dead. By the time I succeeded, it was already too late to let him know. Ironic, isn't it?" Michael sighed. "He's been a patient in an Alzheimer's unit for the past five years."

THE DRIVE TO GREENLEIGH took exactly twenty minutes. Oliver had driven it many times throughout his career, during those long years of struggle with his own failing practice and, later on, to his job at Winthrop Wells's satellite office. The trip had provided far too much time for reflection.

Now he only made the trip for banking purposes. With a population of forty thousand and a dozen banks to choose from, he'd remained carefully anonymous to the plethora of young tellers who came and went over the years. It wouldn't do to become well-known.

His caution had been warranted. Today he'd purchased money orders from five different banks using cash, and there'd been no hint of recognition from any of the clerks. A total of five thousand dollars was now on its way to a bank in the Cayman Islands.

Only this time it wouldn't be deposited in a numbered account. He'd opened a new account and used a name, instead of a number. Not that the "owner" knew about it. Of course, Oliver wouldn't be able to touch the money again. But there was far more at stake, and this step he was taking would provide good insurance. If anything went wrong with his plans, he'd now have the perfect person to blame.

All he had to do now was to reveal some information about the holder of the account, so news of this transaction would have the proper impact. It had been a stroke of luck to find someone who knew so much about her past.

CHAPTER THIRTEEN

"THANKS AGAIN for taking us along last Thursday."
Lauren stretched luxuriously, then lifted her glass of
iced tea in a toast. "It's been over a week, and Hannah is still talking about how much fun she had."

She and Michael were on the patio. Since the trip
to St. Paul they'd fallen into the comfortable habit
of going outside together after Hannah's bedtime.

Now a heavy wash of stars blanketed the sky.
Crickets chirped. From somewhere in the branches
above came the buzz of a cicada. As usual the mos-
quitoes were out in full force, but Lauren had placed
burning citronella candles at the perimeter of the
patio and had sprayed bug repellent for good measure.

"She must have been exhausted to go to bed so
early tonight."

"World record. I couldn't even get her to bed at
eight o'clock when she was a baby." Lauren waved
off a June bug that bumbled against the side of her
chair. "When will your furniture arrive?"

"August thirteenth, unless there's a delay with the
carpeting."

She leaned back and closed her eyes. The day had
grown oppressively hot and humid by late afternoon.
Even now the temperature had to be in the eighties.

"Bertie called and left another message. She confirmed that she'll be back September third and wanted us to know that she's booked a commuter flight from Minneapolis to Briar Lake."

He stayed silent for so long that she thought he hadn't heard her. "Have you given any more thought to staying in Briar Lake?"

She shook her head. Impossible hopes had been dancing at the edge of her mind for weeks now. Finding a teaching position here, finding an affordable house. Putting down roots.

All that was overshadowed by the idea of staying in the same town as Michael with little chance she could ever have him. If he couldn't forgive his ex-fiancée for her involvement in that trial, how would he react to Lauren's embezzlement charges? *I've got to tell him. I've got to give him that chance.*

A dark shadow loomed over her. She hadn't heard him move, but now she looked up to see him silhouetted against the moonlight, tall and powerful as a warrior of old.

He bent forward and braced his hands on the arms of her chair. "I wanted to do this all the way home from St. Paul," he said, leaning closer. "I've thought about it every night since."

She stared at him, transfixed by the intensity of his gaze and by an overload of sheer sensual awareness. With any other man she might have felt intimidated, but this was *Michael.*

He took her hands in his and helped her rise, then looked down at her. She could see his gaze darken. He ran his fingertips down her cheek, lingered at her lips, then cupped the back of her head to pull her closer.

At the first brush of his lips a shiver of anticipation raced through her. She melted against him, needing more, afraid he would stop.

Before, if she'd been asked to describe him in a single word, she would have said *controlled*. That word sure didn't describe him now. His fingers trembled. She could feel the heavy beat of his heart against her chest.

His fierce low whisper rasped across her senses when he pulled back. "You're so very, very beautiful."

There were just four weeks left of summer, and she held no foolish illusions about the future. He wouldn't follow her. She couldn't stay. And no one on the planet would ever make her feel this way again.

She held two fingers to his lips, then caught his hand in hers. "Come with me," she whispered, wishing this night could last forever.

"MOM, ARE YOU AWAKE?"

"No." Lauren opened one bleary eye and peered at the alarm clock. Nine-thirty. She never slept this late, ever, not even—

Realization slammed through her like a freight train. Sitting up with a jerk, she patted the bed linens next to her and sank back in relief. He was gone.

Except...it would have been so wonderful to snuggle close and doze the morning away, to savor the head-to-toe contact of skin against skin. "Can you let Baxter out?"

"He's already outside. I think Michael let him out." Hannah came at a run and threw herself onto the bed. "What's for breakfast?"

"Mmmm."

"It's Saturday morning, so when are you making pancakes?"

Lauren gave up. "Give me a good-morning hug and I'll get dressed."

"I love you, Mom." Hannah wrapped her arms around Lauren's neck.

Lauren hugged her close, marveling as always at the precious warmth and brimming energy of her child. Such a change since the beginning of summer, when Hannah had been too sullen and aloof to allow such affection.

"When did you get so big?" Lauren murmured against her hair. "You should still be a little baby."

Hannah giggled and curled closer as Lauren started humming a lullaby. "I don't fit anymore!"

"Ahhh, but you'll always be my baby." *And there's nothing I wouldn't do to protect you.* With one last fierce hug, Lauren kissed Hannah on the top of her head. "Now scoot, honey, so I can get dressed."

She's my priority, Lauren reminded herself firmly when standing in the shower a few minutes later. Thinking about Michael and impossibly happy endings wouldn't change the facts.

Even while at Briar Lake, she'd never really had a chance.

MICHAEL BACKED the Jag out of the garage and drove it around to the front of the house. He'd picked it up a few days ago and had immediately parked it out of Daisy's reach even though the goat had been on her best behavior for the past few weeks, thank goodness.

Michael debated taking the car out in the country for a spin. In the past, the feel of the Jag's responsive steering wheel beneath his fingertips and the roar of its powerful engine had filled him with a sense of excitement. Now it seemed almost... pointless to go by himself.

Maybe he'd invite Lauren and Hannah to come along. In just a month Bertie would return, and then Lauren and her daughter would be leaving. The thought filled him with sadness.

He couldn't get Lauren out of his mind. If not for the risk of being discovered in her room, he wouldn't have left her bed this morning. She'd been beyond his wildest imagination last night. Passionate, sweet and tender, she'd touched his heart and soul like no one ever had before, breaking down every wall of control he had.

He shook his head, wondering what had happened to his firm resolve to avoid emotional commitments. It hadn't taken long for Lauren and her little daughter to slip right past his defenses. If he wasn't careful...

Across the sweep of lawn beyond the hedge separating Bertie's and Miller's front yards, he caught a flicker of movement.

Miller appeared on the other side of an overgrown section of hedge with a set of electric clippers in hand, expertly sweeping the clattering blades across a ragged section of foliage.

The judge glanced across the lawn at the Jag. Clipped another section. Then he turned off the clippers and looked at the Jag again. Even at a distance his keen interest was obvious.

Perhaps this was a chance to finally mend some fences, Michael thought. "It was my grandfather's car," he called out. "Mint—until the goat got at it."

The judge snorted.

"Want to look her over?"

Miller hesitated. Then he sidestepped through an opening in the hedge and started across Bertie's front lawn. Watching the man's purposeful stride made it easy to imagine him in his robes, presiding over the courtroom with an iron fist.

With any luck, he had a short memory when it came to goats and roses.

The judge halted on the other side of the Jag. His hand hovered above the bonnet, then dropped to caress the gleaming paint. "It's a beauty," he said gruffly. "Great year. I had a '61 E-Type OTS years ago."

Here at last was common ground. Cars. Life would be a lot easier if everyone got along. Michael cocked an eyebrow. "With the outside bonnet latches?"

"And the welded louvers," Miller said with reverence. He circled the Jag slowly, taking in each detail. "My wife never could figure out how to shift it. Oh, she hated that car. I can still hear her stripping the gears trying to get it into first."

"That gearbox was a challenge for a lot of people."

The judge raised his gaze and gave Michael a long assessing look. A corner of his mouth lifted into the barest glimmer of a smile. "Absolutely right. But that just made it more fun, eh?"

Michael grinned as he tossed him the keys. A look of surprise on his face, Miller caught them in midflight.

"Want to take her for a drive?"

"No. I don't think—"

"Why not? It's fueled. It's just sitting here."

"It's a long time since I've been in one of these. You grow old, turn practical—"

"Then this is your chance." Michael reached down and opened the driver's-side door. "Head out of town. Go out on the highway."

Miller hesitated only a second. "Maybe just around the block. Thanks, son."

Michael nearly missed seeing the twinkle in the older man's eye as he slid behind the wheel and settled into the leather seat. Within moments he'd started the engine, flawlessly shifted the car into gear and was heading out onto the highway, driving as carefully as if the car was made of spun glass.

Shooting the breeze about Jaguars wouldn't forge a strong relationship. Michael didn't expect one. But there would be a lot of years ahead when he had his office out here, next door to Miller's place, and he would also be standing at the bar of Miller's courtroom.

With luck, perhaps Daisy's damage to the relationship could now be undone.

"I CAN HIRE someone to do this," Michael said dubiously, looking at the rolls of wallpaper lying on the floor.

Lauren waved away his suggestion. "That heavy furniture arrives in two weeks. You'd never find someone to do the job before it's here."

"Well—"

"You planned on doing just two walls in each room, and anyone can handle that much. It should be a breeze. Want to help?"

"Well…" A scene from an old sitcom ran through his mind. Being draped in sopping limp swaths of paper did not sound like fun.

Lauren looked up at him, her eyes sparkling. She'd tamed that magnificent cloud of red hair into another one of those haphazard knots on her head, but already escaping locks were curling around her face.

She wasn't a classic cool beauty like Gloria. She was much more. Her enchanting hazel eyes and that dazzling smile took his breath away.

"Okay," he said finally, knowing that wallpapering was just another excuse to spend more time with her. "You're sure you know what you're doing?"

"Nope. But how hard can it be?"

THEY HAD THE WALLS sized by noon, with Hannah's help. After that, the job was just a tad harder than Lauren had predicted.

"So 'prepasted' doesn't actually mean it will *stay* on the wall," he observed, watching her slap up a recalcitrant sheet of wallpaper for the third time.

As before, it stayed up for about twenty seconds.

Then slowly, gracefully, it pulled away from the wall at the top and hung down in an ever-widening arc.

She glared at it and jammed her hands on her hips. She'd done that several times already, and there were gray smudges of paste on each side of her jeans. "Maybe I soaked it too long."

"Maybe we should give up?"

"Nope." She pawed through a large plastic bag, then triumphantly withdrew a quart container. "This paste is for the border, but I'll bet it will help get this first piece up. After that we'll try moving a little faster."

Michael helped her measure and cut each piece, then hauled the dripping rolls out of the water tray and handed them to her. Cold and slimy with wet paste, the wallpaper was more than a little slippery. But with each section Lauren grew more adept at positioning and smoothing it out.

"Well, what do you think?" she asked triumphantly, standing back to admire their handiwork. "I think we make a pretty good team."

"Just so long as you do the creative part and I man the preparation." Michael countered. "You did a beautiful job."

She looked down at her damp T-shirt, then held up her hands and wiggled her fingers. "I feel like I've been finger-painting in glue. I'd ask you to kiss me as my reward, but we'd probably be bonded for all eternity."

The T-shirt clung to the ample curves of her breasts, and bonding didn't sound like a bad idea at all. He'd been thinking about that and a whole lot more for the past hour. He gave her a wicked grin. "We could find out just how well that paste works on fabric and skin."

"I don't think so!"

He inclined his head toward the windows. "The blinds aren't up in here, but the storeroom would be okay."

He reached for her and she darted away with a shriek of laughter, but he caught her wrist gently and spun her back.

And just that fast, the playfulness faded.

"I want you so much," he said, gazing down into her bewitching eyes. They looked green now, mysterious as cat's eyes. He slid his hands down her sides and rested them at her waist, then pulled her close.

Her eyes widened. "I can definitely tell just how much."

Her smile turned soft and seductive, and his heart skipped a beat. A rush of adrenaline and sheer hot desire rushed through him, eclipsing all other thoughts. With one swift motion he swept her up in his arms, then carried her into the storeroom and kicked the door shut.

"But Hannah might—"

Michael grinned at her in the darkness as he reached for the doorknob. "It locks."

"And the cement floor—"

"We don't need it."

In the total darkness he undressed her slowly, kissing each newly exposed expanse of skin, savoring the softness and scent of her. "You are incredibly beautiful."

"That's because you can't see in the dark."

He gave a low laugh. "In sunlight or darkness there couldn't be anyone as beautiful. It isn't just what I see, it's what you are."

She wrapped her arms around his neck and kissed him until they were both breathless. And then she undressed him with such deliberate care that he wanted to move away and do it faster himself.

His body tensed as she slowly slid off his jeans and then his briefs. A jolt rocketed through him when she finally took him in her hand.

Kissing her hard and deep, he lifted her to the edge of the countertop and stepped between her legs, then trailed kisses down her neck. She moaned with pleasure as he drew a nipple deeply into his mouth.

Desire slammed through him when she wrapped her legs around his hips. He lifted her away from the counter and drove into her with a groan of pure male satisfaction. His world narrowed to her warmth, her touch, her wildly erotic response.

Swamped by a primitive need to claim her as his, he covered her mouth with his own and kissed her with everything he possessed.

His release was incredibly powerful. But that rush of pleasure paled as he recognized something far more overwhelming. These stolen moments would never be enough.

He'd viewed his lack of emotion over the end of his engagement as an innate inability to love. Now he knew that love had never been part of that relationship. He knew, because he was rapidly falling for Lauren McClellan, and he'd never felt this way before.

He needed her as much as he needed his next breath.

THE CARPET LAYERS arrived first thing Monday morning. By midafternoon the floors were covered in a rich forest-green plush so deep that she just couldn't resist. Lauren slipped out of her shoes and shuffled to the center of the room, then closed her eyes in sheer bliss.

Hannah did haphazard cartwheels, then dropped to the floor to do snow angels in the deep nap. "Look, Mom! They even show!"

Michael leaned against the door frame, his arms folded and ankles crossed. Lauren's heart tripped into a faster rhythm at just the sight of that powerful build and bronze tan. Whenever he held her in his arms, her blood rushed through her veins and her heart ached with all that couldn't be. *You've got to tell him, an inner voice whispered to her night and day.*

"Well, what do you think?" he asked, glancing around the reception area. "Did we do a good job?"

Hannah did a somersault that took her to his side. "It's cool! I love this carpet. It's as soft as my bed!"

From over her head Michael flashed a wicked grin. "What do you think, Lauren? Is it soft enough?"

She couldn't think of anyplace on earth she wouldn't want him. She looked away and focused on the walls. Two were painted white, and the papered walls were a subtle weave of white, ice-blue and gray. "The carpet is perfect with the paint and wallpaper. I love the border you chose."

The strong chemical scent of new carpeting still lingered, and she wondered what this room would look like five, ten, fifteen years from now. Redecorated, maybe, but the large windows would still look out on the lush grounds, and birds would still sing from the branches overhead. Perhaps there would be rows of photographs on the walls, of Michael's children and that boat he planned to buy. Those images of the future sent a pang of loneliness through her.

"Mom?" Hannah took her hand and looked up at her with a worried frown. "Are you okay?"

Lauren managed a smile. "Of course. I'm just a little overwhelmed by how well it turned out."

"I think we ought to celebrate," Michael said. "You two were a great help." He winked at Hannah, then offered Lauren the crook of his arm. "Shall we go?"

Lauren looked down at her faded jeans, baggy red University of Wisconsin T-shirt and paint-spattered orange sneakers. "Wait until I do the animal chores, and then I'll change."

He gave her a head-to-toe glance. "You look just right."

"You do, Mom. Honest!" Hannah practically danced with delight as Michael led the way to the far end of the backyard, with Baxter galloping eagerly ahead.

HANNAH ALREADY KNEW about the surprise, because Michael had told her. He'd even shown her the pictures and asked her advice before deciding which one to choose. She'd felt all warm and funny inside for the rest of the day, thinking about him caring about what *she* thought. And he'd done just what she said!

Now, as they locked the backyard gate behind them and headed for the long flight of rickety wooden steps leading down to the lake, she could barely keep quiet. Back in the yard, Baxter whined, wanting to come along.

"Where on earth are we going?" her mom asked, gingerly skirting a tangle of raspberry vines arcing over the path.

"You'll see!" Michael looked back at Hannah and winked, and that same warm feeling wrapped around her heart.

Bertie must not have used the lake much, because the dock and the boathouse behind her house were both as swaybacked as an old horse, and you had to be careful where you stepped. With a jungle of cat-tails crowding the shore and masses of seaweed that made the water look like watery spinach, Hannah couldn't imagine swimming off the dock.

But that dock led straight to adventure, because tied way out at the end was the most beautiful boat she could imagine.

It was red, but not like any red Hannah had ever seen. It looked as if there were a million red sequins glittering beneath clear glass, so bright that it almost hurt to look at it.

"Oh, Michael!" Mom exclaimed. "When did you get this?"

"It came yesterday. I don't have a vehicle that can pull a boat trailer, so the guy told me he could deliver it after church. What do you think?"

Her eyes lit up. "It's gorgeous. I haven't been on a boat in years! Have you been out in it yet?"

"Nope." Michael led them down to the shore and eyed the dock. "Here, I think you'd better follow me. Watch where you step or you'll wind up in the lake."

At the end of the dock he took each of them by the elbow and steadied them as they climbed into the boat. It bobbed and swayed as they got in, and for one crazy moment Hannah imagined it flipping them into the lake. Knees bent, she quickly sat down on a bench seat at the back and gripped the edge with both hands while her tummy did a few flip-flops of its own.

Michael sure seemed to know what he was doing. He started the engine and let it run awhile, then he tossed lifejackets to Mom and her. By the time they'd figured out the zipper and straps, he had the boat headed out into the lake.

When her tummy finally settled down, Hannah looked over at her mom and beamed. "He wanted a sailboat, but I told him you didn't know how to run one of those."

"Hannah!" Mom looked horrified. "That doesn't mean a thing. This is his boat, not ours!"

"I'll probably find a sailboat later on," Michael said easily. "This was advertised locally, and I thought it might be fun to do a little waterskiing sometime. What do you think?"

"It's beautiful."

"I think it's cool!" Just ahead of the steering wheel were a couple of steps leading down into an open doorway. "What's in there?"

"I don't know." He grinned at her. "Someone must have left that door open. Want to check it out and let me know?"

Hannah stood up cautiously. The floor seemed alive beneath her feet, dipping a little with each wave, but by the time she reached the door she'd straightened and didn't feel quite so leery.

"Wow!" she breathed as she went down the stairs. Cushioned seats lined both sides of the curved hull, and to one side were a tiny sink and stove. Soft lights ran along the low ceiling.

Hannah flopped down on the cushions and wriggled with delight. Her foot hit a crinkly plastic bag. She reached around and started to push it out of the way—and spied a gift-wrapped box inside. For mom?

"What do you think?" Michael called to her. "Was this the right decision?"

"Oh, yes!"

Bracing an arm on either side of doorway, he frowned as if trying to remember something. "I know there was something I needed to tell you..."

Hannah eyed the plastic bag, hoping.

He thought for another moment and then reached for the bag and handed it to her. "I think this is for you, Captain. When you get your sea legs, you can help me at the helm, okay?"

He winked and backed out, leaving Hannah to stare at the bag in her hands. The warm feeling in her heart was now spreading clear to her fingers and toes. *Michael bought me a present!*

The temptation to rip away the paper and bow almost sent her fingers flying, but she stopped to admire the shiny gilt bow and iridescent foil wrapping.

Then she closed her eyes tight and thought about all the Christmases and birthdays when she'd hoped for a present from her dad. But hoping hadn't made things happen, and he didn't love her enough to remember. It hurt being someone so easy to forget.

Her vision turning blurry, Hannah slid her fingers into seams of the wrapping and opened the gift with reverent care.

CHAPTER FOURTEEN

THEY WERE A FEW hundred yards out into the lake when Hannah came running up the stairs with the captain's hat clutched in her hands. The look of delight on her face made his heart turn over. He pulled back on the throttle. "What's the rush?"

She threw herself into his arms so fast she would have knocked him over if he hadn't seen her coming. He hesitated for just a split second, then leaned down to hug her back.

"It's wonderful," she cried, looking up at him with the biggest smile he'd ever seen. "Thank you!"

Lauren rose from her seat at the stern and came over to ruffle Hannah's hair. "What do you have there, squirt?"

Hannah stretched up to give Michael a kiss on the cheek, then released him and displayed her new cap. "Isn't it cool?" she asked, running a finger along the nautical emblem on the bill. Her voice lowered to a whisper. "I sure wish I had a dad like you."

Lauren looked at Michael, a shadow of sadness in her eyes. "That was really nice of you." She reached out to position the cap on Hannah's head, then gave her daughter a loving tap on the nose. "You look like quite a sea captain."

"Does this mean I get to steer?"

"I don't know about that," Lauren said. "How fast does this thing go?"

"Close to forty miles an hour, I think," Michael said. "But I'll stay right behind her. Come on, Hannah." He winked at her as he slid out of the seat and helped her get settled. "Here, you steer like this—" he demonstrated "—and if you want to go faster, you push on the throttle."

She reached for the throttle, her fingers trembling. "Here?" she asked, twisting around to look at him.

"Exactly right." Michael felt a wash of unexpected emotions flood through him. Family. Togetherness. Protectiveness. *Exactly right, indeed.*

He was thirty-six years old. A professional success, respected among his peers. But in all his years he'd never learned just how much he was missing by being alone. It had taken one ten-year-old sprite and her mother to teach him that. And now he couldn't imagine Briar Lake without Lauren and her daughter at his side.

WHEN A DELIVERY VAN from St. Paul pulled into the driveway, Hannah shrieked with excitement and rushed to the front door.

"The desk is here!" she yelled, racing back to the kitchen. "Come and see!"

Another milestone marking the passing of summer, Lauren thought sadly as she followed Hannah outside. The past week had been wonderful. Michael helped with animal chores—except the birds, which made him sneeze. Every evening they all went out on the boat. After Hannah went to bed at night, she and Michael talked—often well into the wee hours of the morning.

They hadn't made love again. Perhaps it was silent acknowledgment that the end of the summer was approaching. Not an hour of a day passed that she didn't long to be in his arms again, just once. But in just three weeks Bertie would return, and then she and Hannah would be on their way back to reality.

Now she found herself wishing for more. Every time she heard Michael's voice, every time he dropped a swift kiss on her cheek or twirled Hannah around in a big hug, she thought about her future and wished he'd be a part of it.

But wishes were a foolish waste of time. Nothing could turn back the clock or change the past.

Michael sauntered around the corner of the house just as Lauren and Hannah reached the moving van, Baxter at their heels. Hannah ran up to Michael and grabbed his hand. "I can't wait to see the desk again! All those neat little places you can hide things!"

He reached down and lifted her into a quick hug as he often did, and she squealed with delight. *Just like the dad she's never had,* Lauren thought, fixing a smile on her face as he approached. How had she ever thought him cold and detached?

Perhaps he'd changed. Perhaps she'd just learned to look a little deeper and see the man beneath the aura of control and sophistication.

In an hour Michael had helped the delivery driver and his assistant unload the furniture and arrange it in his office. As soon as the truck left, he turned to Lauren and grinned. "Well, what do you think?"

"Absolutely perfect," she murmured, studying the room.

The massive cherry barrister's desk dominated one wall, the glass-doored bookshelves flanked the east windows. The conference table, placed at the far end of the room, had ample space for its eight chairs. When two overstuffed leather chairs were delivered the next day, the office would be complete.

Hannah had been searching for hidden cubbyholes in the desk for the past ten minutes, calling out to Michael as she discovered each one.

"I think we should celebrate, don't you?" he said, moving to Lauren's side.

A thrill of awareness shimmered through her, as it always did when he drew near. "To christen your new office?" She managed a teasing glance, hoping he couldn't see the emotion that had to be in her eyes. "Champagne over the prow of the conference desk? Confetti from the ceiling fans?"

"I was thinking more in the line of dinner. Just the two of us. Maybe someplace with music and dancing?"

"Hannah…" She felt his arms come around her, then he pulled her back against the solid wall of his chest. Was that his heart beating, or was it her own?

"Maybe she could go over to Ashley's place for a few hours. Ashley has been here overnight several times when Sue had to go out of town, so I'll bet Sue'll return the favor."

An evening alone with him. The invitation conjured up thoughts of intimate conversation over candlelight and how it might feel to slow-dance in Michael's arms just once more. Soon the summer would be over, so what harm could there be? *Only that you'll care even more,* warned an inner voice.

But that didn't really matter, because she knew that he'd already stolen her heart. There would never be a day in the future when she didn't wonder how he was doing or wistfully imagine herself back here at Briar Lake. For her, it was already too late.

SUE WAS MORE than willing to take Hannah for the evening. "If you want her to stay all night, that's fine," Sue whispered to Lauren as they stood at Sue's front door. Amidst peals of laughter, the girls had already disappeared into Ashley's bedroom.

"Thanks, but we'll be back in a few hours for her. I don't really think we—"

"I've *seen* the way that man looks at you."

Lauren managed a smile. "There's very little chance of anything happening between us, believe me."

Lifting a hand to wave at Michael, who was leaning against the hood of his car, Sue grabbed Lauren's hand and pulled her into the entryway.

"Earlier this summer I tried my best to get his attention. And—I say this with all due modesty—I usually catch the guy I'm after. I may not be able to keep him, or I may not want him after I've got him." She flashed a grin. "But Michael wouldn't even give me a second look."

"He must need glasses."

"No, sugar. I think he needs *you*."

"Hannah and I are leaving Briar Lake."

"That's crazy! He cares about you both. You three could be a wonderful family."

Lauren shook her head as she turned to the door. "It won't happen—and wishes won't change a thing."

HANNAH AND ASHLEY knelt on Ashley's bed and watched out the window as Lauren climbed into the Jag.

"Did you see that?" Ashley sighed. "He opened the car door for her. Just like in the movies. I think he *could* be in the movies, don't you? He's soooo cute!"

Hannah slid a wary look at her friend before turning back to watch as the Jaguar disappeared down the street. Ashley's mom was pretty enough to be in the movies herself, and Ashley constantly talked about how neat it would be if Michael and her mom got married.

The whole idea made Hannah's insides tighten with jealousy. "He would never go off and be in the movies. He's going to stay right here, 'cause he likes my mom a whole lot."

"But you guys are *leaving*," Ashley said, her tone accusing. "If he liked her so much, he would make her stay."

"Well...maybe we'll come back."

"Or maybe they'll both pine away for each other and die." Ashley flopped melodramatically against the pile of ruffled pillows and stuffed animals at the head of her bed.

Ashley watched way too many movies. "I don't think so," Hannah retorted. "My mom says people

should go after what they want and work at it, because we only get one chance to live.''

''My mom wouldn't have to try. If she told Michael she liked him, he'd probably never look at
your mom again.''

''Oh, yeah?'' If Hannah had been a few years
younger and not so grown-up, she would have
shoved Ashley right off the bed. ''So how come my
mom is going out with him tonight and your mom
is stuck home with us?''

Ashley's brow furrowed. ''Maybe because your
mom has to help him work on that office and stuff.
And she cooks...and he has to live in the same
house. Sort of like a return favor.''

The truth of those words wrapped around Hannah's heart like a cold hand. Maybe he *was* just
acting nice because she and her mom lived in the
same house. Maybe her dreams of having Michael
as her new dad were as hopeless as wishing for a
school cancelation the day of a big test.

Ashley, whose moods changed faster than frogs
hopped, now gave her a sympathetic smile. ''Wanna
play Monopoly?''

''Whatever.'' Hannah picked up a floppy pink
bunny and held it out to stare into its black eyes,
then drew it to her chest and hugged it tight.

A HALF HOUR LATER Lauren and Michael were
seated at a window table at The Shores, a softly lit
restaurant along the far side of Briar Lake.

Outside, moonlight glimmered across the lake.
The intimate atmosphere created by dark oak furnishings, burgundy tablecloths and candles made it

seem as if only she and Michael were in the room. Soft haunting strains of classical music rose from a small chamber orchestra seated in the far corner.

Lauren closed her eyes and took a slow breath, savoring the rich buttery scent of the lobster tail and steak on her plate. "If this tastes half as good as it looks, I'll be in heaven," she murmured. "I don't remember the last time I got to eat in a place like this."

She looked up to smile her thanks and discovered that Michael was watching her, his gaze dark and intense. "Is something wrong?"

In the dim light his silvery blue eyes were darker. The shadows gave him a hard masculine look that made him appear larger, more powerful. One corner of his mouth tipped upward. "We haven't had an evening like this all summer," he said in a low voice. "Here we are, living together…"

A woman at a nearby table glanced over the top of her menu at them. "Not living together," Lauren shot back in a stage whisper. "We're simply under the same roof."

He heaved a sigh. "And a strange situation it is. How about you, Lauren? Are you sleeping well at night? Do you ever lay awake and wonder—"

"No!"

He gave a low laugh that sent sensations skittering across her skin. "Me, neither."

She forked up a piece of lobster and dunked it in the melted butter, then poised it before her mouth. "We've handled this in a very mature manner, I think. Two adults, able to share the same space—"

Michael winced.

"—for an entire summer." She eyed him as she popped the lobster into her mouth, hoping he believed every word. She didn't want to see embarrassment and pity in his eyes if he thought she'd come to care for him too much.

"I'd like you to stay."

Lauren's heart teetered at the edge of a towering cliff. "What?"

"Stay here in Briar Lake."

She waited silently, but there was no *Stay because I love you.* Or *Stay because I need you.* Her heart tumbled slowly back to earth. This wasn't a proposal. What had she been thinking? That this attorney would want to marry a woman like her?

"How could I afford to stay?" she asked with a short laugh.

He started to speak, then fell silent.

Dark and large and dangerous in the flickering candlelight, his masculine presence drew her like a hypnotic force. She wanted him so very much. She waited a little longer for him to say something—anything—but the moment had passed.

Lauren felt a piece of her heart break away, and then another as she took a deep breath. "I need a decent job to support Hannah. I have an apartment leased in Minneapolis. My life is in the Twin Cities, not here."

Michael nodded slowly, his dark gaze smoky. Compelling. She felt an undercurrent of anticipation spark between them. In the background, the orchestra began a slow waltz.

With a sigh, Michael rose and offered her his hand. "Dance with me?"

Images of that Fourth of July night drifted through her mind as Lauren walked into his arms. She felt like a leaf borne on a fall wind as he slowly, expertly spun her through the smooth three-quarter rhythm of the dance. If there were other people on the dance floor, she didn't see them. She only felt Michael's large warm hand at her back and the smooth weave of his summer-weight wool blazer beneath her fingertips.

The music went on and on, until they were no longer moving across the floor, but had slowed to an almost imperceptible movement. Michael released her right hand and tucked her head beneath his chin, then folded his hands at the small of her back and held her close.

She knew what he wanted. What they both wanted. But another night in Michael's arms would make leaving even harder to bear.

Long after midnight, after Hannah was tucked in bed and the lights were all out, Lauren curled up in her bed alone and wondered if she'd just missed her last chance for happiness, however brief it might have been.

MICHAEL WANDERED through the downstairs of the old house, unable to sleep as the evening replayed in his mind over and over. They'd had a wonderful dinner. Dancing with her, feeling her warm and pliant in his arms, his need for her had grown with each passing moment.

And not just for one night.

The enormity of that truth had blindsided him—hell, he'd practically proposed to her before he realized what he was doing. With the pain of Gloria's deception still fresh, he was in no condition to be thinking about long-term commitments. After that last debacle, he'd realized that it would be better to go solo than ever risk making another big mistake.

The good Lord knew he wasn't much of a bargain, at any rate. Lauren was better off without the kind of guy who could break an engagement without feeling anything more than a touch of nostalgia.

Now, with her and Hannah asleep upstairs, the house seemed to echo with memories that sharpened his feelings of loneliness and loss.

During late evenings in this house he could still hear Winthrop's booming voice and Bertie's laughter. Could see them at the front entryway, where Win would sweep his aunt into a dramatic embrace worthy of *Gone With the Wind* every time he left for work. In forty years they'd never spent a night apart.

If Michael could have anything on earth, it would be that type of passion and joyous companionship in a lifelong marriage. But some people had a gift for commitment; some didn't.

Maybe when summer ended and he found a place of his own away from this house, he wouldn't feel these constant reminders of the empty places in his soul.

In the study he ran his hand over the spines of Winthrop's old law library. Only Bertie would be so sentimental about books filled with the driest reading on earth. She'd kept every volume, unable to part with anything that reminded her of Win. His glasses still lay on the desk, next to his favorite coffee cup. A picture of the two of them hung above the credenza placed along the wall.

Michael glanced at his watch and sighed. Maybe some leftovers would help him sleep. Flipping off the lights in the study, he made his way toward the kitchen.

Moonlight filtered through the lacy curtains at the front of the house, turning everything inside to shades of gray. As he passed the front entry, his eye was drawn to the door. Below the letter drop an envelope gleamed white in the darkness. *A midnight delivery?*

He paused to scoop it up. There was no return address, no postmark. It was addressed to him in block letters, with *Personal* stamped on both sides. Intrigued, he tore it open and lifted out the single sheet of paper inside, then headed for the kitchen.

By the soft light of the stained-glass lamp hanging over the table, he unfolded the paper. It was a fuzzy photocopy of a newspaper article, probably from a microfiche machine at a library.

Michael froze. The photo was dark. The hairstyle was different. But it was *her.*

And the headline made his heart stand still.

"IT SURE IS NICE of Ashley's mom to invite you over today," Lauren said as she started the car. With a quick glance over her shoulder she stepped on the gas and pulled out of Bertie's circular front drive and onto the highway. "Tell her that I'll take you two to a movie tomorrow afternoon, okay?"

Hannah nodded glumly. "I wish we could stay in Briar Lake forever."

"I know, honey." Hannah brought up the subject nearly every day and Lauren's answer was always the same. *I'm sorry, I wish we could.*

After dropping Hannah off at Ashley's, Lauren drove downtown to her appointment with Kay Solomon. As usual, she parked behind the building and entered by the back door.

Kay met her at the office door and ushered her inside. "So," Kay said as she sat down behind her desk, "any luck with finding a job up here?"

Lauren sighed, staring at her folded hands. "I haven't seen anything that would pay enough once we leave Bertie's place."

"Do you want me to do some checking? I deal with a lot of employers who've hired my parolees."

Lauren sat back in her chair. "Then they would know that I'd been…in the legal system. People would talk—everyone would know."

"I *can* be tactful," Kay said dryly. She thought for a minute. "I do know of a third-grade teacher who's pregnant. She goes to my church and has been talking about asking for a leave of absence from Thanksgiving through the end of the school year."

"Would I have a chance? When I give references from my old job…"

Kay sighed. "After September your record will be clear."

For the first time in three years Lauren felt a flicker of hope. "Maybe I'll pick up an application." She shifted her gaze to the window and watched some crows land on the courthouse roof, envying their freedom. "You know, when I think about the fools who break the law just for the hell of it, I wonder how they could possibly be so stupid. A few days of work and they would have earned that money, but just look at what happens to a life after one is caught. I wasn't even guilty, and my life has been in ruins ever since.''

''Is there a chance your husband would ever admit to perjury and exonerate you?''

''Rick?'' Lauren gave a bitter laugh. ''He'd never risk further legal charges against himself.'' She stood and offered her hand over the desk. ''Thanks for everything.''

Kay gave her hand a warm shake. ''Take it easy, honey. If the past comes up, don't try to hide from it. Things will work out for the best.''

LAUREN HAD JUST STEPPED OUT into the parking lot when an all-too-familiar voice rang out. *Michael.* Her heart skipped a beat as she spun around.

He crossed the parking lot, coming from the direction of the courthouse. With his crisp khaki pants, white polo shirt and loafers he looked like any other guy heading out for lunch. But his dark sunglasses hid the expression in his eyes from her, and as he drew closer, she felt deepening dread. Had he seen her go into Kay's office?

He flashed a cold smile at her and caught her elbow. ''Coffee?''

A shiver of awareness raced up her arm. Or was it fear? ''I have to get Hannah. She's at Ashley's and—''

''She'll be just fine,'' he said firmly, falling into step with her. ''The Sunflower Café is next door.''

"No," she said a little too sharply. Definitely not there. Courthouse workers flocked there every day. Someone might recognize her from her visits to Kay's office—and maybe say something to her in front of Michael.

"'No' to the invitation in general or 'no' to that particular place?"

"I've heard the service is slow…and…it's usually crowded…"

"You'd rather go someplace else." Giving her a curious look, he released her elbow and curved an arm around her shoulders as they walked. "I know just the place."

Usually the weight of his arm on her shoulder felt warm and intimate, reminding her of the night they'd danced on the courthouse steps. Now that magical night seemed years in the past, and the weight of his arm made her feel as if she was being drawn inexorably into a trap.

In a few minutes they were seated in a quaint little coffee shop on Main. Michael removed his sunglasses and tossed them onto the table. The intensity of his gaze sent a shiver down her spine.

"I wouldn't have taken you for a Gingham Cat sort of guy," she said, trying for a lightness she didn't feel as she surveyed the avalanche of lace, dried flowers and artsy craft items vying for every millimeter of wall space around them. "Does this reflect a hidden facet of your personality?"

He batted away a mobile made of pewter hanging next to his ear, then reached with both hands to unfasten it from its hanger and lay it on the next table.

"This was too close by," he muttered, glancing around.

The waitress, a chirpy young thing in a flouncy gingham skirt and tottery heels, brought their coffees and gave Michael a big smile. "Anything else?" she purred, not sparing a glance for Lauren.

"No, thank you," Michael said, seeming not to notice her attention. When the waitress moved away, he eyed Lauren over the rim of his cup. "Where have you been?"

"Here...there...." She gave a little wave of her hand. "Boring errands."

"Why did you come downtown, Lauren?"

He knows. It was as clear as the words on a football scoreboard.

"Maybe you should tell me," she said. Her thoughts slid back to another time. The questions, the accusations. Lawyers who twisted what she said and only looked for guilt. How could she have forgotten that Michael's career was spent doing the same thing?

"I received some unusual mail last night, so today I did a little research at the courthouse." He sighed heavily. "Any idea why your name would show up there?"

Anger rose in her throat, coupled with fear.

"Tell me, Lauren." His voice was filled with regret.

She'd been accused in a court of law and by townspeople on the streets of her hometown. None of it had hurt as much as these questions from a man who had touched her heart.

"Apparently you know already, so what's the

point?'' Remembering Kay's words about not hiding from the truth, she took a deep breath. Her heart pounded in her throat. Maybe—if he truly cared about her—he would believe the truth. ''My ex-husband embezzled thousands of dollars from a school-playground fund. He stole from *children*. And fine man that he was, he testified that I was involved from the start, because he hoped to get a lighter sentence for himself. Since I worked at the school, it was logical that I could have helped him plan the theft.''

''You were tried and found guilty in a court of law,'' he said flatly.

''I was falsely accused and given a deferred judgment. In September my record will be cleared.''

''Why didn't you tell me?''

''And what would I say? How could I ever prove to you that I wasn't involved? You just found out and you already believe I'm guilty.''

''I didn't say that.''

''Give me a break,'' she retorted bitterly.

''Couldn't you have trusted me?''

His expression looked almost sympathetic, but the emotions of the past swamped her, driving away all reason. ''Can you imagine what it's like, having something like this hanging over your head? I lost my job. I lost my teaching license. After trying to make restitution on embezzled funds I never saw, I have nothing left—no home, no money, no career. For most minimum-wage jobs, I can't even get an interview. I have to support my daughter until my license is reinstated. And then…I can only hope that someone, somewhere, will give me chance.''

Michael silently stared at her, undoubtedly thinking about the funds missing from Bertie's accounts.

"I almost told you several times. But this became…a magical summer for Hannah. She loves being here and playing with Bertie's animals. It's been so good for her to be around a man like you, instead of—" Lauren stood abruptly, unable to go on.

"Lauren—"

"This has been very hard on Hannah—frightening and confusing. A child needs to look up to her father. Can you imagine being in second grade and having a dad who stole money from your school? A dad who has gone to prison? Please promise you won't talk about this when she's around."

He reached for her hand, but she twisted away from his grasp. Without looking at the other customers, she walked blindly out of the shop and into the bright, hot sunlight. It took a moment to get her bearings and head in the right direction.

Behind her she heard Michael drop a handful of change on the table and come after her. But some blessed person waylaid him with a question, and she made it to the quiet refuge of her car alone.

His doubt hurt more deeply than anything Rick had ever said to her, dashing the faint and desperate hope that he might have somehow understood and accepted her past.

Fat chance.

She'd promised to stay in Briar Lake through to the end of the summer. Unless he ordered her out of the house, she would keep her word no matter how much it hurt. She could only hope that someday she could mend the ragged edges of her heart.

WITH HANNAH PEERING over his shoulder, Michael pried open the first box of the veritable mountain of boxes piled on the floor of his office.

At least Hannah was still talking to him. Lauren, on the other hand, was now coolly distant and had barely spoken to him in two days. The silence had given him plenty of time to think.

It couldn't be easy for anyone to reveal information about being on probation—especially when one hadn't done anything to deserve it.

If there was anything he was sure of now, it was that her anger was justified. He'd seen the truth in the unwavering way she'd met his gaze, daring him to believe her, and he'd heard it in the painful vehemence in her voice. That stark expression of betrayal had haunted his thoughts ever since. She believed he was like all the others who had doubted her innocence.

Her ex-husband must have been one hell of a bastard—and one hell of a convincing liar.

Twice Michael had tried to explain that while her past was something that needed to be discussed, he believed in her innocence. She'd looked back at him with a sad smile and disbelief in her eyes, then turned away.

Thinking back over the summer, he deserved that and more. He'd been a complete jerk over the power-of-attorney business and everything else. It made him wonder about his subconscious motivation. Self-defense? A need to keep his distance from a woman who touched his heart?

Mid-August had arrived, and there wasn't much time left to repair the damage he'd caused. It was damned ironic to find himself falling in love with a woman he'd managed to drive away so completely.

"Can you believe this?" he muttered. "Five tons of cardboard and packing material for just two computers."

Hannah reached around him to snatch some bubble wrap. She popped several bubbles between her fingers, then folded the sheet over, laid it on the floor and jumped on it.

The sharp report sent Baxter out of the room with his tail between his legs.

"Oops. Sorry, Baxter." Hannah picked up the plastic material and set it aside on the desk, then plopped down on the carpet next to Michael and looked up at him with awe. "Do you really know how to put all these computer things together?"

Setting aside sealed bags filled with cords and miscellaneous literature, he lifted out a monitor and put it on his desk. "I sure hope so."

She edged closer and shook a collection of booklets out of a plastic bag.

"Uh...let's keep all that together, okay?" Michael said. "I need to be sure I can get this right."

Looking crestfallen, she sat back and wrapped her arms around her knees. "Okay."

"Hey, you know what you could do? I'm expecting some mail today, and I'll bet the mailman has already come to the house. Could you go get it for me and bring it here? Just my mail, though. Not your mom's."

"Sure!" Hannah scrambled to her feet and was out the door like a rocket, her braids flying. Before he'd even gotten the first keyboard and CPU unpacked, she was back again with a fistful of envelopes. "Where do you want them?"

He waved a screwdriver in the general direction of the desk. "There's fine."

"What else can I do?"

"Hmm…let me think. Baxter could use a walk. Daisy might like to eat grass on the front lawn, if you hold on to her really tight."

"But I want to help *you*."

He didn't have the heart to say no. He gestured at the keyboards. "One on the receptionist's desk, one on mine."

Nodding, Hannah carefully picked up the slim cardboard boxes holding the keyboards and delivered them, then squatted down on the carpet next to him and waited. After worrying her lower lip with her teeth, she finally looked up at him, and from the fine tremble of her mouth he wondered if she was about to cry.

"Are you staying here forever and ever?" she asked.

He bit back a smile. "That would be a long time."

"Will you ever go anywhere else, like, for visits?" Her tone was wistful. "Like if you missed somebody far away?"

At least three times this week she'd casually mentioned that her mom was a great cook, a hard worker and really, *really* pretty, and then the little matchmaker had given him a hopeful look.

"Hannah—"

A shadow fell across the room. They both looked

up to see Lauren standing in the doorway, backlit by the sun.

"I see you've got a helper." She held out a hand to Hannah, while giving Michael a wary look. "I'm sure she's been a great deal of help, but Ashley's mom invited us for a swim in her pool and lunch, and we're already late. There're leftovers in the fridge if you want to eat here."

"Can't he come along?" Hannah begged.

"I think this is just for us girls," Lauren said, still holding out her hand to her daughter.

"And I need to get these computers set up before I can start loading programs this afternoon. We can all go out on the boat after supper, okay?"

With a mournful sigh Hannah left with her mom. Even before Lauren's car sputtered to life in the front yard, the offices seemed to echo with emptiness. Well, there *was* Baxter, but he was now sprawled on the carpet and had started to snore.

"Some best friend you are," Michael muttered, prying open a monitor carton.

By late afternoon a pile of boxes stood outside the door and both computers were up and running. Another few hours to load software and set up the printers, and he'd be ready for business. The local grapevine had been busy, apparently, because there were several queries on the answering machine already, and at least four people in town had asked about his hours.

He glanced up at the clock on the wall. Four-thirty. Time enough to take a shower, get cleaned up and hunt through the fridge for supper.

As he headed for the door, a pile of envelopes on

the receptionist's desk caught his eye. He fanned through them, saw nothing of interest and set them down.

And then his heart skipped a beat.

He slowly looked through them one more time. It was at the bottom of the stack. Sent by a bank he'd never heard of, addressed to Ms. Lauren McClellan at a post-office box in a nearby town. The typewritten box number had been crossed out and Bertie's street address handwritten at the side.

The postmark was from the Cayman Islands.

This wasn't from a vacationing friend. No one used bank stationery and a typewriter to send holiday letters back home.

Michael's thoughts spun back to the day he'd discovered that Lauren was on a deferred sentence for *embezzlement of school funds.* He thought back to the discrepancies in Bertie's accounts.

It couldn't be.

In Bertie's study Michael sank into a chair and leaned his head against the back, staring at the shadows of the room as memories drifted through his mind.

Lauren's wit and charm. The way she could smile at him and make him feel the world was his. How she was raising a child, so determined to make it on her own. How she'd been so insistent about paying for the damages Daisy had done to his car. His heart told him that she was everything good and positive in his life.

But he'd been wrong before, ignoring the irrefutable truth about Gloria until it was too late. Lauren's embezzlement charges, the missing funds and this new piece of evidence were coincidences too over-whelming to ignore.

Feeling as if his heart had turned to lead, he waited for Lauren to walk in the door.

CHAPTER FIFTEEN

"I THINK WE'RE IN TROUBLE, honey," Lauren teased when they walked in the door. "It's already five, and I haven't even started thinking about what to have for supper."

"Look, it's a card from Aunt Bertie!" Hannah cried, stooping to pick up a scattering of mail under the slot. "'Dear Hannah, Lauren and Michael. I hope you are all having fun in Briar Lake. Have you done lots of things together? I'm having the time of my life. I'm planning some changes for the future and can't wait to tell you all. Love Bertie.'"

"Where's that one from?"

Hannah turned it sideways, then upside down. "I can't read the postmark. The picture shows mountains again. She isn't coming back soon, is she?"

"September third, so we have three weeks left. Though with Bertie, one never knows for sure," Lauren said dryly. "Now scoot upstairs!"

Hannah turned away and trudged up the stairs. Lauren sighed, then toed off her sandals and headed for the kitchen.

She hadn't gone three steps before a deep familiar voice called her from the study.

Michael was seated in one of the matching chairs flanking the fireplace, an ankle crossed over the opposite knee and his arms folded across his chest. A white business envelope lay on the end table at his side.

With a damp swimsuit beneath her beach cover-up, there wasn't any place in the room she dared sit. Just as well—she didn't want to talk to him, anyway. She hovered at the door.

"Come in here," he repeated. His voice sounded rough as gravel and held an undercurrent of anger.

A dizzying rush of fear snaked through her as memories of Rick's countless angry outbursts flooded back. He used to lie in wait for her, too, but he'd always turned the lights off so he could snap them on and startle her.

Damp suit or not, she needed to sit before her knees buckled. She sank in the oak chair at the desk, Michael watching her every move with an intense expression.

He lifted the envelope and tapped it against his palm. "The day I arrived, there was an envelope lying on this end table. An envelope you seemed rather concerned about. Has your summer been... profitable?"

She gave him a startled look, remembering the letter from the Hennepin County Court system in Minneapolis. It had been about the transfer of her probation to this county. Nothing to do with money. "Profitable?"

"Why did you decide to come up here when you could have made more at any number of jobs in Minneapolis?"

Her tension melted as her anger flickered to life. "I told you this before," she said evenly. "Bertie was wonderful to my grandma Frannie and me through the years. I was glad to return the favor any way I could.''

''Know anyone who's vacationing in Cayman Islands?''

''No.''

''Any idea why you'd be getting mail from there addressed to a post-office box in Greenleigh?''

''What?'' she stared at him, mystified. ''I don't have a post-office box there.''

''That's odd.'' He looked down at the envelope in his hands, then said softly, ''The Greenleigh post office forwarded this to Bertie's address, so they obviously know about you. Why would you need the privacy of a post-office box in another town?''

Lauren stood abruptly and stalked over to his chair. ''I think it's a federal offense for you to intercept and open my mail.''

''I didn't. Hannah brought me my own mail, and this was in the stack. I'm just…returning it to you. Open it, Lauren. Prove my suspicions wrong.''

She snatched the envelope from his fingers. ''How could you think I would do anything to hurt Bertie?''

''Well, there's that deferred sentence for embezzlement hanging over your head, for starters.''

Lauren gasped.

''Then there's the fact that you obtained power of attorney over my aunt's assets, and now this. From the feel of the envelope I have a pretty good idea of what's inside.''

Her fingers trembling, she stared down at the neatly typed address, the stamped forwarding-address message angled to one side. Bertie's address had been written over it in an impatient scrawl. "I don't even know, exactly, where Greenleigh is," she whispered. "Why would I have mail sent there?"

"You tell me."

Speechless, she stared back at him, her mind reeling at the implication as she ripped the flap off the envelope. It held a single sheet of folded paper. "So what's this supposed to be? Some sort of treasure I've stolen? A receipt for the sale of Bertie's silver?"

A major credit card fell to the floor next to Michael's foot as she withdrew the paper. She looked at it in shock.

He swiftly picked it up and studied it, then gave her a grim smile. "Do a lot of offshore banking?"

"Offshore what?" Lauren opened the letter with trembling fingers. The letterhead was that of a bank she'd never heard of on an island she'd never visited. The words swam on the page. She blinked, concentrating harder.

The letter welcomed her as a new customer, acknowledged five thousand dollars deposited to her account and instructed her to sign the credit card and keep it in a safe place.

"Five thousand dollars," she choked out. She looked up and met Michael's cold stare. "I don't *have* five thousand dollars. Why would this bank send me a credit card?"

"Come off it, Lauren."

"I don't understand."

"You want me to spell it out. Fine. Offshore banking provides a secure discreet place to deposit funds with tax-free interest. Fixed-interest or time deposits are common, but debit or credit cards can provide easy access to an account. With this credit card, any charges will be deducted directly from your own funds. Close enough?''

Lauren gave a helpless shrug. ''I have no idea.''

He gave a growl of impatience. ''When I found money missing from Bertie's accounts, I couldn't believe you'd done it. Your deferred sentence for embezzlement nearly blew me away, but I got past that. I guess I'm totally naive when it comes to the women in my life.''

''You think this…this Cayman deal is Bertie's money,'' Lauren said flatly.

''You said you used all your savings to repay what your *husband* embezzled from that school.''

She'd never thought a heart could shatter. Even when Rick had betrayed her, she hadn't felt this kind of pain, because she'd lost her love for him so long before that final blow. But now she felt dizzy with the pain of knowing Michael thought her no more than a thief and a liar.

Fear shot through her. *If he believes this, maybe the courts will, too.*

''I didn't take a dime of the school's money,'' she whispered. ''And I've never touched a dime of Bertie's, either.''

''Lauren, the Hennepin County Court system decided there was enough evidence to give you a deferred sentence not so long ago.''

Lauren drew her breath in sharply, her throat raw with fear. ''You think I would do anything to jeopardize the terms of my sentence? I would *never* risk going to jail.''

Michael watched her, his face expressionless, as if he'd heard a thousand alibis and a thousand excuses, and now tuned them out as he would an irritating television commercial.

Lauren plowed on, her mind racing and her heart begging him to understand. ''If anything happens to me, the courts might find Rick and give him custody of Hannah. Believe me, I'd run to Canada with her before I'd let that happen.''

Michael unfolded his arms, but she could still see the cold skepticism in his eyes. ''Money can be a potent lure.''

''Not to me,'' Lauren said bitterly. Another thought hit her like a sledgehammer. ''*Someone* set me up. Was it him?'' Panic clawed its way up her throat. ''My God, if Rick does want Hannah, he could be trying to find an easy way to take custody!''

The door to the library clicked softly shut. Small bare feet ran across the entryway, then pounded up the stairs.

''Oh, no.'' Lauren closed her eyes in horror. ''She must have overheard us.'' Jamming the bank letter into Michael's hands, Lauren spun toward the door. ''Because of your suspicions, my daughter has just learned awful things about her father—things I never wanted her to know. I'll never forgive you for that.''

At the door she hesitated, one hand on the doorknob. She spoke without turning around. ''For your information, I have nothing to do with any account in the Caymans. Figure who did and how to return that money, and I'll pay for your legal services once I get a job back in Minneapolis.'' She took a deep breath and looked over her shoulder. ''And, Michael, when you finally learn the truth, don't bother trying to find me. You've destroyed every feeling I ever had for you.''

HANNAH RAN DOWN the hall to her bedroom, slammed the door shut and flung herself onto her bed. The cockatiels shrieked in surprise. The parakeets flew up against the top of their cage, their wings beating madly against the wire. Baxter galloped up the stairs, then whined at her door.

Backhanding her tears away, she let him in. He curled up next to her, taking up most of the bed, but he was warm and soft and his eyes looked sad and wise, as if he could read her thoughts.

Mom's words about Hannah's dad filled her with terror. What if he came some night in the dark and forced her to leave with him? Memories of his rages were all too real—even after a year and a half.

A minute later she heard a soft tapping at the door. ''Can I come in?'' Mom asked, opening it enough to peek in. ''Please?''

Nodding, Hannah sniffled and nudged Baxter over a little.

Mom sat down on the edge of the bed and gently rubbed Hannah's back. ''Anything you want to talk about?''

Hannah hugged Baxter and shook her head. ''No!'' Talking about what she'd heard would make it all real.

"I'm afraid you might have the wrong idea about what I said downstairs," Mom said gently.

Her breath caught on a lump in her throat, and Hannah swallowed hard. Warm tears trickled down her cheek into Baxter's fur.

Mom gathered her up in a hug and held her tightly. "I'm not going anywhere, sweetie. I'll be with you until the day you go off to college."

"B-but what if you go to jail?"

Mom sighed and hugged her even closer. "There was a big mistake made a long time ago. I was blamed for something I didn't do."

"But you said—!"

"No. That won't ever happen, because I'll never do anything that could take me away from you."

Hannah tried to hold back her tears, but they came, anyway, with huge racking sobs that shook through her until her cheeks and the front of Mom's shirt were wet. "I'm scared."

"You don't need to be, sweetie. When summer is over, we'll go back to the same apartment we had last spring. You'll be in the same school, until we can find a good job for me and have a house of our very own."

Hannah clung more tightly. Her stomach felt like a roller coaster. She tried to shut out what she'd heard, but the scary words loomed over her like a huge black cloud.

Mom seemed to know how terrible she felt. "I'm so sorry you heard me talking about your father. Sometimes…grown-ups feel a lot of anger long after a relationship is over." She stroked Hannah's back. "He and I will never be married again, so don't misunderstand that. But someday…maybe he can be a part of your life again.''

Hannah leaned against her and sniffled.

"He loves you, honey, but he's just a little mixed-up right now."

"I wish I had a dad like Michael," Hannah mumbled against her mom's shirt, feeling too much like a traitor to say the words any louder.

"Maybe someday the perfect dad will come along. Until then, it's just you and me, but we can be happy just as we are, don't you think?"

Hannah made herself nod in agreement, but nothing would be better than having Michael for her dad. She'd tried to give him the idea, but he still hadn't taken the hint. Maybe she'd have to try again.

Sometimes grown-ups weren't very smart.

MICHAEL SETTLED BACK in his chair and stared at the door long after Lauren's footsteps faded up the stairs. He'd pressed her hard. Too hard. But he'd had to make sure. He'd had to protect his heart.

And now his jaded view of life had destroyed any chance of a future with the one woman who could make his life complete. He knew the truth because he'd seen it in her eyes. She hadn't opened that Cayman account. And she would never forgive him for his lack of trust.

A powerful sense of loss filled his chest, followed by a surge of anger at himself. *It doesn't have to end this way.*

Resting his elbows on the arms of the chair, he studied the letter from the bank. Suddenly he remembered other letters with Cayman postmarks—

letters that had fallen at his feet in a small neat living room—and been snatched up by one very nervous man.

Lauren had been set up, all right, and now Michael had a good idea of who had done it. He just needed to find out why.

Slipping the document back in its envelope, he glanced at the clock and then grabbed the phone book lying on the desk.

It was time to make a few social calls on the good ladies of Briar Lake.

MILDRED WALKER met him at the front door of her big old colonial home on the other side of town. He'd called first, but with her car parked in front, its engine running and her bulky purse slung over her forearm, she clearly didn't plan to give him much time.

"I'd ask you in, but like I told you, I'm just on my way to a council meeting downtown," she said, buttoning her black blazer with one hand. "Is there something I can do for you?"

He knew of just one thing that would slow her down. "I'm worried about Bertie."

"Oh." She faltered, then her expression softened. "I'm sure she's having a wonderful time, but I do think it's sweet of you to be concerned. She'll be back in a few weeks."

"Can I come in for just a minute?"

Mildred frowned at her car idling in the drive. "Well...if this is quick. I don't know what else I can tell you."

Mildred's living room was white-on-white, as

stark and spotless as an operating room, save for the bright flower arrangement on the coffee table. The understated decor spoke of wealth. She was the perfect person to ask.

As soon as he sat down, Michael leaned forward, his forearms braced on his thighs and his hands folded. "I don't want to spread rumors by asking the wrong people," he confided, willing her to trust him. "I've found some…discrepancies in Bertie's financial affairs and now wonder if perhaps she's ever said anything to you. Worries, perhaps?"

Mildred eyed him thoughtfully. "What kind of worries?"

"Debts, investments…anyone who's been pressuring her for money, that sort of thing."

"I can't see how you'd think I would know. She and I are friends, but we don't talk about *money*."

"No local people offering investment schemes? Real estate? Anything that would involve substantial payments?"

Mildred's gaze flickered. "I wouldn't have any idea."

"Mrs. Walker, I couldn't locate Bertie right now if I tried, so I can't ask her. I've found substantial withdrawals from her accounts and can't trace where the money went. I'm worried. If someone is using her, preying on her in some way, I need to know."

Mildred stared at him for a long moment. "No, I really can't help you. You'll just have to talk to Bertie when she gets back. Maybe the withdrawals were for some of the local fund drives. Or for those animals." A small smile played across her wrinkled face. "Once she bought an elephant from a traveling circus, sure it was sick and miserable. That thing trumpeted night and day until she found it a new home at a private zoo. Last year she donated a thousand dollars to a family that lost their home in a fire.''

Well, that sounded like Bertie, but those amounts would have been in her old check registers. These latest withdrawals were not, and the bank had refused to give him any information. Michael sighed. ''If you think of anything, let me know, okay?''

Back out in the sunshine, he opened Mildred's car door for her, helped her in, then shut it. He gave her an encouraging smile. ''Have you ever noticed anything unusual happening with your more elderly acquaintances in town? Such as someone trying to befriend them?''

Mildred gave him a sharp look. ''Not at all,'' she said with steel in her voice. ''I would notice if a stranger was up to no good, and Bertie would never fall for such a thing.'' She shifted her car into drive.

''Wait—one more thing. You once mentioned a circle of close friends, going way back to your schooldays. You said the circle had grown smaller in recent years, because some had passed away. Could you give me some names?''

With a snort of impatience, Mildred shook her head. ''There's no use in knowing them,'' she said curtly.

Michael leaned down and rested his hands on the open window of the car door. ''And there's no harm in telling me, if nothing's wrong.''

She wavered, then grudgingly gave him several names. ''These are dear friends who passed away in the last year or two," she said. "Though why you want to know is beyond me. Oliver has watched out for all of us over the years. He'd never let anyone take advantage of his friends. Now please, let me go. I'm late for my meeting as it is."

Michael watched her leave, then climbed into his car and headed for town. Mildred had just given him information he needed.

Oliver! Now everything was falling into place. Michael just hoped he could catch the guy in time.

CHAPTER SIXTEEN

THE NEXT FEW DAYS crawled past, each moment lasting a lifetime. Lauren went through the motions of taking care of Bertie's animals. Watering the plants. Maintaining the house in good order.

At every sound, her heart tripped over a beat and a new rush of anxiety washed through her. Someone had secretly set up that account in the Caymans, and he—or she—was no friend.

Lauren watched Hannah's every move, afraid to let her out of sight. But why would Rick be after his daughter if he'd never cared enough to maintain contact? Who else could it be?

With a cursory goodbye, Michael had left on some sort of business trip early Tuesday morning, leaving her staring after him in surprise. *Business* trip? Or had he just wanted to get away from her?

Their relationship was over. She'd known it from the moment he'd confronted her with that damnable bank letter. She could no more trust him again with her heart than she could change what had happened in the past. But if it had been uncomfortable avoiding each other in the house and maintaining stony silence, the past three days with him gone were ten times worse.

She'd told him she no longer cared, but she'd

been lying. The pain she felt filled her chest until sometimes it was hard to breathe. *Priorities,* she reminded herself firmly *Hannah is your life, not him.*

Bertie had called late last night to announce that she'd caught an earlier flight home, and would be back tomorrow. So now the summer was truly over.

"How are you coming along?" Lauren called up the stairs to Hannah. "Do you need a cardboard box?"

When no answer came, Lauren went upstairs and found her sitting on her bed, with Baxter lying beside her. As usual, he took up practically every inch of space.

"You haven't started packing?"

Hannah shook her head with force. "I'm not gonna."

"Now that sounds more like a five-year-old talking." Lauren ruffled her bangs.

"But I want to stay," Hannah wailed.

Lauren managed a smile. "I know how hard this is. But we knew right from the start that this was only for the summer, right? You've had a great time with Ashley and Baxter and all the animals, but now it's time to think about heading home."

When Lauren's voice broke a little over the last words, Hannah looked up with stark sadness in her eyes. "I think Michael and you and me could have been a real family, if we'd tried harder."

Some things just can't be fixed, and hoping doesn't make love happen. Lauren sat at the side of the bed and drew Hannah into a hug. "We can remember all the good parts of this summer, right?"

Hannah's eyes filled with tears. "How soon do we go?"

"We'll visit with Bertie until Sunday afternoon, and then we'll head home. School starts on the twenty-fifth of August, so we'll have a day or two to get you ready. New shoes, school supplies… maybe a new backpack?"

Lauren rose and pushed Baxter over a few inches, then lifted Hannah's suitcase onto the bed. "Just leave out what you need to wear for the next couple of days, and we'll get the rest packed. That way we can go have some fun, okay? How about if we call Ashley and her mom and go for a picnic?"

Her lower lip set in a pout, Hannah looked at the floor.

Lauren thought fast. "Do you suppose they've ever been to the Minnesota State Fair? We could invite them down for Labor Day weekend and we could all go together."

Hannah nodded, her lower lip trembling.

"Do you want me to help you?"

"No."

With a sigh Lauren looked at her daughter, wishing she could change everything, knowing that everything was out of her hands. Bertie would return and then they would leave. It had been a glorious dream while it lasted.

Only one thing would give her a sense of closure—finding out who opened that account in the Caymans, and why.

MICHAEL DROVE the rented Taurus sedan out of the gas station and back onto Highway 1, then headed north toward Newport Beach.

He had two situations to resolve, and given Rick McClellan's tendency to change addresses, this one had to come first—before the guy disappeared completely. Rick had falsely accused Lauren of involvement in his embezzlement scheme, and both she and her daughter had paid the price.

Michael's own mistakes had ruined any chance for a future with her, but at least he could do this much for her before summer's end.

For four long days he'd been in California, following a trail of addresses and tips from Rick's various landlords and roommates. He'd tracked him from a condo on the beach to a cramped apartment in Pasadena, and then to a duplex in Glendale, with a number of false leads along the way.

At his last stop, one of the neighbors had given Michael this Newport Beach address. "I hope you find him," the guy had said with relish. "If you do, tell him I still want my ten bucks back. He never picks up the phone when I call."

Either Rick couldn't keep a job, couldn't keep friends or was trying to stay on the move. Maybe all three—because more than a few irritated people wanted to know his address when Michael tracked him down.

A wave of heat met Michael as he stepped out of the car in front of a modest one-story home tucked away on a cul-de-sac far from the high-rent district. No ocean breezes ever reached this place, he guessed, glancing at the bikes and toys and old cars littering yards in either direction.

The house was painted a jarring pink, the yard

littered with motorcycle parts and plastic lawn furniture. The sweet scent of gardenias grew stronger as he neared the door. They grew in lush abandon along the house, the scent bringing back memories of the years he'd spent out here as a young idealistic pre-law student.

Michael knocked at the door. Waited, then knocked again with greater force. No answer. *Damn.*

A man sauntered around the corner of the house. Lanky, a good six-foot plus, he wore cutoffs with ragged holes, worn pockets and a loose T-shirt with the sleeves ripped out. Surfer-blond and unshaven, the man would probably catch the eye of most any woman who walked past. He lifted a can of beer in salute.

"Looking for someone?"

"Rick McClellan."

The man gave Michael's briefcase a cursory glance. "Ain't buying insurance, and I ain't changing my religion."

From the looks of him, he probably didn't have either one. "I'm not here to sell anything. I'm here to talk about Lauren McClellan and your daughter."

Rick's beer can halted halfway to his mouth. His gaze slid to the lane beside the house, then back to Michael. "You from the county? If you're trying to make me take her, it won't work. I don't have any-place for her to stay. I share this house with three other guys and—"

"We have other matters to discuss. Can we sit somewhere?"

Eyeing him warily, Rick headed for the backyard

and a couple of deck chairs flanking an old grill. Beer cans overflowed a garbage can next to the patio door.

"We had a party last night," Rick said, gesturing broadly with his beer can. "Haven't got things back in order."

"I'm an attorney from Briar Lake. That town ring any bells?"

Rick was instantly defensive. "I haven't done anything."

Michael leaned back in his chair and hooked an ankle over the opposite knee. "I know, and I'm here to change that."

"Huh?" Rick stiffened and glanced again toward the house. He appeared ready to bolt.

"If you don't talk to me, I'll see that you're talking to the police in less than ten minutes. They'll be a lot less friendly than I am. Your choice."

The man's beach-boy good looks sure suffered when his features turned sullen. "Did Evans send you here? That lying no-good bastard. You can't believe a word he says."

Evans? Suddenly a memory clicked into place.

"Five or six years ago we were up here, and my husband had quite a visit with Oliver out on Bertie's front lawn."

Another memory came into focus—a dim recollection involving Win and Bertie arguing. Now he remembered the topic of their disagreement. *"The man's incompetent!"* Win had roared. Bertie's softer voice hadn't been distinguishable, but Win's response had echoed up the stairwell. *"I just don't trust him, Bertie, but because you want this, I'll give him one more chance…"*

"You and I have quite a few things to talk about," Michael said calmly. "Your connection to Oliver Evans, a matter of perjury and nine thousand dollars. Where would you like to start?"

Rick launched himself out of his chair so fast it fell over with a crash. "I don't have *nine* dollars in my pocket. Who do you think I am?"

"For starters, a father who's way behind on child support and traveled to another state to avoid paying. When a federal grand jury hears that, there will be a warrant for your arrest." Michael gave him a lethal smile, then nodded toward the upended chair. "You might have missed hearing about that law— you were in prison when it passed. Now *sit.*"

He waited until Rick grabbed the chair and sat, then he lowered his voice to pure steel. "You're the father of a little girl who deserves better than she has right now, and you're the ex-husband of an innocent woman who never deserved what she got. I think we need to explore the meaning of perjury, and what it means to your future."

Rick was definitely sweating more than he was before. Giving him a satisfied smile, Michael leaned back in his chair and opened the leather folder on his lap. "Mr. McClellan, we're going to talk."

BERTIE ARRIVED in Briar Lake Saturday afternoon in a taxi filled with suitcases, boxes and bags. Despite her pleasure at seeing her old friend, Lauren's heart broke just a little bit more when the green-

and-white vehicle pulled up at the front door. The summer was over.

Bertie, wearing a bright blue-and-turquoise muu-muu and sturdy walking shoes, charged through the front door and gave Baxter a big hug, then turned and opened her arms to Hannah.

"Hi, sweetheart. You've grown at least six inches this summer!" she pulled back a little and scanned Hannah head to toe, then hugged her again. "Maybe eight!"

Over Hannah's head she smiled at Lauren. "It's great to be back and see you both. Did you have a good time?"

"We think everything is in shape for you here." Lauren managed a bright smile. "I hope we did everything just as you wanted."

Bertie released Hannah and grasped one of Lauren's hands between both of her own, a frown settling over her wrinkled features. "Is everything okay? Are you well?"

Well, my heart is dying, but other than that... "Of course. Hannah, let's help Bertie with her things, okay?"

Bertie let her escape that time, but two hours later, when Hannah was outside playing with Daisy, the older woman came up the stairs to Lauren's room bearing two cups of steaming peach tea and a determined smile.

"Okay, Lauren. Let's hear it." Settling into a small upholstered chair in the corner of the room, Bertie propped her feet on the matching footstool and looked ready to stay put until she had every answer. "It looks like you're in quite a hurry to pack."

Folding the last of her T-shirts and laying it in her suitcase, Lauren spoke without looking up. "We need to get home so Hannah can start school on Monday. We'd planned on her missing the first few days until you got back, but since you're here earlier, we can go."

Bertie clucked her tongue. "What about my nephew?"

"He's been gone since Tuesday. He hasn't called, so I don't know where he is."

Waving her hand impatiently, Bertie leaned forward in her chair with an eager light in her eyes. "I don't want to know where he is. I want to know how you two got along this summer."

Lauren stared back at her, then straightened and put one hand on her hip. "You set me up!"

"I don't meddle," Bertie said primly, lifting her cup for another sip of tea. "Much."

Despite the painful end of her relationship with Michael, Lauren couldn't suppress a smile when she saw the twinkle in her old friend's eyes. "Oh, yes, you do."

"And yet you're packing." Bertie's voice was filled with reproach. "The perfect man, the perfect summer together, and you're heading back to that abominable apartment in Minneapolis. Don't leave Briar Lake, not yet. With time, things will work out."

Lauren felt her smile slip a little. "But without trust, there's not much hope. He couldn't handle my legal history. And—" she swallowed, hard "—he even thinks I took money from your accounts. I swear to you I would never do such a thing.''

Bertie slammed her cup down on the lace-draped table next to her chair. "He thought *what?*"

Lauren felt a shiver of fear race through her. "I swear, I never did anything but pay your b—"

"Don't be ridiculous. I've always trusted you like my own daughter. My nephew is the one I'm upset about."

Her knees started to go weak, so Lauren sank to the edge of the bed. "He had a hard time accepting my deferred sentence. It was worse when he found out I had power of attorney this summer."

"It was logical, since I planned to be out of the country for three months," Bertie snorted. "You could handle any investments or business transactions that came up."

"Well…he figures I wormed my way into your good graces so I could run off with your wealth."

"You'd think he could read people better than that." Bertie threw her hands in the air in disgust. "The boy's a *lawyer,* for heaven's sake."

"I think that makes him more suspicious."

Bertie uttered something incomprehensible, then blushed a little. "Gaelic. I picked it up in a pub somewhere and thought it was a lilting sort of phrase. Didn't find out for days that I was repeating a barnyard curse."

Lauren couldn't help but laugh.

"I did make some withdrawals before I left," Bertie mused. "I donated money to the low-income-children's dental clinic in town and…" She thought for a long moment, her brow furrowed. "I gave to the fireworks fund and started a drive for a new organ at church. The old one is awful, and I'd had enough of listening to those notes sticking on every other hymn. I gave cash, so that's probably where those withdrawals went.''

"Cash?'' The thought of an elderly woman carrying a large amount of cash made Lauren's blood run cold. "Oh, Bertie. That's not safe!''

Bertie waved away her concerns. "I'd run out of checks and hadn't received my new ones yet. It was no big deal.''

"What if someone saw you at the bank? They could follow you out the door and—''

"I was very careful,'' Bertie shot back in an affronted tone as she set down her cup and rose to her feet.

"Do you know of any other large withdrawals made before you left, just so we can be sure everything is accounted for? I'll be glad to help you check your statements, or Michael will.''

"There might have been…something or other.'' Bertie's gaze slid away. "I really don't remember. Shall we go downstairs? I brought you all some things from Ireland and France, and the cutest little—''

"Wait!''

Bertie was already halfway to the door, and this had to be said before she heard it from Michael. Lauren took a deep breath. "A Cayman Islands bank sent a letter thanking me for opening an account. It acknowledged an initial deposit of five thousand dollars.''

Bertie turned, her eyes trained on Lauren's face.

"I didn't open that account and certainly I don't have that much money." Lauren met Bertie's eyes, willing her to have this last bit of faith. "Michael figures it's proof of theft."

Bertie slowly retraced her steps, her mouth a thin line.

"I gave Michael the letter," Lauren continued, "and asked him to deal with it, because I have no clue how this happened."

"The Caymans, you say? A bank?"

"It was a complete surprise to me. I didn't even realize people opened offshore accounts like that."

A silence lengthened in the room, heavy and forbidding. "I didn't, either, until a friend discussed it one evening with me years ago," Bertie said slowly. "None of my other acquaintances have ever mentioned such a thing to me."

"Is he…would he…"

"I don't know. But setting up such an account without your knowledge could have no good purpose." She sighed heavily. "Betrayal by a dear friend is devastating."

"I swear to you—"

Bertie returned to the chair by the window, sat and raised a trembling hand to her chest. "After years of support and kindnesses, this is nearly incomprehensible."

"Should I call 911?" Alarmed, Lauren rushed to her side. "Are you all right?"

Bertie took a shaky breath. "Now and then my angina kicks up, but it's nothing."

"I'm so sorry, Bertie. I didn't mean to upset you."

"It isn't you, dear," Bertie finally whispered, almost too softly to hear. "I can only think of one person who could be involved. I tried to help him through the years...Lila and I both did. It hurts to think I've misjudged him all this time."

Lauren's breath caught in her throat. Her heart pounded. "Who, Bertie?"

The old woman turned her head toward the window and stared out at the leafy branches for a long time. "I can't say, not yet." A faint smile curved her lips. "Poor Winthrop finally gave up trying to teach me the difference between libel and slander—I could never remember. But I do know that I'd best not say anything until I know for sure."

"Maybe I can help somehow, if you tell me who he is."

Bertie turned back toward Lauren and shook her head. "I don't want you involved any further. When Michael returns, I'll discuss it with him."

"Please—"

"No, dear." Her gaze slid away. "I'll take care of it. Right now, I think I need a good long nap. Don't wake me for supper—I'll just have some toast."

At the door she rested one hand on the door frame and then turned back with a smile. "In the midst of all this, I nearly forgot. I have some lovely news to share with you all later."

AT FIVE O'CLOCK Sue called and offered to take the girls to a six-o'clock movie. Lauren looked in on Bertie after they left, then tiptoed down the stairs and stood pensively at the front door. Debating.

Bertie had mentioned Lila—that was the name of Oliver's late wife. The huge portrait of her above Oliver's fireplace had been unforgettable. How many Lilas could there be in a town the size of Briar Lake? And only one male friend of Bertie's had stopped frequently at the house while she was away. *Oliver.*

But why on earth would he open an account in Lauren's name?

Grabbing her car keys from the hall table, Lauren stepped out into the warm early-evening air and headed for her car. She and Hannah were leaving tomorrow, so this might be her last chance to ask a few questions.

LAUREN KNOCKED on Oliver's door. Waited. Then knocked again. She could hear someone moving around inside.

She hesitated. Then knocked a third time.

At last the storm door cracked open a few inches, and Oliver peered out. When he saw her, he drew a sharp breath. "I'm really rather busy this evening. Perhaps you could stop back tomorrow."

He pushed at the door to close it. She blocked it with her shoulder. "I thought you would want to hear about Bertie," she managed. "Or have you already heard?"

At that his gaze met hers. Interest flickered in the pale depths of his eyes, though he still held the door tightly. "Bertie?"

"I need to talk to you about her."

With a sigh of resignation he looked over his shoulder, then opened the door. "Do come in. For just a minute.'' He ushered her inside, then rammed the dead bolt home behind her.

A feeling of unease crawled down her spine like a host of tiny spiders. Now what did she say? *Did you set up an account in my name? Did you give me five thousand dollars?* The local police would surely laugh at her accusations and think she was crazy.

She focused on the ancient white cat curled on the sofa and tried to decide what to say. "Uh... Bertie's back. Exhausted, but glad to be home.'' The words tumbled out of her mouth like a rushing stream. "Isn't that great? I knew you'd want to know.''

Something about the room seemed very odd. She glanced around, trying to decide what was different. It was neat as ever, save for an empty cardboard box and a roll of heavy shipping twine.

Oliver stared at her, his brow furrowed. "I wasn't planning on company,'' he murmured. "I thought you'd be long gone by now.''

She gave him a distracted glance. "No...but we're leaving tomorrow...'' And then she realized what was wrong. The huge gilt-framed photograph of Lila Evans was gone. In the wall behind its usual spot was a small open door revealing a small safe.

"How clever,'' she said, peering at it from across the room. "Is it...''

She glanced down at the floor, where a haphazard pile of shredded paper gleamed in a shaft of sunlight. An eerie sense of dread shot through her when she realized what it was: the photograph of Lila, neatly sliced into hundreds of narrow strips.

Oliver was still watching her, but now the corners of his mouth tipped upward. "I was done with her," he said simply, almost to himself. "She watched over me from the moment we met until this morning, making sure everything was perfect, making sure I couldn't fail. But now I'm *done*."

All thought of confronting him about the Cayman bank fled when she saw the odd light in his eyes. Anything else she wanted to say could definitely wait.

"Well," she said brightly, edging away. "I'm so glad I found you so I could tell you all about Bertie. I know you and she are the best of friends and—"

Surprisingly quick, Oliver slipped in front of the door and gave her an apologetic smile. "It's already locked, I'm afraid. You'll have to stay."

"Oh, I'll bet we can get it unlocked. Here, let me try."

For a man of his age, he had a surprising amount of strength. His fingers digging into her bare arms, he dragged her away from the door and gave her a shove that sent her onto the sofa in an undignified heap.

"Hey!" She lunged forward. He was there before she could move fast enough.

She hit and kicked at him. He seemed oblivious to her efforts. With a few deft twists of that shipping twine, he had her hands tied behind her back. Then he pulled it tight and bound her ankles.

"You know, you're a heck of a lot stronger than you look," she muttered, glaring up at him from beneath the tangle of her hair.

He sighed. "I really didn't want this, you know.

I wish you hadn't gotten in the way.'' He turned and headed toward the bedroom.

''Hey!'' she shouted, twisting her hands within the tight loops of twine. If anything, the twine felt tighter for her efforts. ''This isn't funny.''

He turned and came back to the sofa, looming over her, the light in his eyes even fiercer now. ''Be quiet so I can finish packing. Not another sound.''

''A-and then you'll let me go, right?''

His expression softened. ''I can't ever let you go.''

CHAPTER SEVENTEEN

LAUREN TRIED to give him her warmest smile—no mean feat, given the twine biting painfully into her wrists.

"I'm sure this was just a silly mistake. I only came to tell you about Bertie, and I'll be more than happy to forget about this little...joke."

Clucking his tongue, he shook his head and turned away. At the end of the couch he leaned over and picked up two old suitcases. "I was afraid you'd be a problem. And now, of course, you are."

"But I'm not! You must be really busy, and I really should get back. Michael will be out looking for me any minute, and when Bertie wakes up, she'll see my note on the counter and—"

"*Shut up.*"

Her heart gave a startled leap at his vicious tone. "Do you need help packing? I'm really quite good. I could help you so you can get going faster, and then I can head for home."

He stopped and turned back toward her, his face mottled with fury. "You cannot begin to understand what my life has been like. You won't destroy my future, is that clear?"

"I..." She took a closer look at him and fell silent.

"Good." He disappeared down the hall. Suitcase clasps clicked. Metal file drawers squealed. A door opened and slammed shut. Papers rustled.

In a few minutes he had his suitcases in hand, clearly much heavier now, judging from the stoop to his shoulders. He took them outside, and then Lauren heard a car door slam. She frantically twisted and squirmed, trying to loosen the twine. Without her hands free, she couldn't do more than try to stand and throw herself against the door.

If she could somehow fall *out* of the front door when he came in, she could start screaming bloody hell. With luck, the neighbors had their air conditioners off and their windows open.

The twine tied to her wrists and ankles was drawn too tightly for her to stand straight up. Rocking back and forth, she gained enough momentum for her feet to hit the floor. The cord cut into her wrists and bare ankles, driving her straight to her knees. *Great move, McClellan.*

From outside came the sound of a door slamming. Footsteps scurried up the sidewalk. Turning, she could barely see the front door past the end of the sofa.

The door handle turned.

"You really don't need to bother," Oliver said mildly as he stepped inside and shut the door behind him.

When she saw the gas can in his hand, her heart stopped.

Trussed up like a pirate's hostage she couldn't run. Couldn't even crawl.

If Bertie woke up...or Michael got back...but

none of that would help. Even if they wondered at her absence, they wouldn't start any searches for hours at best, and who would trace her to Oliver's house? *Stall for time.*

"Please...I know you're a nice guy. So what if you're taking a little trip? Everyone deserves a vacation now and then." She wriggled a little. Felt just a millimeter of slack in the cord wrapped around her left wrist. "Your clients will all understand."

He unscrewed the cap on the red plastic gas can. Pungent fumes wafted into the air. "I never planned on a fire," he said apologetically. "I'd wanted a quiet late-night departure. No one would notice my absence for days. But now you know I'm leaving. Someone could trace my steps, figure out where I've gone. I just can't be sure there wouldn't be some evidence left behind."

"I won't tell!"

"No," he said with a small smile. "You won't."

She watched in horrified fascination as he tipped the container and began trailing a stream of gasoline around the center of the living-room floor in a large circle.

He splashed it over her legs. The fumes and prickly sensation of the fuel against her skin sent her jerking back against the sofa. He simply followed her and trailed the stream up her hips and back.

"Hey!" She choked, sputtered as the fumes swirled around her, stealing the air.

He turned and headed for the other rooms, leaving a narrow trail of gasoline on the carpeting as he went. She heard the dull *thunk* of the empty can hitting the kitchen floor, and the return of Oliver's soft footsteps.

He glanced around, then perched at the edge of an upholstered chair at the far side of the room. "Bertie never should have left for the summer," he mused. "There wouldn't have been any trouble if she'd just stayed put."

Her heart pounding in her throat, Lauren wriggled another inch toward the door. "This is crazy! You don't need to set your house on fire to walk away. Just go! If you do this, they'll be after you for arson and murder. You won't make it past the city limits."

He frowned at the pile of shiny strips of photographic paper, the ruined photo of his late wife. "Can you imagine what it was like, all those years? My own practice failed. Bertie and Lila insisted that Win hire me—out of pity—and then I was little more than a clerk to the man everyone loved. An entire lifetime as a nobody, with a wife who made sure I remembered that fact every single day." His face hardened. "Every one of her friends knew, of course. Their condescending smiles were my own private hell. But…they've paid."

Keep talking. Keep talking….

Oliver had poured gasoline over the twine wrapped around her wrists, and both the cord and her skin were slippery. She inch-wormed toward the door, keeping her back hidden from him. The gasoline burned like fire at the raw places on her wrists. Her eyes watered from the fumes. Coughing, she edged farther.

He stood, and stepped carefully across the living room toward the front door. "You can't get out, you know. But perhaps this was all meant to be. We're both under five foot five. With enough charring, the authorities might mistake you for me, and then they'll never look any further.''

Nausea welled up in her stomach, crawled to her throat. If her heart beat any faster, she might just die of heart failure, anyway. "The dental records would never match."

"Good point." He frowned, then twisted off his law-school ring and came back, reached behind her and jammed it on one of her fingers. "Thanks. This might help divert any doubts."

"J-just tell me. I deserve to know. Why go to this extreme? Why not just...leave?"

Reaching into his pocket, he pulled out a book of matches.

"Lila's friends helped make my retirement possible," he murmured. "But not all of them know about it. Yet. I need to disappear. With your criminal record and that account in the Cayman Islands, people might assume you were to blame—especially for Bertie's losses. They'll figure the rest of the money is hidden somewhere else."

"My record? How do you know?"

Oliver smiled. "Never underestimate the powerful need for revenge, my dear. I believe a certain husband of yours was unhappy when you didn't cover for him during his trial."

Lauren twisted her hands harder. Part of the cord slipped. *One hand was free!* Her flesh tore and the gasoline stung as struggled. *More. Just a little more....*

In a split second both hands were free.

From outside came the sound of a car coming to a screeching halt. A car door opened and shut. Heavy footsteps thundered up the walk.

Oliver whirled around and peered out the small window in the oak door, then turned back. His hands shaking, he tore a match out of the book and poised, ready to strike it.

A fist pounded at the door. "Oliver, we need to talk."

"I guess it's too late," he said simply. He unlocked the dead bolt, then pulled the door open and stepped aside.

Michael stood at the door, tall and dark and furious, his eyes pinned on Oliver. Then his eyes widened. "What the hell?"

"Get out!" Lauren screamed. Kicking aside the last of the cords, she lunged to her feet and threw herself at him. "Now!"

And as they both catapulted out the door, the house exploded into flames.

LAUREN DREDGED UP a smile for the hospital's emergency-room registration clerk. Her wrists stung. She reeked of gasoline. She wanted to go home. "Really, all I need is a shower and a little nap," she said hopefully, tipping her head back to look up at Michael.

"No." He stood behind her chair, his warm strong hands on her shoulders. "I want her seen *now*. Not in ten minutes, not in an hour. As her lawyer, I'm extremely concerned that she have prompt and professional care."

The clerk picked up the phone and spoke rapidly

into the receiver. "The on-call doc is with the fella who just came in the ambulance, but it's a slow night and you'll be next," she announced. "A nurse will be here in just a second."

"The older gentleman, the one in the ambulance—is he doing okay? We were in the same explosion and—"

The receptionist shook her head. "I really couldn't say. Perhaps the nurse can tell you."

Back in one of the exam rooms, Lauren perched on the edge of the gurney and glanced impatiently at the clock on the wall. They'd spent a good hour talking to the police back at what was left of Oliver's house, and the ER could take forever. "I need to get back to Sue's—"

"I called and explained. Hannah is just fine. She doesn't know anything about the fire, so she isn't worrying." A dimple creased one of his cheeks. "She did, however, tell me that she missed me a lot, and that you did, too. I keep getting the feeling that she's trying to get us together."

Hannah! "And Bertie—"

"I talked to her. Before I could tell her anything, she told me she's planning to marry again. Did you know about that?"

"Marry?"

"An old family friend she met up with on her trip. She's as giddy as a teenager about the whole idea—plans to travel a lot and tells me she wants me to take over her place so she'll be free to go."

Lauren was speechless.

"But all that can wait till later." Michael paced the narrow room for the fifth time. Then he stopped in front of Lauren and leaned over, bracing a hand on either side of her. His face just inches from hers, he scowled, his silvery blue eyes turning hard and cold as stainless steel. His voice lowered to a growl. "Why in heaven's name did you go to Oliver's house tonight?"

He looked dark and angry and very, very large. And from deep in her heart came the overwhelming urge to grab his shoulders and kiss him till neither one of them could breathe.

He must have read it in her eyes, because his own gaze softened. Cupping one hand at the back of her head, he leaned forward and rested his forehead against hers. "I had to choose where to go first, and I never thought you'd be crazy enough to confront Oliver on your own."

"Where to go first?"

"Tell me why you went to Oliver's."

She slid her arms around his neck and drew him into a long lingering kiss that sent a rush of heat straight to her heart. "We were leaving, and—"

"*Leaving!*" He pulled back and stared at her.

"Hannah and I are leaving for Minneapolis tomorrow. All along I'd had the idea that Rick was trying to set me up so he could get Hannah. But that didn't make sense—he hadn't even wanted shared custody. Then I started to wonder about Oliver after something Bertie said. I wanted a chance to talk to him, because maybe he was the one who'd ruined my one chance for happiness."

Pain flashed across Michael's face, followed by remorse. "I was way too hard on you. I haven't found it easy to trust, given what I do and my history with Gloria. But if it's any consolation, I was only confirming what I already knew—that you weren't guilty of anything at all.''

''Well, you could have fooled me. You made me feel like dirt.'' She looked away and took a deep steadying breath, willing herself not to cry. ''Not that it hasn't been done before.''

''And speaking of that, I—''

Rapid footsteps approached. A tall fair-haired doctor loped into the room, an affable grin on his face. ''Howdy, folks. I hear you were involved in the explosion at the Evans house. What have we here?'' He gently reached out and took Lauren's fingertip, then rotated her hands. ''Nasty rope burns there. Anything else?''

She shrugged.

''Check her back,'' Michael ordered, stepping out of the way. ''Things flew out of that open doorway with a heck of a lot of force.''

''Hematomas over the scapula and thoracic vertebrae. No lacerations, though,'' he murmured. ''How's this?''

She winced.

''And this here?''

''Uh…fine. Really, I just need a bath and a good night's sleep.''

''Hmmm…'' The young doctor scribbled in the chart hanging at the end of the bed, then gave her a big smile. ''Sandy will come in to clean and dress your wrists, and give you a tetanus shot if you're due.'' He cocked an eyebrow.

''I had one last fall.''

"Good. Then I think we'll shoot some film on those ribs, and you can probably be on your way."

"What about Oliver?" She suppressed a shudder, thinking about what might have been.

He closed the chart and stuffed his hands into his lab-coat pockets. "Quite honestly I think he wanted to die in that house. We're keeping him on suicide watch while he's here, and they say he'll be transferred to jail when he's able. There's a deputy in the room with him."

"How badly is he hurt?" Michael asked. "When I went back after him I thought he was dead."

"He's conscious now. He has a concussion and some second-degree burns. Not extensive enough to need transfer to a burn unit, though. We can handle him here."

"Has he been talking about what happened?"

The doctor hesitated, then shrugged. "The police have been talking to him. They seem to have a lot of charges against him, including something back a few months. Another arson case, maybe?" He nodded to them both, then headed out the door.

"The carriage house," Lauren breathed, remembering Michael rushing into the flames. Two fires, two chances he could have been killed. Just the thought sent a wave of anger and sorrow through her. "Does Bertie know about all this?"

Michael nodded. "She took it pretty well once she knew you were okay." He picked up Lauren's hand. "I saw your note on the counter when I got back, then raced to Oliver's place."

"Do you think Bertie knew about Oliver all along?"

"She never expected this. Oliver was always out of his depth as a lawyer, and she regretted insisting that Winthrop take him on as a partner. I gather Win spent the last five years of his life covering for him."

"Oliver said something about old friends supporting his retirement, and that they didn't know about it. That's one reason he wanted to leave town in a hurry."

"I'll bet he did. An inquiry will probably show that he defrauded his elderly clients. He'll be disbarred...though he'll have a good long retirement plan, courtesy of Uncle Sam, at any rate. He could be charged with attempted murder, arson, embezzlement, mail fraud... I don't think he'll see daylight as a free man ever again."

"In a way I feel sorry for him."

"Then consider how he wormed his way into the lives of elderly women—women without families nearby to protect them. I suspected him before I left Briar Lake. After I got back from California, I went straight to the county courthouse and did a little research. He was named as primary beneficiary in four wills in the past two years."

"Did Bertie..."

"She didn't add him to her will, but she did give him interest-free loans through the years, most of which he never paid back. I think Oliver was pretty skilled at garnering sympathy and support from wealthy widows."

"He seems to be a very bitter man."

Michael gave her a grim smile. "Don't waste your sympathy on him. He started that account in a

Cayman bank and made sure that Bertie or I would see the documents. He framed you as an embezzler, in case anyone discovered the money missing from Bertie's accounts.''

Lauren took a sharp breath. "He *stole* from her? From the woman who tried so hard to help him?"

"It appears he managed to gain access to some of her investment accounts and had been filtering off money for some time. He apparently also stole from a trust and failed to pay her settlement monies on a lawsuit he helped her with a couple of years ago. The insurance company paid, he pocketed the money, and he told her the claim had been denied."

"She didn't figure it out?"

"Bertie has a warm heart, but she was getting suspicious. When you and I showed up for the summer, Oliver must have seen his schemes were at great risk."

A nurse popped in. "Sorry to keep you waiting. I'll be in as soon as I can."

Michael waved her away. "Take your time."

"Michael! That could mean a two-year wait in an ER!"

"There are things to be said, and this way you can't rush off until I'm done."

A corner of his mouth tipped up, but his eyes were somber, filled now with longing and a touch of uncertainty. A flicker of hope came to life within her as she looked into his eyes.

"I've had time to do a lot of thinking over the past week. I've got to ask you something, Lauren, but I've also got information for you that might change your plans for the future. I'm just not sure whether to start with the question that's most important to me, or the information that will make it easy for you to say no.''

Lauren's heart tripped over itself. ''I could save you time by saying yes and nothing else matters, unless you're just going to ask me if I'll move the car.''

With a shout of laughter he bent down and slowly, sensually, settled his mouth over hers, as if there were no other people for miles, as if they were alone in the dark.

His touch was at once seductive and gentle, recklessly possessive, as if he wanted to mark her forever as his and never let her go. And then he stepped back and looked down at her.

The raw love and need and that flash of uncertainty in his eyes filled her heart until it felt as though it might burst.

She reached up and laid a hand against his cheek. Why had she ever thought him cold and aloof? He was everything she could possibly desire. He was strength and caring and a deep sense of honor, a man who could weather the assaults of surly neighbors and cantankerous goats with good humor. One who treated her daughter with exquisite tenderness.

''Michael—''

He kissed her again, a long searching kiss that claimed and sought, sending heat through her until she felt as though she was in that burning house. She could feel the swift beat of his heart against her chest, and the tremble of his hands as he cupped the back of her head and held her close. This was beyond desire, beyond anything else in her experience, a need so deep and essential that it was more important than her next breath.

He broke the kiss and took a deep ragged breath, holding her close. Then he stepped back and shoved his hands in his back pockets. "I didn't tell you where I was going this week, because I didn't want to give you any false hopes."

Lauren lowered her head and closed her eyes, reliving the long days when she'd thought he had left because he didn't want to be around her at all and was eager to have her out of his life.

"I found Rick."

Startled, she jerked and nearly fell off the gurney. He reached forward to steady her, then dropped his hands.

"You *what?*"

"I believe in you, Lauren. I didn't go searching through your past to find evidence of guilt. I went back to prove you innocent."

He reached into a hip pocket and withdrew a folded sheet of paper. "I know you feel Hannah is better off away from him. I agree to an extent, though there may come a time when she really needs to make a connection. But there's no reason she shouldn't be receiving child support from him. He owes it, and maybe facing a little responsibility will be a good thing."

Michael handed Lauren the paper and she unfolded it. The top listed Rick's current address and phone number, his social-security number and the addresses of two siblings. "What—how did you get this? I lost track of his brothers a couple years ago and had no idea how to track Rick down after that."

He shrugged a shoulder. "He and I had a little…talk. He seemed to get a bit smarter as the conversation continued. With this current information, the authorities can go after him in California. If nothing else, they can garnishee his income, his income-tax returns or his bank accounts. You should never again have to struggle to support your daughter."

"Thank you," Lauren whispered.

"He…" Michael paused, as if he didn't want to go on. "He and Oliver kept in contact over the years. Apparently Oliver had helped him figure out how to set up accounts for hiding the embezzled money. Rick returned the favor this summer by giving Oliver a newspaper article about your trial—which was slipped under my door. He also gave Oliver information about your deferred sentence and provided your social-security number so Oliver could set up that bank account in your name."

"Rick swore he'd find a way to get back at me," Lauren whispered.

"There's something else." Michael stopped and eyed her with concern. "Are you okay? Do you need to lie down? I can get the nurse—"

"No, no, I'm fine." Lifting her chin, she forced herself to meet his worried gaze and smile. She'd been through worse, heaven knew. She could get through this.

"Read farther down."

She looked at the paper in her hand, now crumpled at the edges by her clenched hands. Smoothing it against her thigh, she tried to focus on Rick's familiar looping scrawl. "My, God," she whispered. "Rick...admitted everything?"

"He has admitted, in his own hand, that he perjured himself in a court of law by claiming that you were involved in the embezzlement of those funds. At the bottom there are the signatures of two witnesses, to avoid any question later on."

Stunned, she could only stare at the paper as the past few years flashed through her mind. The humiliation. The loss of her job at the elementary school. The cramped apartments and rattletrap of a car, the lessons and trips and pretty clothes she hadn't been able to give her daughter because she had lost everything.

"How on earth did you manage this?"

"Well...I told him that I had absolute proof that you weren't involved. I reminded him about the laws involving lying under oath, and the fact that he could be prosecuted fully, now that he'd been found. In practical terms such prosecutions aren't common, but it was enough to convince him. I told him that if he cleared your name now, it was unlikely that the matter would be pursued further."

"Will it?"

"Probably not. I did warn him that you had a lawyer and a powerful judge as friends, and causing you any sort of difficulty would mean far more trouble for him than he could imagine.

"A *judge*?"

"Miller."

"Judge *Miller*?"

"Hey, he's mellowed quite a bit." Michael glanced at the papers in her hand. "A copy of these documents and a letter are on their way back to Minneapolis. Though your deferred sentence is nearly up, I plan to make sure this entire situation is resolved as soon as possible." He smiled, though sadness lurked in his eyes. "You should have your teaching license reinstated very soon, Lauren. Your name will be clear and you'll be able to apply for any teaching position you want.

A flicker of hope caught, then grew inside her. "Free to go anywhere, right?"

"That's right."

"A new life. My career back. *Anywhere!*"

He stared down at her, the light in his eyes fading. "Anywhere at all." He turned toward the door.

"Tell me about your evidence."

"What?"

"You told Rick that you had absolute proof of my innocence."

"I didn't tell him what it was." When Michael turned back to her, he fixed his gaze on the wall beyond. The raw emotion in his eyes nearly made her weep. "My evidence is that you and your daughter have become part of my soul. I tried to keep from loving you by holding on to my doubts, but inside I always knew the truth. I would trust you with my checkbook, with my possessions, with my life."

He smiled a little then and finally met her eyes. "All very minor points, when you already hold my heart in your hands."

The hospital gown was…breezy. That nurse could return anytime to finally bandage her wrists and take her to X-ray. But if she didn't reach him in the next second, Lauren's own heart might just explode.

She launched herself off the gurney and threw herself into Michael's arms, tears and laughter crowding out all rational thought.

"Now about that question," she managed after breaking away from a searing kiss.

Michael laughed, then caught her in another deep kiss that sent flames clear down to her toes. "I love you, Lauren. I want you more than anything I've ever wanted in my life. I want to be a good father to your daughter, and I want to be with you until the day I die. Will you marry me?"

When she pulled back and looked up into his eyes, she saw all the trust and love and faith that she'd ever hoped to find. "Absolutely."

Then she kissed him back with all the joy in her heart.

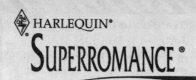

HARLEQUIN®
SUPERROMANCE®

You are now entering

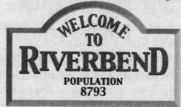

WELCOME
TO
RIVERBEND
POPULATION
8793

Riverbend...the kind of place where everyone knows
your name—and your business. Riverbend...home of
the River Rats—a group of small-town sons and
daughters who've been friends since high school.

The Rats are all grown up now. Living their lives and
learning that some days are good and some days
aren't—and that you can get through anything
as long as you have your friends.

Starting in July 2000, Harlequin Superromance brings
you Riverbend—six books about the River Rats and
the Midwest town they live in.

BIRTHRIGHT by **Judith Arnold** (July 2000)
THAT SUMMER THING by **Pamela Bauer** (August 2000)
HOMECOMING by **Laura Abbot** (September 2000)
LAST-MINUTE MARRIAGE by **Marisa Carroll** (October 2000)
A CHRISTMAS LEGACY by **Kathryn Shay** (November 2000)

Available wherever Harlequin books are sold.

HARLEQUIN®
Makes any time special ™

Visit us at www.eHarlequin.com

HSRIVER

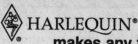

You're not going to believe this offer!

In October and November 2000, buy any two Harlequin or Silhouette books and save $10.00 off future purchases, or buy any three and save $20.00 off future purchases!

Just fill out this form and attach 2 proofs of purchase (cash register receipts) from October and November 2000 books and Harlequin will send you a coupon booklet worth a total savings of $10.00 off future purchases of Harlequin and Silhouette books in 2001. Send us 3 proofs of purchase and we will send you a coupon booklet worth a total savings of $20.00 off future purchases.

Saving money has never been this easy.

I accept your offer! Please send me a coupon booklet:

Name: _____

Address: _____ City: _____

State/Prov.: _____ Zip/Postal Code: _____

Optional Survey!

In a typical month, how many Harlequin or Silhouette books would you buy <u>new</u> at retail stores?

☐ Less than 1   ☐ 1   ☐ 2   ☐ 3 to 4   ☐ 5+

Which of the following statements best describes how you <u>buy</u> Harlequin or Silhouette books? Choose one answer only that <u>best</u> describes you.

☐ I am a regular buyer and reader
☐ I am a regular reader but buy only occasionally
☐ I only buy and read for specific times of the year, e.g. vacations
☐ I subscribe through Reader Service but also buy at retail stores
☐ I mainly borrow and buy only occasionally
☐ I am an occasional buyer and reader

Which of the following statements best describes how you <u>choose</u> the Harlequin and Silhouette series books you buy <u>new</u> at retail stores? By "series," we mean books within a particular line, such as *Harlequin PRESENTS* or *Silhouette SPECIAL EDITION.* Choose one answer only that <u>best</u> describes you.

☐ I only buy books from my favorite series
☐ I generally buy books from my favorite series but also buy
   books from other series on occasion
☐ I buy some books from my favorite series but also buy from
   many other series regularly
☐ I buy all types of books depending on my mood and what
   I find interesting and have no favorite series

Please send this form, along with your cash register receipts as proofs of purchase, to:
In the U.S.: Harlequin Books, P.O. Box 9057, Buffalo, NY 14269
In Canada: Harlequin Books, P.O. Box 622, Fort Erie, Ontario L2A 5X3

(Allow 4-6 weeks for delivery) Offer expires December 31, 2000.   PHQ4002

COMING NEXT MONTH